STORMY LOVE

by

Carlene Rae Dater

WHISKEY CREEK PRESS

www.whiskeycreekpress.com

Published by
WHISKEY CREEK PRESS

Whiskey Creek Press
PO Box 51052
Casper, WY 82605-1052
www.whiskeycreekpress.com

ISBN 1-59374-326-2

Credits
Cover Artist: Nora Baxter
Editor: Karyn Cheatham

Printed in the United States of America

Dedication

~~For Dennis - always.~~

Prologue

Amelia Island, Florida, 1979

A vicious pain stabbed the woman's side, making her slow to a walk. She was so intent on getting to the boat she nearly missed seeing the small form sitting in the middle of the vast lawn at the side of the house near the woods.

"Hey, Jilly-bean, what are you doing here by yourself?" Overhead the late afternoon clouds were gray and angry looking. There must be a storm heading inland. She had to hurry. "Why aren't you at Alice Mae's house?"

The tiny girl peered up from where she sat on the ground, shading her eyes against the hot Florida sun with her hand. "She won't play with me no more, Mama." Tears spilled down her cheeks. She sniffled, wiping her eyes with the back of a dirty fist. "You play with me, Mama?"

The woman glanced over her shoulder and bit her lip. Her long ebony hair whipped around in the freshening sea breeze. "I, ah, can't right now, sweetie. I have to run an errand. I'll walk you back to Alice Mae's house." She reached down and drew the child to a standing position.

"Can't. Her mama said I should go home and not come back. I'm a bad girl."

The woman squatted in front of the child, her eyes wide with confusion. "But why? What did you do?"

"Nothing, Mama. I promise. Alice said I'm bad 'cause I don't have no daddy. Why don't I have no daddy, Mama?" More wet tears wandered down chubby cheeks.

"Oh, baby, you had a daddy. Remember? We talked about it. He's in heaven, helping the angels watch over little girls like you." She knelt on the ground and gathered the child in her arms. "Don't you ever let anyone say you're less than perfect. Come on, Jilly-bean. I'll walk you back to Auntie's house so she can watch you for a couple of hours."

She rose and took the child's hand, pulling her across the wide expanse of lawn. They skirted the white latticework gazebo and followed a path through a flower garden blooming in riotous colors.

"Auntie told Alice Mae's mama she going to Jacksonville. She said business." Midnight curls jumped when the child nodded her head emphatically.

Indecision halted the woman in her tracks. Her searching eyes scanned the woods. How had they found her so fast? She inspected the vast expanse of lawn, from the big Victorian house to the forest surrounding it. "Doesn't matter now, I'll bring you with me. Come on, hurry. We're going to go for a nice ride in Auntie's boat. Won't that be fun?" She started off across the grass toward the snowy expanse of the beach, dragging her child along.

"Mama, you're going too fast. Carry me."

"I can't, honey. You're too heavy. You're a big girl now, almost four years old."

The woman hurried toward the water, her daughter's fingers clasped tightly in her own. The child's pudgy legs pumped frantically to keep up. By the time they reached the dock, they were both sweating, panting, out of breath.

"Jump in, Jilly-bean." She hoisted the child over the rail and placed her on the center seat of the dinghy. White caps flashed, rolling toward shore as the breeze grew stronger. Palm trees along the sandy beach swayed in the stiffening wind. The woman searched the horizon before lifting the rope off its mooring and clamoring into the boat. She wiped her sweaty palms along the sides of her cotton skirt and gnawed at her trembling lips.

This wasn't the best idea with a storm brewing, but she didn't have time to come up with a better plan. She had to get her daughter away from their pursuers.

"Here, sweetie, crawl into your life preserver." The woman knelt awkwardly in front of her daughter in the rocking boat. She slid the girl's arms into the orange life preserver. With a snap she fastened the straps.

Row after row of waves smashed the boat, ramming it into the dock. The woman fumbled under the seat then peered into the locker. Both of the spaces were empty.

"You wear a jacket too, Mama. Them's the rules." The child smiled, parroting her mother's oft-repeated warning.

Glancing once more toward the trees, the woman saw two burley men emerge and start toward them—moving fast. Metal glinted in the waning sunlight when one pulled an object out of his coat pocket. She hoped it was a pair of binoculars, but feared it might be a gun. They both wore dark clothing and had hats pulled low on their faces and looked very menacing.

The men would reach the dock in seconds. Her stomach cramped. Her gaze flew around the dock scrutinizing the area for a weapon. There was nothing. It was up to her. She had to protect her child. Escape was their only hope.

"Guess mine's at the house. Don't worry, sweetie. The seat cushion floats. We'll be okay. We're only going for a short ride." Placing an oar against the dock, she pushed with all her strength. The dinghy lumbered out into the water. Sweat poured down her face.

Wrapping the starter cord around her fist, she yanked. It took three tries before the motor turned over. Salty spray spattered her face, burning her eyes, blurring her vision. She opened the throttle wide. The boat jumped, slamming into the rolling surf, bouncing over whitecaps. The sun disappeared behind furious gray clouds. The wind grew stronger. Angry waves barreled in.

"Slow down, Mama! I scared!" The child fought to hang on, grasping at the side of the bench. In the distance, the afternoon freight train hooted and wailed as it chugged over the bridge. "Too much noise! I scared!"

"I'm sorry, baby," her mother shouted above the rising din. "We're going to go out a ways into the bay, then circle around to town. Mama's going to find a nice policeman to help us." A gust of wind snatched her words out of her mouth. Thunder rumbled, lightning flashed. Black squall clouds trampled across the sky, dumping a torrent of rain. The boat floundered in the strong waves.

The dinghy rounded a protected outcropping of land into the open sea. The full fury of the storm lashed at the boat. The motor dipped in and out of the water, sputtered, then died. Wave after wave hit the vessel. The woman braced herself in the stern of the boat, ripping at the useless motor cord. She struggled to shove the oars in the locks. She succeeded, but her efforts were futile against the raging weather.

"Stay where you are, baby." She smiled to hide her terror from her child. "I'll move over and hold you. We'll be all right. The boat will drift to shore." Watching to gauge the waves, the woman fought to stand. Two giant waves hit the boat broadside, one right after the other. Before the woman had a chance to grab a handhold, she catapulted over the side.

Above the howling wind, the child heard the terrible sound of her mother's head hitting the side of the boat. Viscous red fluid fanned out around dark hair, in a crimson halo.

Huddled in the middle of the boat, the child screamed, "Mama!"

Chapter 1

Amelia Island, the present

Jillian Bennett hunched over the steering wheel of her rental car to peer through the windshield into the late afternoon gloom. Gale-driven rain slashed across the narrow two-lane highway, wind howled, straining to crawl inside the car with her. Just when she thought her journey couldn't get any worse, a sign at the side of the road advertised, "Marsh Bridge, one mile".

"Oh no," she groaned. Bad enough to be caught in a rain storm, in a strange car in an unfamiliar part of the country. Now she had to fight her fear of the water and drive across a bridge. The urge to nibble at her cuticles was almost overwhelming. She'd just managed to break herself of the bad habit and didn't want to start again. Jillian shook her head, afraid to let go her death-grip on the steering wheel. She couldn't help wondering for at least the nine-hundredth time how she'd gotten herself into this mess. She wasn't the least bit brave, yet here she was traveling alone, thousands of miles from the familiar. Well, she had no choice. It would be a new beginning.

Slowing down, she rotated her head to relax the tense muscles. She had a knot in her stomach the size of a beach ball, and a muscle near her eye twitched in rhythm with her heartbeat. The soft jazz playing on the radio did little to ease her nervousness. A huge semi rode up on her bumper, blasting its horn. She pulled as close to the side as she dared. When the truck pulled around and lumbered ahead of her, her car rocked in its wake.

"Okay, okay, I can do this." Jillian bit down on her lower lip hard enough to taste blood and eased onto the bridge. She kept her eyes focused on the rear of the blue truck in front of her. The tires shimmied across the waffle-patterned metal plates on the road. A gust of wind pushed the car sideways a few inches. Jillian's heart jumped into her throat. Below her in the water, not far away, a wooden barge tooted its horn. Even with the car windows closed tight, the smell of rotting fish and salty water oozed into the car.

After cresting the bridge, she descended the other side. Sweat trickled between her breasts. A headache thrummed in her skull, reminding Jillian she hadn't eaten anything since the meager lunch on the plane. She should have stopped for a meal when she called the attorney from the airport in Jacksonville, but she'd been in a hurry to miss the storm. Once she located the bed-and-breakfast and got settled, she'd grab a sandwich and a cup of strong coffee.

A sign at the side of the road read, "Welcome to Amelia Island, Florida, Population 21,000. Fernandina Beach 10 miles ahead." Relief flooded her weary body, her spirits lifted. She fumbled for the map at her side to check it once more in the waning light.

The map of the town at the northern end of the island showed well-marked streets clustered around the harbor. It should be an easy place to explore. Why not drive by for a quick peek at her property? Ever since Jillian had received the letter from the law firm informing her that her great aunt had left her a Victorian house on Amelia Island, her imagination had run amok. She had vague memories of a sunny, sandy place when she was small, but didn't really know if she was remembering this place or some other beach. She had no clue why an aunt she didn't recall had left her a house. Whatever the reason, she was ready to start a new life with a new business in the house. Her toes itched to get moving and curiosity gnawed at her.

The lights of an oncoming car pierced her eyes. She threw her hand up to dim the glare. Fatigue pulled at her. Tomorrow would be time enough to survey her new kingdom. She chuckled at the idea of rambling around in a huge old house. After years of living in an apartment in Denver, the idea was almost incomprehensible.

She got all twisted around driving. By the time she reached the outskirts of Fernandina Beach, full darkness covered the area. The closer she got to the ocean, the louder the storm howled. Jillian shivered, wishing again that she'd kept her heavy winter coat in the car. Instead she had thrown it in the trunk in anticipation of warm March air in Florida.

Closer to the ocean now the scent of salt water slipped into the car, teasing her. Neat houses on tiny plots of land lined the road. The nearer she drove to the center of town, the larger the homes. Through the gloom she spotted a stately Victorian, then a second larger one, and her excitement grew.

Mrs. Cantrell had told Jillian her bed-and-breakfast would be easy to find. "You can't miss it!"

Maybe in the daytime in the sunlight when she was wide awake, but on a dark rainy night, exhausted, Jillian could barely read the signs. She knew her own house stood a few blocks from the B-and-B so she'd be able to walk there in the morning, hopefully in sunshine. She drove from street to street until she became thoroughly lost.

Low tree branches swayed in the wind. The radio in her car crackled with static. She reached over to snap it off, brought her eyes back to the road, slammed on the brakes and screamed.

A man scuttled diagonally in front of her car. She skidded to a stop inches from the ragged topcoat draped over his body. Fluffy gray hair sprouted from his head. A gust of wind flattened his matching beard against his face. He held both palms up in front of him like an Old Testament prophet endeavoring to hold back the tide. His mouth fell open. Jillian saw most of his teeth were missing. His shadowy eyes were wild.

Before Jillian could react, he disappeared into the forest. She huddled in the seat, terrified. Her eyes probed the edge of the woods, but he'd vanished. She was sure she hadn't hit him and he didn't move like he'd been hurt. Still, perhaps she should check. When she'd stopped shaking, she looked all around the area, but saw no one. She got out of the car and hugged the door, ready to spring back inside. What was happening to her? Only a day from her previous life, and already she was taking chances. Deep in her heart she knew she should stay in the car, but she had to find out if the old man was okay. Jillian took a few steps toward the dark curtain of trees. She couldn't see a thing.

Wet hair plastered against her face, obscuring her vision. Her clothes were drenched. A gust of wind sent shivers down her spine. In the distance she heard the mournful wail of a train. For some reason, it scared her. Nothing to do now but go on. Jillian would report the incident to the police when she arrived at Mrs. Cantrell's B-and-B. Jillian pushed the ebony hair out of her eyes.

Someone gripped her elbow and whirled her around. She came nose to neck with a man dressed all in black. Jillian tilted back her head. She was only five-feet-four, and the man towered over her by at least a foot. He had the long, lean body of a runner or serious athlete. Jillian's weary mind flashed on the statue of David.

He pulled her an inch closer and she gazed into his eyes. They were jet-black, depthless, and gleamed in the wavering light from the street lamp. She felt herself being drawn into their intensity, helpless to move. Parallel grooves ran down the valley between his nose to the corners of his firm sensual lips. Raindrops glistened on his hair like snowflakes. He had streaks of gray amid the ebony curls coiled around his ears. Never very good with ages, Jillian pegged him to be somewhere in his thirties.

"What the hell are you doing here?" His voice came out low and rusty, like he wasn't used to speaking or he had a cold. His midnight eyes pinned her. She stood unmoving; words failed her. She couldn't believe it, but she felt like melting into the power of his strength, then her anger surfaced.

"Take your hands off me." She pulled her arm from his grasp, stepped back—right into a water-filled pothole. If he hadn't grabbed her again, she would have fallen over.

He pulled her toward his body, then gently leaned her against the car. "I asked you what you're doing out here alone. Do you have any idea how dangerous this part of town is?"

"I almost hit an old man with my car. You must have seen him." A faint aroma of Canoe aftershave drifted over with a gust of wind. It reminded her of Craig—but she pushed the thought out of her head. That part of her life was finished, done, kaput.

"I haven't seen anyone but you wandering around in the middle of the street waiting for a car to plow into you." He stepped closer and sniffed. "Have you been drinking?"

"No, of course not." Tears hovered behind her eyes, straining for release. She wouldn't give him the satisfaction. "I'm on my way to Cantrell's Bed-and-Breakfast. I got confused. Then, this man appeared from nowhere. I slammed on my breaks, but he ran off into the woods, before I could see if he was hurt."

He lifted his eyebrow and crossed his arms over his broad chest. "Cantrell's is only three blocks from here."

An icy chill crept into Jillian's bones. Tired and hungry, her frustration escalated by the minute. "I'm lost."

A sardonic smile crept across his face. "Do you always have this much trouble reading a map, lady?"

The idea of popping the guy right in the nose was appealing, but she stood alone on a dark side street in a strange town in front of a man she didn't know. It probably wouldn't be a smart move. She pulled herself up to meet his gaze and glared.

"I am perfectly capable of reading a map; I simply lost my way in the rain. I inherited a house here. It's the reason I came to Amelia Island... If you'll excuse me..." Why on earth was she explaining things to this idiot? She had her fingers on the car door when he stopped her.

"What house? Where?"

"Thornton House at 536 Broome Street."

Lightning flashed, thunder boomed. The wind howled through the trees like an animal in pain. Jillian gazed up into the stranger's face. His thick black eyebrows drew together in a straight line. His broad hands anchored both shoulders in a firm grip. He spun her around. "You aren't too lost, lady. Thornton House is right behind you."

The sky lit up, crackling with lightning. Nothing could have prepared Jillian for what she saw. She squeezed her eyes shut, shook herself before opening them again. This couldn't be her house—her future. Her stomach cramped with despair.

She could almost hear her dreams shattering around her. Jillian slumped against the car in shock, her tears mingling with the raindrops.

* * * *

While the woman was staring at the derelict house, Detective Seth Falconer slipped away and faded back into the woods. There was no sign of the old guy; he'd gotten away again, thanks to the stranger. Seth wiped cold rainwater from his eyes and peered at her from behind the tree. The rough bark nibbled at his cheek. She stood there, staring at the house. He shoved his frigid fingers deep into the pockets of his blue jeans. The sodden fabric did nothing to warm them. His windbreaker was soaked through and his feet had been numb for hours. His holstered gun dug into his lower back, adding to his misery.

"Who are you, lady? What's your game?" His whispered words disappeared into the wind.

Seth had been closer tonight than at any time before, almost had his fingers on the guy's sleeve when her headlights had swept down the street, distracting him momentarily, allowing the man to escape. Had the old bum been there to meet her? But then, why almost ram him with her car? Why did she say she had been hunting for Cantrell's B-and-B? Probably thinking fast, to throw him off guard.

A gust of wind blew twigs off the trees. Wet leaves skittered along the street; a drop of icy water snaked under Seth's collar, running down his back. Enough. He was tired, drenched, and totally discouraged. Time to go home, fall into a hot shower and slug down a cold beer. The woman had ruined a good bust and Seth wasn't sure when he would have another opportunity like this one.

A train whistle blew in the distance. Nearby a dog barked twice before stormy silence filled the night once more. He stole one more look at the woman. The streetlight swayed overhead alternating light and dark. She pushed a handful of sopping hair out of her eyes. She straightened her back, mumbling to herself, then her chin came up.

"Feisty, aren't you?" Seth mumbled. He couldn't help but smile. Even her disheveled state couldn't hide her loveliness. Raven hair framed a heart-shaped face. Her skin was pale and flawless. Her eyes were dark too, luminous. The kind of eyes a man could drown in. When he'd grabbed her arm he smelled the faint fragrance of lilacs. She was slender, reed-like, but he could tell she had a core of steel inside her. It did not lessen her femininity, instead made her more appealing.

Easy boy, Seth thought. He slipped back behind the tree. She had to be part of what he suspected was drug activity that had gone on in the old house. His captain didn't agree, but Seth was working on his own time, determined to prove it. Why else would she be there? In the middle of a storm, in the middle of the night, in the middle of...what? It was his job to find out.

Seth zigzagged between trees to where he'd hidden his truck. He stopped for a moment when he saw the woman slide into her car; the overhead light flashed on. Her inky hair glistened like polished ebony, and her full lips pouted over opalescent, even teeth. She said she would be staying at Letty Cantrell's B-and-B, she must be checking directions. He'd wait until morning then go have a chat with Letty, better still, with RaeJean the housekeeper. Maybe she could fill him in on the mysterious new owner of Thornton House.

* * * *

Jillian pushed soggy strings of hair out of her eyes with shaky fingers. Salty tears streamed down her face blending with icy raindrops. She blinked and gawked again. This two-story clapboard house nestled in a copse of moss-covered trees could have starred in a horror film. The siding hadn't made acquaintance with a paintbrush for years, probably decades. She could see where several slats had pulled away from the building, curling outward in the moist air. Most of the windows on the first floor were boarded up, and those on the second story were missing glass panes, open to the elements. The chimney leaned at a raffish angle. She watched several roof tiles lift, then dance across the rough surface, before they pirouetted and sailed off into the night.

In the woods an owl hooted. The wind moaned, whispering leafy secrets though tall tree branches. Jillian shivered, finally coming to her senses. She opened the door of her rental car, scrambled into the driver's seat and locked the door. She had been standing in the dark, freezing, in front of an abandoned house, where at least two strange men lurked about. Fatigue had rendered her mind to mush. While she sat for a moment, panic raged through her. She was so alone in the world with no one to help her.

Jillian decided to suck it up. She took a deep breath and fumbled with numb fingers for the overhead light. Twice she swatted at the switch before a soft glow again filled the interior of the car. She reached for her map. Her moist touch left soggy ripples on the edge.

"Okay, okay, if this is Thornton House, I should be able to go down to the corner, turn left, I'll be right in front of Cantrell's." It was only three blocks away, just like the man had said. Jillian could almost feel eyes staring at her out of the darkness. With a click she flicked off the map light and stared at the dark woods, but didn't see anyone. She turned the ignition, the car rumbled to life.

"Man, it is dark out here," she said. With a start she realized she hadn't turned on the headlights. Jillian peered into the gloom and flipped on the headlights before easing down the empty street.

In less than two minutes, she found her destination. For the first time since she'd departed the security of the airport in Jacksonville, she had a bit of luck. A parking space stood waiting right in front of the B-and-B.

In sharp contrast to 'her' house, Cantrell's was exactly the way she'd pictured it. The streetlight's glow bathed the Victorian in rays of warm amber. Also two stories high, it was a scaled-down, prettier version of Thornton House. Lights shined from all the windows on the first floor, illuminating the front porch. Jillian struggled to open the car door until she realized she hadn't unlocked it. She must be tired. She'd never been this ditzy in her life.

The rain had diminished to a soft mist. Jillian trudged up the walk, plodding in puddles of water, through the gate of the white picket fence surrounding the place. She shook like a dog coming out of water before knocking on the front door. Before her knuckles left wood, a woman snatched it open.

"Are you Jillian?"

"Yes. Mrs. Cantrell? I'm so sorry I'm late."

"Call me Letty. Why, sugar, where have you been? You should have pulled in here hours ago." The plump woman standing before Jillian took her arm and drew her into the foyer. Her frosted blond hair was teased up into a rigid style reminiscent of the 1980's. Her skin was rose petal smooth, a friendly smile decorated her face, and she smelled like peppermints.

"I was so worried about you, I was ready to call the authorities. Did you have car trouble? Mercy, you look like a half-drowned pup." The words dripped out of her mouth like warm butter trickled on grits.

Letty pulled a clean white handkerchief out of the sleeve of her lavender pants suit and handed it to her. Only then did Jillian realize water had been dribbling off her clothes all over the aqua tiles in the entry. She'd been so fascinated at the cadence of the woman's words she'd lost her own train of thought. Letty sounded like a road company version of Blanche Dubois.

"Oh, I'm sorry. I'm dripping all over. Yes, I'm Jillian Bennett. I'm afraid I became a bit lost in the rain."

"No matter, honey. You're here how. Where is your luggage? Still in the car? Give me the keys. I'll have Malcolm fetch it. You must remove those wet things before you catch your death. Are you hungry? It's just the two of us now, Mal and I, we been waitin' dinner for you. Surely it must be hours since you ate." While she chattered away, Letty Cantrell took the proffered keys, clasped Jillian's elbow and pulled her through the doorway into the parlor. She disappeared and Jillian heard her thundering up stairs. In less than a minute she was back, and continued talking like she'd never left the room. "'Course most B-and-B's don't serve dinner, but I want my clients to experience more of the ambiance of this wonderful old house. Don't you agree?"

Jillian kept her mouth shut, allowing herself to be led. Inclusive dinner had been one of the main reasons she'd chosen this B-and-B. She hated eating alone, especially dinner, and figured it was worth the extra money she'd be paying.

A cheery fire burned brightly in the fireplace, drawing Jillian to its warmth like a heat-seeking missile. Sighing in contentment, she held her cold fingers in front of the fire.

"Here, sit right in front of the fire, warm yourself, sweetie." Letty pulled a navy blue-patterned wing chair up close to the embers, draped an afghan around Jillian's shoulders and handed her a towel for her hair. Jillian disappeared under the towel and slipped her feet out of her sodden shoes. She brushed her frozen toes along the worn Oriental carpet while she rubbed her hair dry.

"Can I bring you a cocktail before dinner? A libation to warm your bones? Mal and I had some nibbles to tide us over till you arrived, so we can wait a bit."

The smell of roasted beef wound its way into the room. Hunger grabbed Jillian's growling stomach. If she drank on an empty stomach she might pass out, or at the least need a nap. Still, it would help to defrost her. "A brandy, if you have it, please."

Letty splashed amber liquid in the bottom of a glass and gave it to Jillian. She filled her own snifter half full before walking over to perch on the arm of the couch. Jillian realized the peppermint smell was breath mints. She opened her mouth to speak, but before the words emerged, they both heard the front door slam.

"Where do you want me to deposit this luggage?"

Jillian swiveled. A man stood silhouetted in the doorway. She almost dropped her glass. For a second, she could have sworn Craig stood there. Then the figure stepped into the light.

His massive shoulders filled the doorway. Sprinkles of rainwater dotted the burgundy polo shirt he wore above neatly pressed khaki pants. He walked into the room with nonchalant grace, and held his hand out to Jillian. She reached out, and found her own hand engulfed in his warm grasp.

"You must be Jillian. Hi, I'm Malcolm Winters."

His firm mouth curled slightly upward, on the edge of laughter. He had thick tawny-gold hair, and eyes the color of kiwi fruit. A dusting of freckles trailed across a nose that had been broken at one time without being set correctly. It gave him a raffish appearance Jillian would have found nearly irresistible, if she'd been in the market for a man. Which she wasn't.

"You mind puttin' Jillian's bags in the blue room?" Letty said. "We'll be eatin' just as soon as RaeJean serves the food. Time for a quick drink if you want." She turned toward Jillian again.

"Do you mind if I run up and change clothes? I'm sopping wet and it will only take a second." She put her snifter on the end table and stood.

"Oh, silly me! Course not, sugar, go right ahead. It's at the top of the stairs, second door on the right. We'll wait for you right here in the parlor."

Jillian squished up the stairs and nearly collided with Malcolm in the door to the bedroom. He'd set her luggage inside the door. Did you tip him? Thank him? What?

"I, ah..." The words didn't make it past her blue lips. Even in her worn out state Jillian couldn't help but wonder why Letty was using Malcolm as servant.

"Here's your key. I'll see you downstairs." He closed the door and was gone. Jillian barely looked at the room as she walked out of her shoes and pulled off her soggy clothes. From her suitcase, clothes flew everywhere as she hunted for something to wear. She found a gray sweatshirt, blue jeans and warm socks. They would have to do. She quickly towel-dried her hair, put on the dry clothes and tennis shoes, and clomped back down to the parlor.

"Tell me, Jillian honey, what ever made you decide to vacation to the island in early March? It's nice all the year round, of course, but much nicer in late spring or fall." Letty tilted her head back and a healthy slug of brandy disappeared down her throat.

"Oh, I'm not vacationing, I'll be moving here." Jillian picked up her glass, took a sip of the liquor and coughed. Her eyes watered and she blinked. She cleared her throat before starting again. "I inherited a house from my great aunt, Felicity Thornton."

Letty's half-empty glass slipped from her fingers, smashing to pieces on the fireplace hearth.

Chapter 2

"I'm not cleaning that up." A middle aged African-American woman stood in the doorway, arms crossed, lower lip thrust out. "You wanna eat, you'd better come. Everything's getting cold." She strolled off down the hall.

Malcolm dashed to Letty's side and knelt beside her chair, staring into her eyes. "Are you all right? Did you cut yourself?

"But, Thornton House—" Letty winced as her words were cut off. Jillian couldn't be sure, but she thought Malcolm had squeezed Letty's arm—hard. But why? What possible difference could Jillian's inheritance make to Letty? A chill rippled up Jillian's spine that had nothing to do with being cold.

Malcolm murmured words into Letty's ear. Jillian couldn't make them out. He patted Letty's shoulder and helped to her feet. "Go on, show Jillian to the dining room. I'll pick up the glass." Malcolm guided her toward the door.

"Yes, of course, dinner. Oh, dear, I don't know how that happened. Perhaps I'm hungrier than I thought." Letty drew a lace handkerchief out of the sleeve of her pantsuit and used it to dab at her forehead. "Thank you, Mal." She reached out and drew Jillian to her feet.

Jillian wasn't surprised she seemed unsteady on her feet; she'd obviously already had too much to drink. Jillian regretted her decision to stay at this bed-and-breakfast, rather then one of the chain hotels in town.

"Mercy, gal, you're all skin and bones," Letty said. "We're gonna have to fatten you up a bit."

Together the women walked across the front hallway to the dining room opposite the parlor. Three places had been set on a long table that could easily accommodate ten diners. The china pattern was simple but exquisite. Wine-filled crystal glasses gleamed in the light cast by two candles flickering in alabaster holders at the center of the table.

A platter of sliced roast beef rested on a warming tray. Mounds of fluffy mashed potatoes peaked in a bowl alongside a basket of warm rolls. A tureen of gravy, salad, a bowl of mixed vegetables all sat waiting. Hunger grabbed Jillian again. She couldn't wait to dig in.

"Here, darlin', you sit on this side opposite me. Malcolm is the only male in the house right now, so we'll let him sit at the head," Letty tittered as she pulled out her chair.

Malcolm slipped into the dining room and stared at Letty once more. He sat down and started passing food around.

"I believe I mentioned before, this is not the height of our tourist season. That's why there's only Malcolm and you in residence at this time. Wine, honey?" Letty asked.

"No thank you. Water is fine for me." Jillian filled her plate and took a bite. The roast beef melted in her mouth. She had to restrain herself from shoveling in the food. Feeling hot eyes on her, she brought her head up to find Malcolm staring at her.

"For a minute I thought my imagination had run amok. Your eyes are two different colors, aren't they?"

Heat flooded Jillian's body; she looked down at her plate. She'd always been self-conscious of her eyes. Why did she have to be such a freak of nature?

"Um, yes. Kinda weird, huh?" All her life she'd been teased because of her eyes. Not bad enough she had dark hair surrounding her fair skin then this mixture of light eyes, one blue and one green. She bit her lip. No doubt about it, her appearance was unusual. She couldn't help but wonder again what Craig had ever seen in her.

"I think they're gorgeous. Don't you, Letty?"

Letty had been pushing food around with her fork, clearly lost in thought. Her wineglass was empty. She tipped the bottle to refill her glass. "Oh, yes, they're lovely. Tell me, Jillian, how did you come to inherit Thornton House? I been living on the Island for near ten years and never knew Felicity Thornton to have any family or heirs."

"I'm not sure of all the details myself. I have an appointment with a lawyer tomorrow. He should be able to explain everything." She wasn't about to tell strangers about the certified letter that had arrived at her apartment out of the blue, informing her she was an heiress. She almost snorted at the thought. She'd inherited a damp old house but nothing else, no doubt. Letty's voice brought her back to the present.

"I know most folks in town, which lawyer you seein'?"

"George Bannerman." Jillian poked at the gravy-covered potatoes before scooping a mound into her mouth.

"He must be the new man over on Front Street, been here about five years. How'd you meet him?"

"Now, don't be so nosy." Malcolm reached over and patted Letty's hand.

Fatigue battered Jillian. Her head hurt, and her body yearned for sleep. It took all of her will power to be civil to her hostess. "I received a letter. Now, if you'll excuse me. I'm exhausted. I'd like to go to bed."

"Why certainly, sugar. I do believe I'll retire too. It's been an exhaustin' day." Letty walked none too steadily out of the dining room and headed up the steps with Jillian in her wake.

She dragged her feet along up the central staircase trailing Letty into the second bedroom on the right. Letty opened the door and walked inside. Jillian realized she had forgotten to lock it.

"I call this the blue room, honey. Best room in the house." Letty crossed the periwinkle carpet to open the bathroom door. "I see you found the bathroom. Should be enough towels, but if you need anything, my room is right across the hall, so you come knock, hear?"

"Yes, thank you, Mrs. Cantrell."

"Now, now, it's Letty, honey. When I hear Mrs. Cantrell, I look over my shoulder for my mother-in-law. Breakfast is anytime between seven and nine. I probably won't be up, so just go on into the kitchen and tell RaeJean what you want." With a wiggle of her fingers, Letty backed out, closing the door behind her.

Jillian locked the door, then rummaged around in her suitcase until she found her nightie. Too tired to worry about a clean face or teeth, she removed her clothes, pulled the pink cotton nightie over her head before collapsing face down on the bed.

Off in the distance before sleep descended Jillian heard the lonely wail of a train whistle. It sounded strangely familiar.

* * * *

"Look who the cat dragged in." Sergeant Murphy Johnson stood behind his desk at the Fernando Beach Police Department. "You catch any bad guys last night?"

"Nope. Caught a cold, I think." Seth Falconer blew his nose and headed for the coffeepot. "I got close to nabbing the old guy, but a strange broad chased him away."

"Hmm, interesting. D'ya think she's part of the drug gang?" Johnson snagged a powdered donut from an open box sitting near the refrigerator.

Seth helped himself to the last glazed donut and sat down with his breakfast. If he didn't start eating better, he'd develop a gut like Murphy's.

"She said she's the new owner of Thornton House."

Murphy pulled out a chair and sat across from Seth. A trail of powdered sugar meandered down the front of his dark blue uniform shirt. "She a Yankee Gal?"

"I don't know." Seth shrugged. "How can you tell? Lack of magnolia blossoms behind the ear? No honey dripping from the mouth?"

"Well, hell boy, did she sound southern?" Murphy asked. "Or sorta like you—like you grew up next door to the Kennedy clan."

"First of all, I do not have an accent."

Murphy snorted, spraying powdered sugar across the desk.

"But if I did, of course I'd sound like a Kennedy. I was born in Boston after all." Seth slugged down the rest of his coffee and stood. "Captain in yet?"

"Yeah, he rolled in 'bout twenty minutes ago."

"I'll go touch base with him, then I think I'll wander over to Letty Cantrell's place, see what I can dig up on her new guest."

Walking toward the back of the station, Seth's mind was filled with a dark-haired woman. Could she be involved in his investigation? He could still feel the soft curves of her body when she'd pressed against his. She had seemed so vulnerable that he wanted to protect her. He tried to push the thought of her exotic colored eyes out of his head before he knocked on the captain's door and entered.

"Sit down, Seth. We need to talk." With his head down, Captain Burgess kept moving papers around his desk. He refused to meet Seth's eyes.

* * * *

Jillian stopped on the landing of the outdoor stairway that led to the lawyer's office. She dabbed a tissue across her brow. After the thin dry air of Colorado, the humidity here made her feel like she was groping through molasses. She'd only walked six blocks from Letty's, but already felt like she needed a bath.

She stared out at the marina at the end of the street, partly out of curiosity, partly to delay her meeting with George Bannerman. Jillian wanted to find out about her past, but she was frightened. What if she discovered something bad? Relatives who were criminals, or evidence of disgusting genetic diseases?

Boats of every size and shape bobbed and shimmed on the ocean in the breeze. Even five blocks from the water, Jillian could hear the rigging clanging against metal bridgework. The tangy smell of fish mixed with salt water assailed her nose. She drew the moist air into her lungs. Yesterday's rain had left the cloudless sky gin-clear. Plastering a brave smile on her face, she knocked.

"Come on in," a deep male voice on the other side of the door commanded.

She pushed open the door and stepped inside. A large orange tabby got tangled between her feet, tripping her. The cat screeched. Jillian lurched, stifling a curse as she fell forward. Before she could hit the floor, a man's strong arms caught her.

"Mercy, we haven't even met and already you're falling for me." He quickly set Jillian back on her feet.

"I'm so sorry. I didn't see the cat. Is he okay?"

"Oh, it'd take more than a squished tail to upset old Lucky."

They both turned to where Lucky crouched behind a cardboard box. Part of his right ear was missing, his upper lip curled back with scar tissue in an apparent sneer. The butter-scotch colored fur on his body stood out in patches scars and dotted his skin.

"Lucky?" Jillian was positive this had to be the ugliest cat she'd ever seen.

"Yeah, I figure the poor old guy has been through so much he must be lucky. He turned out to be a stray. Somehow we adopted one another when I moved in here." He gave her a disarming smile. "George Bannerman. You must be Jillian."

"Yes, it's nice to meet you." She glanced around the room in wonder. "I hope I didn't catch you at a bad time. Are you...moving?" The square one-person office was a mess. Files full of papers from metal cabinets had been thrown all over the floor. The desk rested on its side, a banker's lamp had been broken, spilling green glass all over the carpet.

"Nope, burglars broke in last night." Bannerman scratched at his thinning straw-colored hair. His pale eyes appeared perplexed. "They completely trashed the place. Can't imagine what they thought might be of value in here. I don't do criminal work. Mostly wills, estate planning, routine matters. Nothing exciting." When he smiled, the gap between his two front teeth, combined with his freckles, reminded Jillian of the old television puppet Howdy Doody. George Bannerman was as warm and friendly as Mom's apple pie.

"Have you called the police?"

"Yes. They said an officer would be by this morning. I'm not supposed to touch the door or windows till they can dust for fingerprints." George turned in a slow circle. "Why don't we sit on the couch while I search for your file?" The sunshine fled from his face as he scratched at his head.

Find the file? Had she come all this way for nothing? Jillian perched gingerly on the frayed purple-velvet couch, obviously a relic or a thrift shop buy. A maverick spring poked her in the butt. "Can I help? Oh, is it all right to touch these folders?"

"Should be. I have to arrange this mess back into some kind of order or I can't do business.

"Is it a regular file folder? Anything unusual about it?" Jillian stood, searching the mess.

"Should say Thornton on the file tab." He knelt and started pushing folders into a pile.

Spotting an empty carton behind the desk, Jillian took it over to where Bannerman squatted. "Here, why don't you set things in here after you go through them, then later you can return them to the file cabinets."

"Why, what a good idea! Thanks."

Together they stacked files for almost half an hour. Panic hovered in the back of Jillian's brain. Each time she placed a heap of folders in the box, her tension rose. What if they never found her file?

"Do you remember anything of the details?" Jillian paused, trying desperately to make her brain work. "Did you have a duplicate?"

"No, no, only the one file. Golly, I don't know what I'll do if it's gone." He walked to a closet to retrieve a dustpan and broom. By the time Bannerman had swept up all the glass, they still hadn't found her file.

Fighting back tears, Jillian returned to sit on the couch. Her stomach hurt and her head whirled. What would happen to her now? She'd have to give up and go back to Denver, or someplace.

"Perhaps if we could reschedule for later in the week, I might be able to find it. I think the taxes were paid for the..."

Jillian started to stand, but a bit of tan caught her eye. "Do you think that's it?" She pointed.

George strode over and pushed the desk a few inches. A corner of beige jutted out from under the furniture. Carefully, pulling a millimeter at a time, he extracted the papers. "Got ya, you elusive devil! Here it is! It must have gotten shoved under the desk during the break in."

George pulled a handkerchief out of his pocket to wipe his sweaty forehead.

"Are you all right?" Jillian asked. She searched the room for a phone. The man looked ill.

"Oh, yes, thank you." He walked over squatted at the opposite end of the couch before opening the slim file. He ran his finger down the center of the page. Jillian held her breath. She didn't have a good feeling.

"Now, I told you in the letter I sent, the main portion of the will consists of Thornton House. The insignificant amount of money that remained was eaten up in private investigation fees in an attempt to find you." He gazed up at her with watery eyes. "Matter of fact, I was about to give up, turn the whole estate over to the state when you called. You barely squeaked by the deadline."

"I'm confused, Mr. Bannerman. Why did Felicity Thornton leave her house to me?"

"Why, she was your great aunt, of course. Don't you remember her?" George's eyebrow ascended toward his receding hairline.

"Are you positive you have the right Jillian Bennett? As I told you when I phoned from Denver, I've never been here before." Her heartbeats sounded loud in her ears. The plane ticket had been her means of escape, but she'd had to make sure. "Have I?"

"The PI firm that found you was quite positive, it's all very legal. Actually, Ms. Thornton's previous law firm hired and funded them. I was a bit, ah surprised myself when I received the letter that they'd found you.

"As to the island, it's no wonder you don't remember; you were too young. According to Ms. Thornton, you spent near the whole summer here with your mother the year you were three."

The sound of angry bees buzzed in Jillian's ears and black spots swarmed before her eyes. Her stomach knotted. In spite of the heat, she felt cold.

"My mother?" She clutched at the arm of the sofa to keep from falling over.

"Whoa, are you okay?" George reached out to grab her arm. "I am so sorry. I thought you knew."

"I've always known I was adopted, but my parents told me my mother had died in childbirth." Jillian moistened her dry lips. "Do you have any information about her—my birth mother? Is she still alive?"

"Oh, dear, I don't believe so, but I don't know. Maybe the letter will give you more information."

"What letter?" Jillian's thoughts whirled with confusion. This was too much information too fast.

George dug into the back of the file then started to give Jillian a sealed business-sized envelope. He pulled back, holding onto it.

"I'm sorry, I guess I'm not thinking straight what with this break-in and all. May I see some identification, Ms. Bennett? To be sure I'm dealing with the right woman."

"Of course." With shaking hands, Jillian pulled out her driver's license. "Will this do? I don't have a passport. Never needed one."

"Yes, sure fine." Bannerman wrote down her license number on a piece of paper, then let her take the sealed envelope. "I imagine Felicity wrote you a chronology of your family or something like that." He dismissed the envelope with a shrug and fished in his pocket until he came up with a ring filled with keys. He shuffled through the mess until he came to the ones he wanted. "This is the front door key. I made a copy of it in case yours is lost. I hope you don't mind." He slid one off and gave it to Jillian.

"Certainly not. I'd feel better if you have a key to the house too."

"I'm not sure what this other one is. Perhaps it opens a door in the house." With a shrug, he gave her the second key.

She placed the keys in her pocket while the envelope rested on her lap. It lay there like a dead manta ray. She touched the edge of it gingerly. What secrets did it hold? More importantly, did she want to know?

George cleared his throat before beginning. "From what Ms. Felicity told me, she lived all her life on Amelia Island. She inherited the house from her daddy. She never married. Her only sister, Laurel, moved out west to attended college in Los Angeles. She married there… Ah, here it is—Alan Brown. Felicity and your grandmother Laurel weren't real close, had sort of lost touch over the years. I believe they had some kind of falling out." George stopped to peruse his notes.

"Your mama, Melody, was born in California, but Felicity had never met her. Your mama showed up on her doorstep one day with you in tow."

A cold chill settled in Jillian's heart. "What about my father?"

"I'm sorry, there's nothing in here about him. I'm not sure if Ms. Thornton had any information." Bannerman's pale face flushed. He lowered his attention to the papers again.

He must think I was a bastard, just as my adopted parents did.

Jillian felt a soft touch brush against her ankle. She glanced down to find Lucky perched there, staring up at her. He'd been hiding in the bathroom while the cleanup was underway. "Hey, sweetie, want a hug?" She gingerly stroked the top of his head. The cat rubbed against her ankle. Jillian had always adored animals, always wanted a dog, a cat, a hamster, any critter to love when she was a child. Her mother never let her have a pet.

"Oh, mercy, he'll get you all dirty. I think he needs a bath," George declared.

Lucky did emit a rather strong odor, but Jillian didn't care. She continued to caress his head and back. She needed time to think. The cat curled up and started doing a credible imitation of a motorboat.

"What do we do next, Mr. Bannerman?" Jillian asked. Lucky licked Jillian's fingers with his raspy tongue. "You mentioned a deadline. What does it mean?"

Bannerman dropped his gaze and shuffled through the papers. "No mortgage on the house, of course. It was paid off years ago. Ms. Thornton took care of my fees, so you needn't worry you owe me anything. The taxes have been paid by the estate, but only until March 30th, in two weeks. You'll need to pay property tax as well as the homeowners insurance if you want to keep the house."

Shocked, Jillian kept her mouth shut and bit the inside of her cheek. Two weeks? What could she possibly do in two weeks?

Bannerman stood, signaling the end of the meeting. "You can take possession immediately, although I'm not sure you'll want to stay there. Thornton House needs, ah, a bit of work."

"A bit of work? Mr. Bannerman, I've seen Thornton House, it needs more than a bit of work. A few sticks of dynamite would be better." Jillian continued to stroke the cat to hide her trembling hands. Her breakfast churned in her stomach. "I had planned to convert the house into a B-and-B, but I know now it's not possible. How much is it worth? I don't have much money. Can I sell it? Obtain a loan?"

"Oh, dear. You could try, but you've seen the place. I doubt any bank will issue you a substantial loan. It will require a lot of money to fix up." George scratched at the side of his face. "I guess you could simply not pay the property tax and let it go to the state for back taxes."

Jillian sat for a moment in confusion. "What about the land, is that worth anything? All those trees."

Bannerman shuffled papers around again. "I seriously doubt it's worth much," he said, not looking at her. "But of course you could check. And there aren't as many trees as you'd think. The whole island was a forest at one time, now it's just thick patches between properties. All those old oaks and Spanish moss make it appear like a real forest."

Jillian patted the top of Lucky's head once more. "I guess I have some thinking to do." She picked up the envelope, grabbed her purse and pushed herself up.

"Here, let me give you one of my cards." Confusion skittered across his face before he stooped down to snatch a business card off the floor. "I'll write my home number on the back in case you have any questions." He patted her shoulder in a friendly way. "I'm sorry things haven't worked out better for you. But, you can always go home, put all this behind you, right?"

Jillian turned to hide her tears from him. "Right. Thank you for all your help, Mr. Bannerman. I'll be in touch."

Without a backward glance, she fled down the stairs. If only she could go home, but of course, she couldn't.

Her adopted father had been killed in an accident at the factory where he worked, and her mom had suffered with a bad heart condition for years and couldn't work. Jillian had dropped out of college, got a part time job and cared for her mother fulltime. When her mother passed away, Jillian had no choice but to find a job to support herself and chip away at the mountain of debts left my her mother's illness. Still, why had she focused all her energy on her job—her man?

She'd met Craig Hamilton her first day on the job as a teller at the bank. She had planned the employment to be a stopgap before continuing college. Things hadn't worked out quite that way.

Craig was the bank administrator, and had asked her out for a drink at the end of her first week. She was so alone and lonely and fell for him hard and fast. When she found out he was married, she'd broken off the relationship. But Craig left his wife, got a divorce and begged Jillian's forgiveness. Of course, she took him back; she loved him and planned on a future together. Instead of a bridge back to college, her bank job had turned into a career. Craig had helped her advance to manager—to keep her near him she now realized. Whenever the conversation had turned to marriage, Craig stalled her, saying he'd married too young and wanted to experience the life of a bachelor for a while.

In the meantime, he'd kept her isolated, without friends. He convinced her they didn't need anyone else. He kept telling her what an important man he was as an excuse for the many times he had to cancel their plans for client meetings. Jillian suffered through holidays and vacations alone, always with the promise that eventually they would be together.

Jillian had always understood how busy Craig was, but suspicion reared its ugly head during the last year of their relationship. Longer meetings, more and more canceled dates until Jillian barely saw her lover outside of the bank. Frustration boiled over on Jillian's twenty-eighth birthday. She had just received the registered letter from the lawyer informing her of the inheritance. She had read it again and again, her heart soaring with the possibilities. The two of them could marry, move to Florida to make a new start.

He'd promised to take her out for dinner to celebrate her birthday. Instead she waited at her apartment all night for Craig, alternating worry with fury. The next day she managed to corner him alone in his office.

"Where were you last night, Craig? I was so worried when you didn't come over or call. We were supposed to go out for dinner for my birthday. I called your apartment near midnight, but you didn't answer. Where were you?" she demanded again. Anger made her body vibrate from head to foot.

Craig had run a manicured hand along his blond razor cut hair. "Lower your voice immediately."

Without thinking, she obeyed him like a naughty child. She lowered her gaze and nibbled at the cuticles of her ragged nails.

"Stop that."

Her hands flew behind her back.

"I'm sorry about last night." He walked around his large mahogany desk, lowering himself into his black leather chair. He sat silently for a moment, his fingers tented before his face "I guess we need to talk. I'll come over after dinner and we'll straighten this all out." The smile on his lips never made it to his peridot-colored eyes.

Jillian held her ground. "No Craig, we settle this now." Her stomach churned, but the registered letter in her pocket gave her courage. She started to pull it out, to share the good news with him, but hesitated. Something was very wrong with their relationship and she had to find out what it was.

Craig heaved a large, dramatic sigh. "Okay. Close the door please, Jillian." He stood and walked to the large window, his gaze fixed out over the city of Denver. With his hands behind his back, he bounced on the balls of his feet, before turning to face her.

"There's no easy way to say this, Jillian. I'm getting married again. I was with my fiancée last night."

Jillian felt like a bowling ball had been rammed into her chest. She doubled over, gasping for breath. She managed to flop into a chair before she fell to the ground.

"Oh for crying out loud, don't be so dramatic. Surely you must have realized I'd marry again."

"But, you're supposed to marry me!" Tears ran off Jillian's cheeks, wetting the collar of her blouse.

At least Craig had the good grace to blush. "Yes, I know we talked about marriage at one time. I shouldn't have kept leading you on but you must realize, Jillian, I could never marry you."

He started to pace across the floor. Too stunned to speak, she clenched her jaw and waited. "I'm forty-two," he continued. "I want to have kids before I get any older."

"I want a family too, Craig." The words slipped by her lips in a mere whisper.

"Jillian, I am sorry, but I couldn't possibly have children with you. I have the Hamilton name to think of, you know."

"What, what do you mean?" Gray dots appeared at the edge of Jillian's vision. The sound of a million bees filled her ears.

"You're adopted, Jilly. Who knows what your parents were like? Your mother could have been a drug addict, a prostitute. She probably had no idea which man fathered you. I couldn't possibly expose my children to an unknown background." He threw his hands in the air. "I mean, those weird eyes of yours. I couldn't take the chance my kids might have features so—odd."

Her lips refused to move and her palms grew clammy. She simply sat staring at Craig until her mouth finally moved, allowing her to speak. "Who?"

"Who what? Oh, whom am I marrying? Linda Gillette, the daughter of Lou Gillette, he's an attorney. Fine family...good people." Craig cleared his throat. "She, ah, graduated from Vassar last year." The idiot had pulled out his wallet and handed it to Jillian. The photo showed a gorgeous young woman, smiling into the camera. Her long blond hair fell in a cascade to her shoulders. Perky blue eyes crinkled at the camera. She even had dimples.

Jillian had pulled herself out of the chair and thrown the wallet at Craig's head. "You bastard." She left the office and ran to the ladies room where she'd vomited until nothing remained in her stomach. Then mustering every ounce of dignity she possessed, she walked away from the bank and Craig forever, vowing never again to depend on a man for anything.

Jillian's life had changed in an instant and she wasn't sure what to do. After three days cowering in bed, weeping, hunger had forced her up. In her mailbox she found an envelope from the bank with a final paycheck. Sadness engulfed her when she realized that not one person from the bank had called to check one her. Thanks to Craig, she had no friends to worry about her. When she picked up the skirt she'd been wearing the day she learned of Craig's betrayal, the letter fell out of her pocket. With nothing for her in Denver, Jillian had decided to move to Florida and start a new life.

* * * *

The third time Seth had sneezed in the captain's face, the man suggested he go home and rest until he got rid of his cold.

"Not much new you can do unless we find out if the woman is connected in any way. Beat it." He moved his capped ink pen around on the desk in lazy circles. "And Seth? Remember, you have two days to uncover new information before we close the investigation." The captain kept his eyes downcast. He knew how much it meant to Seth.

Great, Seth thought. That was all he needed on top of his cold.

Seth hated being sick, but felt so rotten, he knew he wouldn't be much good until he recovered a bit. But he didn't have much time either. He walked out of the police station heading for the drugstore for cough medicine, canned soup, and a couple of paperback action-adventure novels to see him through this bout of illness. Depression dragged at his heels. He'd spent so much time on this case and now he might have to give it up, unsolved.

Traffic was sparse on Main Street. While he waited for the light to change, he glanced toward the ocean. His heart stopped. On a bench in Water Front Park sat the woman from last night, the Yankee Gal. Now he'd started thinking of the woman as the Yankee Gal, too. Without hesitation he trotted across the grass to where she sat staring toward the sea.

Her dark hair whipped into a whirling froth around her creamy cheeks. She had something grasped tightly in her hands. Unhappiness radiated from her like a dirty cloud. Pity rose in Seth's chest. In the fresh morning light, she looked even lovelier than he remembered. He hadn't been hallucinating last night; her eyes were two different colors, one smoky blue the other sea foam green. Without warning, he sneezed.

She cringed against the bench then her eyes grew large. "You! Why are you spying on me?" She jumped up, her fists balled on her hips. A lavender envelope dropped from her lap to the ground. "If you don't stop following me, I'll go to the police!" A pale blue blouse and navy skirt hugged the curves of her perfect body.

"Don't flatter yourself, lady. I'm not following you." Seth crossed his arms to keep from reaching out to touch her. "Last I heard, this is a free country. I can go wherever I want."

Her mouth opened then snapped shut. Her lips were glossy and tempting. Before Seth had a chance to speak and tell her he was a cop, she stomped off. Overhead an angry seagull swooped, screaming, to snatch up bits of bread resting by the picnic table.

"Hey, you forgot something." Seth picked up the envelope; part of the flap was ripped open. His heart leapt into his throat. Everyone in town had known of Felicity Thornton's obsession with the color lavender. People used to see the woman wander around in shapeless lavender outfits. She'd worn heavy silver jewelry, carried a cheap silver purse, and even donned silver lace-up tennis shoes for her walks around town. The envelope had to have come from Felicity. Two words in spidery script flowed across the parcel: Jillian Bennett. At least now he knew the Yankee Gal's name. If only he could see what was inside. He lifted the torn piece but couldn't see anything on the folded paper.

"Give me that letter." She stood in front of him. Fear streaked across her face as she snatched the envelope from him, turned and ran.

He watched her as she fled across the uneven grass. He had to think of a way to get to know Miss Jillian Bennett better and find out what the envelope contained. They certainly hadn't gotten off to a good start last night. Today had been even worse. Damn this cold. His brain wasn't working worth a damn and his thoughts were all fuzzy.

Jillian reached the curb and stepped off without checking for traffic. A large black car with tinted windows came out of nowhere, heading right for her.

"Jillian!" Seth sprinted across the grass and grabbed her arm. He whirled her into his embrace a few seconds before the car would have hit her. It came so close he felt the kiss of hot air as it sped by.

"Let me go! What do you think you're doing?" Anger flashed from her odd eyes. He could smell her perfume, a flowery feminine scent. The top buttons of her blouse had come undone, exposing the soft swell of her breasts above her white lace bra.

"You fool, didn't you see the car? It almost ran you over." He could feel her heartbeat pulsing under his fingers where he grasped her arms.

"Please. You're hurting me." Bright tears sparkled in her eyes. Her voice emerged low, choked with emotion. Instead of letting her go he wanted to enfold her in his arms to keep her safe. She pulled away, breathing hard. She turned and shot across the street, then slowed to a jog and disappeared into the crowd of tourists milling about the downtown area.

He'd been so busy rescuing the woman he hadn't had time to read the license plate number of the fleeing car. Was it a near miss or had someone just tried to kill Jillian Bennett?

Chapter 3

Jillian hardly remembered the walk back to Cantrell's B-and-B. The letter squatted in her purse like a present under the tree on Christmas morning waiting to be opened. But was it a gift she wanted? Jillian was dying to find out the contents, but feared what it might reveal. What if she discovered she owed people money? Perhaps she was the child of a drug-addicted woman? Her father might have been a criminal, or could even be in jail. She had started to open the envelope just before that man had startled her. Now she wanted to be sure she was alone before she tackled it again.

Cantrell's was empty when she walked in the front door. Only the sound of RaeJean vacuuming in the back of the house greeted her. She climbed the stairs and went into her room. Inertia pulled her to the edge of the bed. She sat there, staring at the lavender parcel, unable to move, until her stomach growled. It had been several hours since RaeJean had fixed her a poached egg with toast for breakfast. Lunch wasn't included in the price of the room so she'd have to find a place in town to eat. First things first. She'd remove these foolish pantyhose, and jump into the shower. Everyone she'd seen in town had been dressed casually.

She decided she would grab a sandwich in town, then sit in the lovely park by the water to read her letter in peace. She was dying to find out what the letter contained, but still reluctant that it might be bad news. She laid a pair of blue jeans and plain blue T-shirt on the bed to wear.

She stood in the shower, with cool water soothing her body, her mind a kaleidoscope of swirling thoughts. Much as he irritated her, Jillian couldn't remove the dark-haired stranger from her mind. After all, he'd saved her from getting flattened by a car. She really should be nicer to him if he showed up again. Still, it was strange running into him last night then again today. He didn't even know her, but kept turning up. She couldn't help wonder why.

Warm water trickled down between her breasts. She remembered the feel of his hard muscular body pressed against hers. When she thought of his curly black hair and heavily muscled arms, her nipples grew hard.

"Okay, Jillian, enough!" She didn't even know the guy. He was probably married with six kids. She didn't have time for romance. Her trip to Florida marked a new beginning for Jillian. She would be an independent woman first, learn to make her own decisions, and worry about love later.

Jillian turned the cold water on full blast for an instant before toweling off and getting dressed. When she passed through the downstairs front hallway, she saw a display rack filled with brochures advertisings activities in the area. She pulled out a map of a self-guided walking tour of the Victorian mansions. Of course she planned on going back to see her house in daylight. But not before she ate and read the letter. She hoped there would be an explanation in the text to explain the retched condition of Thornton House. The thought of going into the house alone gave her the willies. She was depressed enough right now.

Jillian headed for Main Street in search of portable food. Two blocks from the ocean, she stopped at a sandwich shop.

She bought a BLT and iced tea and took them outside to sit in the warm sunshine at one of the outdoor tables.

Jillian forced food into her mouth, munching while she watched a parade of people pass by her table. Many had dogs on leashes. Pain pierced her heart. She'd always wanted a dog. Craig didn't like animals, so she'd never had one after she had gotten a place of her own.

The few bits of sandwich she'd managed to eat set in her stomach like a rock. Jillian disposed of the remains of her sandwich in the trash and headed for the park.

Anticipation got the best of her at last. Seated once more at the same bench in the park she'd occupied that morning, Jillian pulled the letter out of her purse. Overhead seagulls screeched as they dived into the water, fighting for morsels of fish. They sounded like quarreling children. She ran her fingernail under the remainder of the flap and carefully lifted it. In the middle of the sheets sat a tiny key. She put it in her pocket, took a deep breath, started to read.

Dear Jillian,

By the time you read this, I will be dead. I am so sorry I never had the chance to see you grow into the beautiful young woman I know you are today. You are probably already married with children of your own. I hope so. I made a terrible mistake by thinking there is only one true love in life, and thereby missed having a good marriage and children. Don't wait too long. Grab happiness with both hands and never let go.

Enough of an old lady's ramblings. Because you are the last of the Thorntons, I have left the family home to you. I hope you will care for it and cherish it as generations before you have.

I'm not sure how much you remember of Amelia Island or Thornton House, but you and your dear mother spent the summer with me the year you were three. I grew to love you both so much. From the first day, your mother remained very agitated and fearful. I tried to gain her confidence, but she only told me there were men searching for the two of you. She made me swear on my mother's grave, if anything happened to her, I would surrender you for adoption and cover your trail so well that no one could ever find you.

This part I hope you do not remember. Your sweet mother drowned at the end of August and we feared we'd lost you, too. The local authorities found you sitting in my dinghy near shore two days later. You were terrified, dehydrated, filthy and starving, but you were alive. While I nursed you back to health, you clung to me like a frightened limpet. Whenever I left you, you screamed at the top of your lungs. I wanted so to keep you with me, dear Jillian, but I remembered your mother's fear and my promise to her.

My attorney helped me arrange for a private adoption. The couple came here, to the island, and stayed with me until you were comfortable with them. They seemed like nice people, I hope they were good to you. When they took you away, they took a part of my heart with them. But I knew I had made the right decision. Not three weeks later, two men came here asking about you. Thank goodness I could say with a clear conscience, I had no idea where you were. They hung around, snooping for a few weeks and finally left me alone.

Now for the hardest part of this letter. Starting in my late '70's I had a series of strokes. The only reason I mention them, dear Jillian, is because while you lived here, your mother and I hid something in Thornton House I know you will want. I know that it, whatever it is, is of vital importance to you. Unfortunately since my health has deteriorated, I cannot remember where it's hidden. I urge you to make haste in searching Thornton House. I believe after my death that others will come to search for the same thing. I do not want you to lose a big part of your heritage.

Please forgive an old lady for letting you down. Know this, your mother loved you very, very much, as did I. Do your best to keep Thornton House in the family, but if you cannot, let it go and proceed with your life. I wish I had. The enclosed key is for safety deposit box 92 at the First National Bank in town. I've left a special treasure for you there, I wish it could have done more.

Good luck, dear Jillian, and God's speed.

With love,

Felicity Antonia Thornton

By the time she finished reading the letter, Jillian's face was awash with tears. A kaleidoscope of thoughts flew through her mind. If only she could remember her mother or the time they had spent here. At least now she knew her mother hadn't given her away, but had loved her very much. Jillian's heart twisted with pity. Her mother had died so young.

Now she had an explanation for her life-long fear of water, too. Ever since she could remember, Jillian had been terrified of a body of water larger than a bathtub. She'd never forgotten the summer vacation when Papa had decided it was time she learn to swim. She had just had her sixth birthday.

"Are you sure? She's frightened." Her mother's worried eyes had peeked out from under a straw hat.

"Nonsense, Mother, it's time she learned. Isn't it, my goofy-eyed girl?"

He'd carried Jillian shrieking with terror to the end of the dock, and thrown her into the lake. She screamed and sank like a rock. Papa had snatched her back out of the water and carried her to their cabin where her parents tried to calm her. Finally her mother had to call for a doctor to sedate her. They had almost been asked to leave the resort for child abuse. He never again tried to teach her to swim.

A couple walking by stared at Jillian, then hurried on. Jillian yanked a tissue out of her pocket to scrub the tears from her face. She didn't have time to digest all the information in the letter right now. She had to go to the bank.

* * * *

Seth thrashed around, struggling to free his arms. Sweat poured off his body. He gritted his teeth, but nothing seemed to help. Off in the distance he could see his sister Melinda reaching for him, crying, screaming out his name. With one mighty tug, his arms popped free, he turned and flopped to the floor. The restraining sheets fluttered down on him. He shook his head to clear the last vestiges of the nightmare that haunted his sleep. As usual when the dream came, guilt followed. Today had been no different. He should have been able to save Melinda, even though he wasn't on the Island when she died. She was his baby sister and somehow he should have been able to keep her safe.

Seth stood, tossed the sheets back on the bed, and stretched to get the kinks out of his weary body. It had been more than two years since his sister Melinda had died from a drug overdose while on vacation on Amelia Island. The whole family had been shocked because Melinda never had anything to do with drugs, didn't even drink alcohol. How could it have happened? Seth vowed he wouldn't rest until he found the answer. He quit his job with the Braintree, Massachusetts police force and moved here to investigate her death. When he heard of an opening on the Amelia Island force, he signed on and hadn't looked back.

He missed his family—called and wrote them frequently—but he'd only been able to afford one trip back. All of his seven siblings were married now, having kids of their own. His girlfriend, Sarah, had promised to wait, but when his long vacation drifted into an obsession, she turned to another man.

The Yankee Gal reminded him of Melinda. The dark hair, petite curvy figure, creamy skin, but of course, the eyes were different. He'd never seen anyone with such unusual eyes.

Scratching at his chest hairs, he wandered to the bathroom to shower. Seth chuckled as he adjusted the faucets. He wanted to chat with Letty and find out what she knew about the Yankee Gal. He couldn't imagine what she might have to do with the drug action in the house, but still he had to find out.

Seth wiped the steam from the mirror before lathering his face and scraping off his whiskers. In the bedroom, he stepped into clean jeans and pulled a T-shirt over his head. The nap had done him a world of good. He felt almost human now, his cold all but gone. Once he filled his stomach, he'd be ready to confront Letty to pick her brain for information about the woman.

Padding to the kitchen, Seth opened the refrigerator to find, once again, he'd forgotten to shop for food. Four cans of Bud Lite sat along side white cartons of leftover Chinese takeout on the center of the shelf. When he opened the top of one carton, a malodorous odor wafted out. He chucked it in the trash, deciding to eat in town once again.

Seth checked his pockets—keys, wallet—and his holstered gun. He shut the apartment door behind him and trotted off toward town. He intended to find the answers to solve his sister's death.

* * * *

"Here we are, box number 92. If I could have your key, Ms. Bennett?" The bank manager smiled.

Jillian's fingers shook so much she almost dropped the key before she managed to place it in his hand. The man inserted it along side his and pulled out the metal box. He held the receptacle out in front of him like it held the Crown Jewels. She wished it did. Together the two of them walked into a room the size of a double telephone booth. He placed the container on the table.

"I'll leave this with you. When you're finished, come find me so we can return it to the safe." He backed out, shutting the door behind him.

Jillian stood staring at the case like it was a cobra ready to strike. Wiping her moist palms along the sides of her jeans, she stepped forward and lifted the lid.

A packet of photos rested inside, barely taking up enough room to justify the price of the rental. Jillian let out a steady stream of air. She hadn't even realized she'd been holding her breath. Her shoulders slumped. She felt the faint beginning of a headache crawl up her neck. Jillian had hoped the box contained money, stocks or gems—anything of value that might help her out of her predicament. She'd cut all her ties in Colorado and had to stay, at least for a while. She was woefully short on funds and had to come up with property tax money in two weeks. Her luck remained consistently bad.

Gingerly, she slid the photos out of their packet. There were only twelve. The color images had been shot outdoors in what was obviously an arid region. The background consisted of sand and sparse vegetation. The first picture revealed a beautiful dark-haired woman wearing shorts and a halter-top, standing next to a tall Saguaro cactus. The next showed a tiny adobe-style house, once again with the woman in the foreground. She rested on her knees in front of a scrubby garden full of bright flowers and more than a few weeds. The close up highlighted the woman's face and Jillian gasped. She might have been staring at herself in a mirror. Except that the woman's eyes were normal, both brown.

"Mama." The word came out in a sigh. Tears blurred Jillian's vision. She had to stop to clear them before she could go on. Two more photos revealed the broken-down shack that had been upgraded into a modest home. Not another human being or building could be seen in the background, only miles of desert dotted with cactus. Far in the distance, a ruddy mesa stood guard against the brilliant aqua sky.

In the next picture, the woman stood sideways, fingers framing her huge protruding belly. She glowed, and looked positively ecstatic. A couple more shots of the woman and house, now a scruffy dog of indeterminate ancestry lounged at her feet.

Only two pictures remained. Now a man stood by the front of the house, his head thrown back, laughing. The dog pulled at a rubber toy he held. Reluctantly Jillian pulled out the last piece. These pictures were the only records she had of her real parents. She gasped. A buzzing sound filled her head. It showed the close-up of the man holding a baby. He smiled right at the camera, his wild black hair blowing in a stiff breeze. His eyes were two different colors, one blue, the other green.

* * * *

Seth trailed the last French fry through the blob of catsup on his plate before popping it into his mouth.

"More iced tea, Seth?" The waitress hovered by his table with a pitcher in one hand and his check in the other.

"No thanks, Gloria. I'm stuffed." Seth pulled out his money clip and dropped bills on the table. "Everything tasted delicious, as usual."

He slid out of the booth, looked out the window and noticed the Yankee Gal coming out of the front door of the bank across the street. She glanced his way before dropping her head. He could see her eyes were red and blotchy, like she'd been crying. Her shoulders were rounded with defeat, her unhappiness broadcast for anyone to see. Seth sat watching her shamble off down Main Street. He had the strongest desire to go to her, take her in his arms to shut out the world and make the hurt go away.

While he watched, a man peeled himself off the building alongside the bank and ambled after the woman. He'd been leaning there reading a newspaper. *I guess I'm not the only one interested in the Yankee Gal,* Seth thought. He hurried outside.

Chapter 4

Jillian walked down the street aimlessly. All around her groups of people went about their business, some laughing and having a good time. The handsome man in the photo had to be her father. Could he still be alive? How would she ever find him? She didn't even know his name.

But from the sound of the letter, Jillian's great-aunt didn't know anymore about her father than she did. Her aunt had medical problems and might not have remembered at all. No, the only choice Jillian had now was to search the house for her hidden treasure. She didn't have much time. She'd need a huge treasure to fix up Thornton House. Felicity had been poor, so the treasure probably wasn't money. What else could it be? If only she had a friend to go to for help, advice, a shoulder to cry on.

Once more she halted, causing a teenage boy on a skateboard to swerve around her.

"Watch it, dude." He gave her the finger and kept going.

Jillian examined the street behind he. She had the creepy feeling of being watched. All she saw were three middle-aged ladies loaded with shopping bags getting into an SUV, a tourist wearing a horrid bright-print shirt, and a young woman pushing a baby carriage. Jillian marked her suspicion up to her ragged nerves and lack of sleep. She had to stop dawdling, hurry to the house and start searching to find the treasure, whatever it was.

The honk of a horn brought Jillian to a standstill. She'd almost walked out in front of a car again. Once the vehicle had gone by, its driver scowling at her, she crossed the street. On the corner stood a stately Victorian home. White filigree porches decorated the front of both stories of the beige house. Black shutters framed all the bright clean windows, and two brick chimneys were visible on the red roof. From the plaque on the corner of the house Jillian could tell it was part of the walking tour. Why couldn't her house look like this one?

Jillian knew she should hurry to her house to start hunting before it got any later, but curiosity about what she might find, or worse—not find, made her hesitate. She pulled the brochure out of her purse. She would love to see all the houses but not today. She stopped in front of Addison House and watched a young couple emerge from the front door, smiling. A happy couple enjoying their vacation, or perhaps their honeymoon.

Jillian turned away and walked down the street. She should be on her honeymoon with Craig, not here worrying about her future. Craig, the rat, had gone to Maui on his honeymoon.

Jillian took a breath and stopped once more. Long shadows angled across the lawn of the oddly shaped Fairbanks House. A cool breeze whispered along her bare arms, reminding her that even a Florida winter could be chilly in the afternoon. Barely glancing at the beige house, she picked up her pace. No way did she want to be in Thornton House after dark. She continued along the streets, her mind a whirl of thoughts.

The bleat of a car horn bumped Jillian back to the present. She found herself standing in front of Thornton House. How long she'd been staring at the place she couldn't tell. Dragging her feet, she walked up the rotting steps and stepped gingerly over gaps in the wooden porch. She took the key from her pocket, inserted it in the lock and opened the door. A strong gust of wind sizzled along the back of her neck, lifting her hair. The trees tops danced in the freshening breeze. She could almost swear she heard a voice moaning her name.

"Jillllliiiiiaannnn."

* * * *

Seth played caboose on the three-person parade traveling along the sidewalk. The man following Jillian didn't have to be careful. She was oblivious. Once again a car had almost hit her as she wandered through town. Seth couldn't imagine what was going through her mind, but she seemed terribly unhappy. He had to find out how she fit into this whole mess he was investigating.

From his hiding place a half block away, he saw her walk carefully up the rickety front steps of Thornton House. The man following her strolled by, eyes front, head down, never glancing her way. Didn't matter, she was still unaware that anyone was tailing her.

Seth watched the guy cross the quiet residential street. The man hunkered next to a huge tree and quickly scanned the area before he pulled a cell phone out of his pocket. When he'd reached for the phone, the wind flipped his Hawaiian shirt up and Seth saw a holstered gun at the back of the guy's waistband. Could he be guarding the Yankee Gal? Or getting ready to kill her?

Activity around the house had slowed to a trickle in recent weeks. Seth couldn't figure out why. Had the Yankee Gal brought money for more drugs? Maybe the gang had found another place to stash its poison before sending it north. He ground his teeth in frustration. This case had been his life for over a year. He wasn't about to lose it now.

Seth saw Hawaiian Shirt flip close his phone, pocket it and mosey his way. Seth bent over, pretending to tie his shoe as the stranger walked by. When he was a block away, Seth ambled after him. Seth couldn't confront the woman now. He'd catch up with her later at Cantrell's B-and-B. Right now it was more important to follow the follower to see where that led.

The guy was easy to follow. His bright patterned shirt stood out among the sparse crowd on Main Street. Seth could see the man wore dress pants and wingtip shoes. The stalker hesitated at the corner, then crossed Center Street before he sauntered down Second Street toward the Hampton Inn. It fit. This guy wasn't the B-and-B type. Seth decided to kill time at the Palace Saloon with a quick beer then he'd go check up on the stalker.

He stepped inside the door of the Palace Saloon, let his eyes adjust, then took his usual place at the end of the bar—information central for the town.

"Pour me a draft, will you, Willie?" Seth pulled out his notebook and a pen.

The bartender placed a frosty glass on a coaster in front of Seth and walked down to the other end of the bar to serve another customer.

In an economy of words Seth jotted down the man's description: Around six-foot tall, trim, brown hair mixed with gray, probably late forties—about fifteen years older than Seth, no obvious marks or scars he could see. He had no idea on eye color since the man wore sunglasses. Seth had noticed a flashy diamond ring on his right pinky when he was using the cell phone. He could be mob muscle. The idea sent a chill down Seth's back that had nothing to do with the air conditioning in the Palace. If the guy was a hit man, the Yankee Gal didn't stand a chance.

* * * *

Jillian tiptoed into the dark house, slipping the key into her pocket. She decided to leave the door open, hoping some heat would penetrate from outside. She was surprised by how cool northern Florida could be in late winter.

She breathed in short, shallow gasps. Nervous sweat trickled down her sides. The round central hallway had doors leading off of it, like spokes in a giant wheel. Most of the once-beautiful parquet floor tiles were missing; the rest were chipped and filthy.

Stepping with care, Jillian walked through an archway into a large room. Dim light penetrated the gloom through the boarded up windows. The bare floorboards were warped and stained. All the furniture and draperies were long gone. Jillian could see the outlines in the faded wallpaper where pictures once hung. A massive fireplace dominated the outside wall. The smell of mold mixed with animal droppings made her gag. Soot and ashes had blackened the white marble mantle to an almost uniform gray color. Jillian stood in the middle of the room, rubbing her arms against the chill. She'd make a list of things to do before coming back tomorrow for more exploring; and she'd bring a sweater and a flashlight.

She retraced her dusty footprints into the entrance hall and went into the former dining room. The remains of a crystal chandelier, festooned with spider webs, hung crookedly from a tarnished ornate chain. Jillian glanced around the empty room, then closed her eyes imagining what it must have been like at one time. There would have been a long rosewood dining table with sixteen matching chairs. She scrunched her eyes more, surrendering to her dream world. Candles flickered on the table while from above a massive sideboard, wall sconces glowed, casting dim light and causing muted shadows to dance around the room. She could almost see Scarlet at one end of the table, with Rhett scowling at her from the other.

With a sigh, Jillian pried her eyes open to survey the dismal room again. There wasn't enough money in the world to restore this house. A tear slid down her cheek.

A scratching noise froze Jillian in her tracks. Her mouth grew dry. Moisture dotted her upper lip. She stood alone in a huge, empty house, and no one knew she was here. Holding her breath, she crept to the window and peered out. She sagged and breathed a sigh of relief. The branch of a tree was scraping against the window. The gnarled tree bowed toward the house. A good wind could bring the whole thing crashing into the dining room. Well, she couldn't worry about it now.

Pushing on, Jillian toured a library, its shelves bare, the kitchen, adjoining pantry, and maid's quarters with tiny bathroom. She pried open a warped door near the pantry and stared into the dark hole of the basement. Chilled moldy air wafted up to greet her. The wooden stairs leading down into the cellar had long ago rotted away. Jillian shivered and slammed the door shut. It was like looking to the Black Hole of Calcutta. Even if there had been stairs, no way was she venturing down there.

The silhouettes crawling across the floor grew dim. Time to leave. Jillian hurried toward the front of the house. Back in the main hall, something soft brushed against her head. She let out a yelp and swiped away a glob of spider web.

"Oh, yuck, disgusting." She pulled the sticky froth off her face with a shudder. When she brushed her T-shirt she deposited a black trail down the front.

"I cannot do this now. Tomorrow I'll start early, do a thorough exploration." Then what? She was too dejected to worry about it. Leaning against the wall of the stairway, Jillian rummaged around in her purse until she found her old checkbook. She ripped a deposit slip out to jot down a few items: flashlight, batteries, paper towels, a sandwich and soda for lunch.

Jillian stopped to run her finger over the name of the bank on the deposit slip. With her banking experience she knew she could probably get a job locally. She really didn't want to work in a bank again, it would remind her too much of Craig, still it was all she knew. She shuddered and shifted her weight. The wall behind her moved.

Chapter 5

Terror rippled through Jillian, her heart hammered in her chest. She staggered back staring at the gaping panel. A secret passage? Could this be where Felicity hid the treasure?

Outside the wind picked up once more. It moaned through a hundred cracks in the house. Jillian took a step closer to the opening. Above her, a floorboard snapped. She froze. Silence, then another noise, closer to the top of the stairs. Out of the corner of her eyes, she saw a gray blur. A rat ran over her foot. She screamed and flew out the front door. She slammed it and her fingers shook so hard she could barely turn the key in the lock. She ran to the sidewalk, afraid to look back. She had the creepiest feeling she would see eyes staring out at her from a front window.

By the time she'd traveled the three blocks to Cantrell's, her nervous sweat had dried on her clothes. The sun had slipped closer to the edge of the horizon, bringing fresh breezes in from the sea. Now she was stiff with cold.

Jillian dragged herself through the gate and up the steps to the front door. Her teeth chattered like castanets. She eased inside, hoping to hurry to her room without being seen. She wasn't in the mood for Letty's small talk tonight. Jillian stopped and sniffed. Smelled like chicken on the menu for dinner. She had her foot on the first stair when the sound of laughter stopped her.

"I swear, Seth, you could charm the birds right out of the trees. Why, if I was ten years younger, I'd set my cap for you myself." Letty's sugary voice filled the house. Curious to see to whom the woman was talking, Jillian tiptoed toward the parlor. A board squeaked and Letty saw her.

"Jillian honey, there you are. Come on in here." She came over. "There's someone I'd like you to meet."

Jillian shoved the sweaty curls off her forehead then stared at her grimy fingers in disbelief. Looking down she saw muddy streaks decorating her shirt and jeans. The toes of her sneakers where covered with dust. What the hell, she thought. Things couldn't be much worse. She brought her head up, thrust her shoulders back and walked into the room.

Sitting on the couch was the man from last night and this morning. His tousled dark hair shone in the light from the fireplace. Muscles bulged under the sleeves of his yellow polo shirt and the fabric of his jeans pulled tight over brawny thighs.

"Jillian honey, I'd like you to meet Detective Seth Falconer."

He stood up and held out his hand. He towered over her.

Detective? He's a cop? Jillian wanted to smack the grin off his face for scaring her so. Instead she marched up to him and stuck out her chin.

"Detective Falconer, I'm Jillian Bennett. Would you please tell me why the hell you've been following me?"

Seth Falconer grinned. "Hate to disappoint you, Miss Bennett. I told you before, I'm not following you."

"Mercy, how excitin'." Letty actually clapped her hands like a child. "Is our Jillian a famous criminal, Seth?" She drained her glass before strolling to the liquor cart. "Fess up now, Jillian, are you a wanted woman?" The bottle clanked against the glass as she poured, then she returned to Jillian. "Here, drink this brandy, have a seat. You must be all done in." Letty handed her a glass. "Your hands are like ice cubes. Mercy, girl, you're going to have to learn to carry a sweater or jacket with you in the evening. It's winter."

Once again, Letty had changed the topic, leaving Jillian's mind awhirl. She collapsed into the wing chair with her brandy snifter then popped up. "Oh, I'm filthy. I'll ruin your chair."

"Don't worry about dirtying the chair, honey, it'll clean."

Confusion fogged Jillian's brain. A wanted woman? What had Letty been babbling about? She stared at the handsome man. "Why would you think I've done anything illegal, Letty?"

"Well, because Seth is a police officer, of course. He helps to keep Amelia Island free of the criminal element." Letty batted her eyes at the man. "Don't you, Seth?"

Jillian sat back on the chair. She had no idea why a cop would be following her, and it made her nervous.

"Yup, I'm afraid so." He picked up his beer stein. "And I'm not following you. Last night I was hunting for my neighbor's cat when I found you standing in the rain like a drowned muskrat. This morning," he stopped to sip from his glass, "I was on my way to breakfast."

He refused to meet her eyes. She saw a faint flush on his face, and alarm bells pealed in her head. She simply did not believe in coincidences.

"You've obviously never lived in a small town, honey. Places like the Island, everyone knows everyone, and their business." Letty took another generous slug of her drink.

RaeJean came to the doorway, her lower lip thrust out. "Dinner's ready. Best come while it's hot, I ain't got all night, you know."

"You'll stay and dine with us, won't you, Seth?" Letty emptied her glass.

"Thanks, but I have plans. Maybe another time." He rose. "Ms. Bennett, nice to meet you."

Jillian merely nodded as he walked out of the parlor. She heard him in conversation with RaeJean in the hallway.

"Hey, RaeJean, how's Marcus doing in Atlanta?"

"He's great, Seth, straight A's. And the college girls," RaeJean giggled, "they're lining up to date my handsome boy." Their voices faded until Jillian heard the front door close.

"I'm going to run upstairs to change for dinner," Jillian said.

"No need, sugar. It's just the two of us. Malcolm's off somewhere." She let her fingers drift through the air. "Doing research, I believe."

"Research? For what?" She'd wondered how the man could afford to stay here without working.

"Oh, he's a writer, gonna do a book about the Island. Fiction, I believe, but of course, you have to detail the history correctly. Amelia Island is an interesting place." Letty's attention was clearly ebbing. "Malcolm's novel is about pirates, Spanish galleons, treasure, maybe the old fort." She shrugged. "Best hurry up, gal, or the food will be cold."

Jillian dashed upstairs to her room and washed up. She wanted to talk to Letty and hoped all the booze would loosen the woman's tongue. Quickly pulling on a clean shirt, Jillian headed to the dining room.

RaeJean's crunchy fried chicken melted in her mouth, the biscuits were airy, the gravy creamy and smooth, the vegetables crisp. Jillian dug in. Letty sat opposite her at the long table, drinking wine and pushing a few morsels around her plate.

Jillian stopped chewing to sip her iced tea. "Have you known Detective Falconer for a long time, Letty?"

"My mercy, no. He only came to our island a couple years ago. He's from Up East—Boston I believe."

"I thought he sounded different from everyone else around here." Jillian speared another chicken breast. "Why is he interested in me, Letty?"

Letty's gaze drifted off. "Why?"

"Yes. I still think it's curious the way I keep running into the man, even in a town this small. What did you tell him about me?"

"Just the facts, ma'am." Letty hooted out a phony laugh. "You'll find our town cops keep their fingers on the pulse of the community. Most everybody round here thought Felicity Thornton was the last of her line, so we were surprised when you said you'd inherited the house."

"But how would anyone in town know about me?" Jillian hid her shaking hands on her lap. She never liked being the center of attention.

"Shoot, honey, RaeJean heard us talking about your house last night, probably told a few friends."

"I 'spect your lawyer-man told a few folks." She emptied her glass then refilled it.

Jillian couldn't imagine how the woman managed to stay upright with the quantity of booze she had in her.

"What difference does it make, sugar. You aren't in trouble with the law, are you?"

"No! I've never even had a parking ticket." Thoughts of the proper Craig flitted into her mind. He would be horrified if he thought she might be under police scrutiny for whatever reason. To hell with him.

Letty popped a tiny piece of biscuit into her mouth. "What you gonna do about that gigantic old house, honey?"

"I don't know." Her stomach full, Jillian sighed and propped her elbows on the table. "My first thought was to turn it into a B-and-B, like yours. Since I've seen the place..." Jillian shuddered. "Now, I have no idea. It will take a fortune to renovate the place." She wasn't about to tell Letty that she only has two weeks to come up with money for insurance and property taxes or she'd lose the house. "I stopped by to peek inside today. It's a dump. Tomorrow I want to go over the house, see if there's anything I can sell. I just don't know what to do."

Tears massed in her eyes, threatening to spill out. She hadn't cried this much since Craig's betrayal. Time to call it a night. Jillian pushed herself up from the table. "If you'll excuse me, Letty, I'm going up to my room."

"Sure, sugar. Sleep well. I'll see you in the mornin'."

Jillian passed RaeJean in the front hall on her way to the stairs. "Great meal again, RaeJean. Thanks."

Surprise flitted across the woman's face, then she smiled. "You're mighty welcome, Miss."

Once in her room, Jillian shoved a pillow behind her shoulders and settled on the bed. Opening her notebook, she glanced over her finances. She needed to find a cheaper place to stay while she explored her options. Cantrell's was wonderful, but pricey. Ferndandina Beach was a tiny tourist town. There wouldn't be many job openings, at least not one paying enough to support her. Maybe she should explore Jacksonville.

She removed the map of the Island from the pocket of her jeans. There were other towns on the island, large hotels, golf resorts. She grabbed her bank deposit slip for scratch paper, and added 'local newspaper' to her list. She pulled the lavender envelope out of her purse to reread the letter. Nothing new jumped out; her predicament remained the same. She shoved it back into her purse. Too weary to even brush her teeth, Jillian threw her clothes on the floor, pulled the covers over herself and flipped off the light.

She slept in a dreamless coma, not waking until nearly nine. She hurried through her shower, jumped into her clothes, making sure to add a sweater, then shoved her room key and wallet into her pockets, along with a pencil and small notebook. No need to take her purse. She planned to explore the house most of the day. Jillian thrust the purse in a dresser drawer. She locked the bedroom door behind her and hurried downstairs to the kitchen.

"There you are. I was about ready to go up and see if you were still breathing." RaeJean stood near the backdoor, a black plastic purse looped over her arm. "You sit yourself down. I'll make you something to eat."

"Oh, no, you're ready to go. I can make breakfast. I only want some coffee and toast anyhow."

RaeJean thumped her purse on the counter, took an apron from the back of the door and tied it around her waist. "No, you aren't going to have just toast; you'll eat a proper breakfast. Girl, you are nothing but skin and bones. I made pancakes for Mr. Malcolm this morning and I have plenty of batter left." With an economy of motion, RaeJean bounced from refrigerator to stove to the warming coffeepot.

"Can I help?" Jillian pulled out a kitchen chair.

"Orange juice in the fridge, fresh squeezed today. Help yourself while the griddle is heating."

Jillian poured a tumbler of juice and brought it to the table. "This is delicious!"

"Should be. I picked the fruit off a tree in the back yard this morning."

RaeJean flipped the stack of pancakes onto a plate and deposited it in front of Jillian. She arranged butter, syrup and jam on the table.

"I'd like to talk to you about something, if I may," Jillian said. She dug in and let the doughy sweet mess slide down her throat, groaning with pleasure.

"'Bout what?" RaeJean asked.

"Letty said you've lived your whole life on Amelia Island. I wondered if you might have known my great-aunt, Felicity Thornton?"

"Why sure, I knew Ms. Felicity real well. I'd be glad to talk some about her, but I don't have time right now. I have a doctor's appointment." She stood by the door, waiting.

"No hurry. I'll catch up with you later." Jillian popped another bite of pancake in her mouth. "You go on, I'll clean up my mess. It's my fault I slept so late."

"You're a sweet child. I'll be back by noon." With a wave, she turned and walked out the door.

Through the kitchen window Jillian watched birds chasing one another in the orange trees while she finished her meal. She cleared the table before rinsing and placing her dirty dishes in the dishwasher.

Puffy white clouds drifted across the sky, a breeze riffled the hedge along the street. Jillian tossed the sweater over her shoulders and headed toward town. She might as well return the rental car. Everyday it cost her money she couldn't afford to lose. She was already running low on cash.

* * * *

"That's all I've managed to find out so far." Seth finished his oral report to Captain Burgess and sat back in his chair. He didn't mention how attracted he was to the woman. How when he'd seen her enter Letty's last night, her thin arms blue with the cold, the cuticles of her ragged fingernails chewed to the quick, he wanted to take her in his arms and protect her. She looked like a child who had played too long in the sandbox. Streaks of dirt festooned her shirt and cobwebs hung off her jeans. When her incredible eyes met his, he saw dark circles of fatigue smudged under them. Seth didn't think she had any idea how beautiful she was, even in her disheveled state.

"Don't you agree?" Captain Burgess stared at him with a smirk on his face.

"Sorry, what did you say?"

"I said, maybe you could ask her out to dinner, or invite her for a walk or something." He shook his head. "The Yankee Gal must be something else. I haven't seen you this flustered since you spotted that movie star filming down here last summer. If she's going to have this effect on you, maybe I should do the interrogating." He wiggled his thick gray eyebrows at Seth.

"What, and have your wife blame me? No way, I'll follow through."

Burgess tapped his pen on the desk. "I'll fax Denver PD to see if they have any info on her, but I seriously doubt she's involved. Right now, I'm more concerned for her safety. If the drug gang thinks she muscled into their territory, they might attempt to harm her."

Seth broke into a cold sweat. Visions of his sister on the slab at the morgue flashed through his mind, her skin the color of marble, the dusky tinge of her lips and fingernails. He stood abruptly and grabbed his jacket from the back of the chair. He'd be damned if he let those animals kill another young woman.

"I have a feeling she'll want to go back to Thornton House to explore it in daylight. I'm going to check on the stalker then head over to the house to see if I can help her." With a wave, he walked away.

Seth hesitated in front of the station to check his watch. The Yankee Gal should be safe at ten o'clock in the morning, but still, he'd better hurry.

It only took him two minutes to get to the Hampton Inn. He walked through the double doors of the motor lodge, scrambling for a good excuse to inquire about one of their guests. As he reached the counter, he saw the very man he was interested in jogging down the steps from the second floor. Seth turned his back and walked to the bookshelves near the fireplace. The man exchanged pleasantries with the clerk at the front counter. A moment later he heard the outer door creak. Seth waited a few seconds then walked up to the desk.

"Hi. Hate to bother you but I think I just spotted a friend of mine go out the door. Wasn't that my old buddy Bill Miller from Atlanta?" Seth gave the clerk his most disarming smile. The young woman was probably a part-timer. He didn't know her.

"No sir, his name is John Smith, from Savannah." The phone rang. "Excuse me?"

He nodded his thanks before leaving. No sense in trying to worm any more information out of her.

Seth hurried outside in time to see a long black car with dark-tinted windows pull out of the parking lot. He snatched his notebook from his pocket and jotted down the Georgia tag number.

"John Smith from Savannah, my ass," he murmured. He headed up the street toward Thornton House to check on that Yankee Gal, Miss Jillian Bennett.

* * * *

Jillian shifted the brown paper grocery bag to her other arm while she inserted the key in the lock. She'd purchased everything on her list at the drugstore, even remembering to add a pair of rubber gloves to keep the worst of the filth off her skin. On her way to the house, she had stopped at a deli to buy a sandwich and can of soda for lunch. The coke would be warm in a few hours, but it didn't matter. At least she wouldn't have to interrupt her search to go to town for lunch. And eat she would. When she'd slipped on her size four jeans this morning, they were noticeably loose.

While she and Craig were together, he'd always made sure she ate—too often she forgot. He'd make sure she had her mittens in winter and pour her cool drinks in summer after she'd come in from jogging. In retrospect, she realized he'd treated her like a child and a convenient mistress. "And I let him."

Jillian walked into the parlor and set the bag of food on the mantel to keep it out of harm's way. She'd seen a lot of mouse droppings on the floor and didn't want to share her lunch with any critters.

The first order of business was to explore the panel she'd discovered yesterday. She walked into the dim foyer and down the short hallway, her heart beating madly. Wouldn't it be wonderful if she found the treasure so easily?

"Fat chance, not with my luck," she murmured. Overhead a board squeaked. She froze, held her breath till she almost fainted. She stood motionless for a minute, then sucked air into her lungs. "Jillian, stop being silly! This is a very old house. It must be full of creaks and groans." Squaring her shoulders, she marched to the panel.

It still hung askew, so she pushed against it. The plank fell inside the stairwell with a thud. She waited, but heard nothing from above. She clicked on the flashlight and trained the beam into the darkness under the stairs. The space was empty except for a few million dust bunnies, enough spider webs to drive an arachnophobic crazy, and an old string-less tennis racket. She probed every corner of the space with her light, but couldn't see anything else. She was disappointed but not terribly surprised.

Jillian turned away from the gaping hole. She had no idea where to start. Once again she heard the snap of an expanding board. She decided to tackle the second story of the house to see what was making the noise.

She tested each step before putting her weight on it. "Dummy, you should have told RaeJean where you'd be today in case of an accident. You could fall and lie here for months before anyone found you." The very idea chilled her. Letty knew she planned to explore the house, but if she'd been drinking, would she remember?

Jillian reached the top of the stairs and sent her light beam down the hallway. A single window high at the top of the stairs let in a little light, but it was still darker up here than on the main floor. A faded runner lay down the center, its colors dulled to a universal gray. Doors along both sides of the hallway were closed. Jillian grasped the first doorknob and opened the door.

A blast of wind smacked her in the face and tried to wrench the door away from her. The square space had served as a bedroom. A broken window had been boarded up, but gaps allowed the weather to blow in. A large water stain on the floor indicted the glass had been missing for a long time.

Jillian stepped back into the hall and closed the door before she moved on. She opened three more doors, all bedrooms, all empty, and two bathrooms. Old-fashioned clawfooted tubs with trails of reddish-brown leaking from the faucets dominated both. The neglected fixtures were streaked with rust. She had no doubt the rest of the rooms were empty too.

Growing increasingly depressed, Jillian grasped the knob of the next room. It refused to open but the lock plate looked new. She stood for a moment then pulled out the key ring. Sure enough, the shorter key fit the lock. With a click the door swung open. It was very heavy and when she gave it a thump she heard the dull clang. It had been reinforced with metal.

When she entered the room, her mouth dropped open in surprise. The large room was flooded with light. A huge four-poster bed sat against one wall, with a well-used fireplace opposite it. Instead of a bedspread, the bed had been covered with a gorgeous multi-colored quilt. White muslin curtains edged all four windows. Jillian stepped inside to investigate.

A door to her left led to a bathroom. The fixtures in this room were modern. Off to her right, the sitting room had been turned into a makeshift kitchen. It contained an apartment-size refrigerator, hot plate, and good-sized microwave oven. An ice cream table with two chairs rested against the wall. Other than a coating of dust, the room's occupant might have run to the store and could return at any moment.

"It's a tiny apartment." Her words echoed, bouncing off the high ceiling of the room. It had never crossed her mind where her aunt had lived before her death. Jillian sort of assumed she'd been in an apartment closer to town or senior residence of some kind.

Jillian walked to the window and peered out. Dark clouds roiled in the sky and the wind had picked up. The view was spectacular. She could see the tops of houses, a thick stand of trees, and off in the distance the sparkle of water. She hadn't realized the house set so close to the ocean. Looking down, she saw the back lawn had been neglected like the rest of the house. It had been much larger at one time, before nature had encroached. She could still see a faint path leading from the back into the woods. She felt a funny fluttery sensation in her chest. A long-buried memory tried to surface, but before Jillian could grab it, it slipped away.

When she sat on the edge of the bed, a cloud of dust rose. She sneezed. Of course the room was dusty. It hadn't been occupied in over a year.

An old rotary-style phone rested on the nightstand next to the bed. Jillian picked up the receiver, but there was no dial tone. Thoughts scrambled around in her brain like demented mice. Obviously her aunt had been living in the house. Would she, Jillian, be brave enough to do the same? It would allow her to search the house faster, as well as saving her scads of money. She noticed a pile of rope by the corner window. On closer inspection she saw it was a fire ladder. Good idea in this musty old house with only one door leading out of the apartment.

A nineteen-inch color television perched atop of the bureau opposite the bed. One whole wall consisted of bookshelves, crammed full of paperbacks. An avid reader herself, Jillian was drawn to the shelves like a magnet. Romances and mysteries dominated the group, with a few biographies thrown in. She made a mental note again to check out the local library for information on the history of this house and the island. Perhaps that would give her some clues as to the whereabouts of her treasure. She could ask Malcolm, but there was something about him she didn't trust.

She'd think about this while she continued to explore. Time was growing short. She examined the hall door, glad to see a deadlock had been installed; the wood was reinforced with steel. Nonetheless, her elderly aunt had been living alone in a house that a five-year-old could have broken into with no trouble.

Jillian removed the key from the lock, exited the room and pulled the door closed behind her. With a twist of the wrist, she locked the door and pocketed the key.

Only two doors left to check, the one at the end of the hallway next to her aunt's room and the one directly across from the apartment. When she turned the knob on the end door, it didn't budge. She tried again, rattling the knob hard and yanking at it.

"Need help?" A male voice said so close in her ear she felt his breath.

Chapter 6

Jillian shrieked in surprise. Outside a clap of thunder echoed her scream.

Seth jumped back, his hands clapped over his ears. "Take it easy. I'm not after your fair white body. I only wanted to make sure you were okay. You seem to need a lot of rescuing."

Jillian huddled against the door. Anger replaced fear. "Don't you *ever* do that again. I almost had a heart attack. What are you doing here, anyhow?" She wanted to kick him in the shins, or higher, for scaring her.

"I figured you'd want to check the place over in daylight, so I came over to see if you wanted company." He glanced around the gloomy hallway. "You are kind of isolated here."

"How did you get in?" Jillian crossed her arms, furious at the intrusion.

"The door was open. I guess you didn't shut it tight when you came in. This is a creepy old place and from the clouds in the sky I'd guess another storm is headed inland. I wanted make sure you hadn't fallen or gotten yourself locked in a closet or something. I'll leave if you like."

She was unsure if she wanted him to stay or leave. Why did he keep turning up? Did he know something about the house he wasn't telling her? Dark clouds scudded across the little window, turning the hallway into a dismal tunnel.

"I can take care of myself."

"I'm sure you can." The lopsided grin on his face denied his words. His adorable dimples jumped into his cheeks. "How about I give the door a shake before I leave? It's probably just stuck."

With a nod, Jillian bit the inside of her lip. She slid to one side, out of his way. Seth grabbed the knob and pulled with all his strength. The muscles of his back bunched up; the sight of his butt in tight blue jeans made Jillian's mouth go dry. No doubt about it, from top to bottom, the man was a hunk. Instead of giving him a swift kick, she wished he'd take her in his strong arms and protect her. Jillian gave herself a mental shake. Nope. Time to become an independent woman.

"I think it's locked. Do you have a key?"

"No, but maybe there's one in here." She unlocked the apartment door and walked inside.

"Wow." The policeman stepped in then did a slow turn to observe the entire place. "I had no idea this was here." His face reddened. "I mean the rest of the place is such a mess."

Jillian wasn't sure how much information to share with the stranger, even if he was a cop. An incredibly sexy cop. "I'll have to check with my lawyer, George Bannerman, but I believe my aunt probably lived here until her death." She studied the humble furnishings. "I doubt she had much money. She sold off most of the furniture just to survive." Jillian's heart ached for the lonely old woman she never knew.

"Any reason you want to look behind the next door?" He walked to the window, pushed the curtain aside and peeked out. He moved like a panther at midnight. "Actually, I think it must be the door to the attic. Not enough space for a room there."

"No reason. It will keep, I guess. I've been exploring a bit, but so far all the rooms are empty." She plopped on the bed, wanting to cry again. If only she had someone to advise her, tell her what to do.

He seemed to be reading her thoughts. "Searching for anything special?" Seth leaned his long frame against the doorjamb, his hands shoved in the pocket of his snug jeans.

Cute, but nosy. "No, Mr. Falconer, I'm simply exploring my house. Why?"

He seemed to hesitate, then shrugged. "Just curious."

"You certainly are. Is there any particular reason you've been quizzing Letty Cantrell about me? Or is it an occupational habit? Have to check out every new person in town."

His eyebrows moved together in a frown. "No, I don't inquire about each person who crosses the bridge. Only those I find standing in the rain in the middle of the night, claiming to be lost, Ms. Bennett. I thought you might have escaped from a locked ward somewhere. It's my duty to keep the island safe."

Jillian had the urge to stamp her foot, except she was sitting down. She couldn't slap him; he was the law.

"Your precious island is safe from me, Mr. Falconer. If I remember correctly, I didn't invite you into my house. Unless you have a search warrant, you may leave." She stood, brought her chin up, attempting a tough demeanor.

"It's Detective Falconer, but since you're one of us now, you can call me Seth. And lady? I wouldn't dream of staying where I'm not wanted." He wheeled about and stomped out. She could hear him thundering along the hallway and down the stairs. With a tremendous crash, the front door slammed.

Jillian ran down the hallway and skipped down the stairs. She flipped the lock then tested the door.

"I know I shut that door." If she did decide to move in here, she'd have to make sure the first floor was secure. Even with a metal door on the apartment, she didn't relish the thought of anyone walking into her house at will, even an attractive policeman.

* * * *

Seth jammed his fists into his pants pockets and hunched against the cold wind blowing off the ocean. As he jogged toward the police station, a fine mist covered his face and bare arms. He'd handled the situation all wrong, alienated her instead of getting close to her. He'd have to figure out a way to get back on her good side so he could get back inside the house. He didn't dare use his burglar picks on the front door again.

He glanced both ways on Center Street before trotting across. A few brave tourists in plastic rain slickers strolled about, peering into shop windows. When the rain started coming down in earnest, Seth ran. He would return to the station, check the license plate, then regroup his thoughts. He knew Captain Burgess was losing patience with his investigation. A snort of derision escaped. He didn't really blame the man.

Seth yanked open the door and walked into the outer lobby of the precinct, knowing he had turned up nothing concrete, and didn't have a clue how to proceed. When he'd come to the Island two years before to claim his sister's body, he had been positive there was a gang of drug dealers based in Thornton House. He had been sure Melinda never took drugs, but, for some reason he'd never determined, she'd died on the grounds of Thornton House. The cause of death was an overdose of Ecstasy. When he questioned Felicity Thornton, she was very confused and didn't seem to be in touch with reality. She died shortly after that. He also questioned all the neighbors. No one had seen anything suspicious or perhaps didn't want to get Felicity Thornton in trouble. There was drug activity all up and down the coast of Florida and the house had easy access to the water.

"We need suspects, evidence—something for an arrest, Seth," Captain Burgess had said.

Hunches and suspicion did nothing. He had apprehended a couple of low-level dealers in the woods behind the house last summer, but they'd both denied all knowledge of how the drugs had come onto the island or where they were stashed.

At one time, all the acres of land between Thornton House and the ocean had belonged to Felicity Thornton. She'd sold it off a few parcels at a time. Trees and scrub brush had overtaken the once-lush lawn. Now the woods between Thornton House and the ocean were dotted with tiny houses, some merely shacks. It was possible that was where the drug deals took place.

Murphy Johnson sat with his feet on a pulled out desk drawer, talking on the phone. He waved as Seth headed for his own desk.

Maybe it was time to reassess the whole problem, Seth thought. *But not until I can get into the house once more.*

And, not until he came to know Jillian better. Like an itch that won't be satisfied, she'd wiggled under his skin.

* * * *

Jillian wiped her grubby palms on the edge of her T-shirt. She'd worn the rubber gloves until they got hot and slick, then pulled then off. She'd have to buy wet wipes and paper towels to deal with the dirt. Off in the distance she heard the grumble of thunder. Through the cracks in the windows, she heard the sound of the wind picking up and sighing in the trees. The pit-ter-pat of fresh rain spattered against the windowpanes.

Since the policeman had stormed out, she wandered from room to room with her flashlight, poking into closets and drawers. The house was huge and she had no idea where to start searching for the hidden treasure. Some rooms she searched were filled with light while others were dark airless tombs. She'd been hoping to find the key to the attic, but so far all she'd found was the recipe for pecan pie handwritten on a yellowing card, four twisted metal hangers and a purple velvet hair ribbon. Certainly not a fortune or any hint of her past.

She had one more room to check—the one opposite her aunt's apartment. With a sigh of resignation, she opened the door and peered inside. The windows had been boarded up here, too, and gloom filled the space. Jillian took a step back, ready to close the door when movement in the corner of the room caught her eye. Her mouth went dry with fear. She floundered backward, ready to run while she aimed her light at the corner. An old bunched up sleeping bag cowered in the corner. Did it contain a person? The trickle of air from between the boards caused the edge to move ever so slightly.

On tiptoes, she crept closer, poised to turn and run. Old food wrappers and an empty soda cup lay near the sleeping bag. The waxy blob of a burned down candle rested on an overturned wooden box. A fusty unwashed odor rose from the makeshift bed. Clearly someone had been sleeping here.

Jillian's shaky light pierced the corners of the room, sliding around and coming to rest on the closet door. She licked her lips, strode over and snatched open the door. A dark blue, moth-eaten man's cardigan sweater hung neatly on a single hanger—the only piece of clothing in the entire house. The mystery of Thornton House deepened. How did this relate to her Aunt Felicity's hidden treasure? She backed out of the room and firmly closed the door.

With determination, Jillian inspected each of the rooms again. She banged on walls and jumped on the floor to see if any of the boards were loose. She found nothing further.

Hunger finally forced her to the first floor. She retrieved her lunch from the mantel and sat on the edge of the fireplace hearth. It was peaceful and quiet here, and the only sound she heard was the patter of soft raindrops smattering against the window. She consumed the sandwich hungrily and sipped warm soda between bites. With a sigh of contentment, she leaned her head against the rough stone. Maybe she'd been hasty in kicking the policeman out. He seemed like a nice enough guy. The sight of him in tight blue jeans molded to his firm butt refused to leave her mind. Or the way he tossed over-long ebony hair out of his eyes. Maybe he only wanted to help her. Would she ever bet able to trust another man? It was too late now.

Rummaging around in her pocket she found the stubby pencil. On the empty brown lunch bag, Jillian started another shopping list. Then she added, *Call Bannerman, re: utilities.* Even if she didn't move in, it would be a good idea to have the phone available. Would they connect it for only two weeks? Then she added to the list: *bucket, soap, sponges, garbage bags.* Money was in short supply, but having electricity and water would help in her search. Meanwhile, she'd clean her aunt's room. If she got to the place where she could no longer afford Cantrell's, she could move in here.

Cold air leaked into the room through cracks in the windows. Shivering, Jillian pulled her sweater on. Okay, she had to admit that she was terrified of living alone in this house, especially after finding the ratty old sleeping bag. Could she do it? Did she have any choice?

The rain intensified as the afternoon wore on. Darkness invaded the room. She ambled into the library and poked at several shelves. She spotted a piece of paper stuck between the boards and her spirits rose. As she carefully worked it free, she hoped it wasn't another recipe.

She plopped on the floor. With the ends of her fingers, she smoothed the paper out. It had been ripped out of a newspaper. Excitement flooded through her. A clue! Jillian flicked on the flashlight to read both sides of the print. She flipped it over, scanned a few words then turned it back.

"Rats." It was a very old ad for a Maytag washer on sale at Sears. She had no idea how long it had been there—or why. Squiggles of fear shot thought Jillian. What if her aunt had been a bit senile toward the end? She had had a series of strokes, so it was possible. Maybe what she'd hidden, like this advertisement, had been important to Felicity but to no one else.

The reflected flash of lightning zigzagged across the room. Thunder crashed. Jillian jumped up and shoved the paper into her pants pocket along with the recipe. Enough. She would go back to Letty's and indulge in a long bath after she called Bannerman. Hopefully, the utilities could be turned on immediately. But if not, she still had work to do at the library, or the local newspaper, researching the house. Jillian was determined to find out more about her this house and mother's death. Should she waste the time? She'd make the time, it was important.

An image of the laughing man holding the baby flashed into her mind. The man with eyes like hers, her father. Could he still be alive somewhere? How could she ever hope to find him?

Glancing around the room once more, Jillian brushed the dust off her butt and dug out the front door key. She walked into the foyer. The hallway floorboards creaked and groaned. Outside the wind continued to pick up, moaning and crying.

Jillian opened the door and stepped outside with relief. She locked and tested the door. *Maybe I should add a gun to my list,* she thought.

She felt a presence and whirled around. The minute she turned, a flash of light blasted her eyes, followed quickly by a second then a third. She ducked and would have run back inside but the locked door stopped her. Jillian hunched against the splintered wood, rubbing at her eyes to clear them of the afterglow. She heard heavy footsteps running down the front walk, but her vision was too blurry to see anything except the retreating back of what appeared to be a tall man.

* * * *

"Someone to see you, Seth." Murphy stood in front of Seth's desk waggling his eyebrows. When he stepped aside, there stood Jillian Bennett, soaked to the skin, looking mad enough to chew rusty nails.

"I want to report an assault." She crossed her arms and thrust her chin out.

All the air whooshed out of Seth's lungs. He jumped up and hurried around the desk. "Are you all right? Do you need a doctor?" He wanted to wrap her in his arms, but the sight of her face stopped him in his tracks. "What happened?"

"Some, some *man* took my picture!"

Seth sagged against the desk with relief. She hadn't been hurt. "Jeez, last time I checked that's not against the law. Poor man was undoubtedly overcome by your," he reached out to wipe a smudge of dirt off her chin with his thumb, 'beauty.'" He couldn't help but chuckle. Even in her disheveled state she was a knockout.

She actually stomped her foot. Dust swirled around her like dirty snowflakes. "It's not funny! First I find you sneaking around my house—"

"Wait a damn minute—"

"Then when I left a few minutes ago, some idiot took several pictures of me!"

"What did he say? What'd he look like?" Seth pulled a legal pad out of a desk drawer. Thoughts of John Smith from Atlanta dashed through his mind, but he kept his mouth shut. Trouble seemed to follow the Yankee Gal like a lost dog, so it was possible two men were stalking her or even a woman. Besides, he didn't want to lead her.

"I don't know. I couldn't make him out; the camera flashes blinded me. By the time I could see again, he was gone." She ran her fingers through tangled hair, detaching a few sticky cobwebs. They drifted down to join the dirt on his desk.

"Are you sure it was a man?"

She hesitated, cocked her head and squinted. "No, but it sounded like a man. Heavy footsteps and he was tall."

"Have a seat. We'll figure out what's happening. You want a cup of coffee or a soft drink?"

"Coffee would be wonderful." She glanced around before sitting in the chair on the other side of his desk.

Murphy had been hovering a few feet away, grinning like an idiot, and taking in the whole scene.

"Murph, you mind getting Ms. Bennett a cup of coffee?"

"Sure boss." A smarmy grin was plastered on his face as he sauntered away.

Seth fiddled with his pad of paper, unsure what to ask her first.

"Why do you think a woman might have taken my picture?"

At this point, he didn't have a clue. "You'll have to help me on that one. Who all do you know on the Island?"

"No one." She brought her finger to her mouth, about to nibble the cuticle, studied her dirty hands, stopped and returned them to her lap. She kept her eyes downcast, lost in thought. With a little shake she raised her head. Her eyes met his. "Mrs. Cantrell from the B-and-B, her guest Mr. Winters and, of course, RaeJean. She's nice. That's it. Oh, George Bannerman my lawyer, but I've hardly talked to the man."

Her unusual eyes swam with moisture. He couldn't help but think she'd be tougher if she'd really been involved with selling drugs. Of course she could be a good actress. He simply didn't know her well enough.

"I'm not too worried about random walk-by photo shoot, but if you'd feel better, maybe you should return home to Denver for a while, come back later."

"I can't. There's nothing for me there anymore." The words came out in a tiny voice, almost a whisper. She seemed so alone. His cop instinct kicked in and all thoughts of drug dealers fled from his mind. No way could this woman be involved.

"Here's your coffee, Miss." Murphy set a steaming cup in front of Jillian and stood there. Seth wanted his coworker to leave so he could be alone with Jillian.

"Murphy, would you mind checking the latest report sheet? Ms. Bennett said someone surprised her at Thornton House and took some photographs. I think it might be kids messing around. See if anyone else has had a problem, okay?"

Murphy nodded, walked over and sat at his desk.

"I have an idea. How about we go out to dinner tonight? We can kick a few ideas around." Out of the corner of his eye, he saw Murphy almost falling out of his chair in an attempt to eavesdrop. All the more reason to hustle Jillian out of the office. She might open up, be more trusting in a casual atmosphere.

"Oh, I don't know." She held up her grubby fingers, "I'm filthy. I think I'll clean up and just stay in tonight."

"Nope. I insist. We got off to a bad start. I know things don't seem too good right now, so I'm going to treat you to the best seafood dinner on the east coast, well south of Boston anyhow." Seth stood and eyed his watch. "Why don't you go back to Letty's, and I'll pick you up at seven. We can talk about who might want photos of you and why."

Over the top of Jillian's head, Murphy gave the thumbs up sign before picking up his phone to make a call.

Jillian seemed to relax. "Oh... To discuss my case. Sure... That would be fine." All business now, she stood. "Thank you for taking the time to help me, detective." She turned on her heel and headed for the door.

"Damn fine looking woman, even in the Pigpen disguise," Murphy said. "Kinda skinny though. You taking her to Captain Jacks?"

"Yeah." Seth stood at the window watching Jillian walk down the street, her eyes on the pavement, unaware of her surroundings. She looked like a lost child and he wanted to be the one to help her find her place.

* * * *

Jillian dragged her muddy feet into the front hallway of Letty's place. She felt like kicking herself. Why on earth had she agreed to go to dinner with the cop? Obviously he had some kind of hidden agenda. She didn't feel alert enough today to pick his brain. Still, she needed a friend and having one in law enforcement wouldn't be bad. She'd tell him about the sleeping bag in the upstairs room. It might be important. Didn't hurt he was so darn cute, either.

"Mercy, did you bring the whole garden home with you?" RaeJean stood near the dining room.

"Nope, only part of the front lawn. I'm sorry, I'll clean it up."

"Don't worry about it. It will only take me a second."

As Jillian walked toward the stairs she pasted a wobbly smile on her face. "I won't be here for dinner tonight, Rae-Jean. I'm going out."

"Why honey, you look all done in. Can you rest a bit first?" Her dark eyebrows came together in a scowl. "Who you know taking you out to dinner? You best be careful, girl."

"It's not a date, more of a…" Her brain flailed around for the correct word. "…business meeting. I think I'll be safe. Seth Falconer is taking me out."

"Oh, he's a fine man, a fine man, Miss Jillian."

"I'm going to soak in the tub, maybe take a nap. I don't know where my alarm clock is, would you knock on the door about six? If it's not too much trouble."

"No trouble at all, honey. You have a nice rest."

Jillian fumbled with the key to her room. Her cold fingers felt stiff and alien, like they didn't belong to her. Once inside, she walked to draw the curtains against the cloudy light still seeping into the room from the window. When she passed the bureau she noticed a drawer gaped slightly ajar. Fear stabbed at her. She pulled it open all the way. Her purse was where she had left it, but the letter and packet of photos were gone.

Chapter 7

"RaeJean! Where's Letty?" Jillian flew into the kitchen out of breath. "I knocked on her door, but she didn't answer."

"Mercy child, what's the problem? You all right?"

"Someone's been in my room!"

"Sure, I went in there this morning to make the bed and tidy up. Here, honey, sit. I'll pour you a cup of coffee. You eat lunch today?"

"Yes, I'm fine. No, I didn't mean you, I mean someone who doesn't belong."

"What's all the commotion?" Malcolm Winters stood in the doorway. Jillian was struck again at how much he resembled Craig. Today he had on a burgundy polo shirt. The outfit showed off both his muscles and blond masculinity. A hank of hair rested in the middle of his forehead. He casually reached up to push it back. It flopped down again.

"Ms. Jillian says someone has been in her room. You see anyone wandering in the house who doesn't belong?" RaeJean stood by Jillian's chair protectively.

"No. Are you missing anything? Money?" he asked. "I'm sure Letty will compensate you for any loss."

"Two other rooms filled up today," RaeJean said, "but I don't think you have to worry about them. The honeymoon couple from Atlanta hasn't been out of the room since they checked in this morning." She chuckled. "The older lady I put on the first floor 'cause she said she can't climb stairs. I doubt she'd be poking in your room."

"I'll go see if I can find Letty. I think she had a hairdresser's appointment today." Malcolm's voice faded down the hallway.

"The front door is always unlocked during the day, but my mercy, honey, I think I would have seen a stranger poking around. Mr. Malcolm's been here most of the afternoon, too." She patted Jillian's shoulder. "What are you missing?"

"A letter from my Aunt Felicity and some photographs. They wouldn't be of interest to anyone else." A shiver shot through Jillian. Unless someone wanted to find out what might be hidden in the house.

RaeJean poured herself a cup of coffee, added a generous amount of cream and two spoons of sugar. "Maybe you misplaced them. You're tired, not thinking straight. Want me to go up with you to help you search?"

"No, thanks anyhow. I guess I'll go back, lie down for a while, maybe catch a nap." She stood on wobbly legs. "Too much time spent alone in a spooky house is making me nervous. Wake me at six, okay?"

"Sure, sugar. Have a good rest."

Jillian used the railing to pull herself up the stairs. Her bedroom door stood open the way she'd left it. She walked inside, closed and locked it. For extra measure, she placed the vanity chair under the doorknob.

Stripping off her clothing, Jillian walked to the bathroom, nibbling at her lip. Who on earth would have come into her room? Who cared about her and her connection to Thornton House? She'd have to ask Seth at dinner. He'd lived here for a while and knew most of the people she'd met so far.

A gush of warm water spilled into the tub. Jillian hunted under the sink, found some bath oil and dribbled a few drops into the bath. The scent of roses wafted through the small room. While she waited for the tub to fill, she strolled to the dresser for clean underwear. There, sitting next to her purse, were the letter and photos.

* * * *

"I know they weren't there before, Seth." Jillian sat across from him in a booth at Captain Jack's Seafood restaurant. Seth was glad he'd made a reservation because, as usual, the place was packed. The sound of soft classical music drifted over the conversation of hungry diners. They were seated in a corner booth, in a dim, quiet corner.

Jillian's pink-tinged face was free of makeup, and she wore only a dab of gloss on her pouty lips. Her fingers clasped the glass of white wine as if it were a lifeline.

She wore a light blue turtleneck sweater that brought out the color of her eyes—both of them. Black slacks were molded to her firm body and he realized she wasn't thin at all. On the contrary, she was perfect. All he could think of was licking the droplet of amber wine clinging to the side of her full mouth.

"Did you hear what I said?" She brought the glass to her lips.

Seth pulled his mind back to the conversation with reluctance. "Letty's nosy, are you sure she didn't do it?"

"Right now I'm not sure of anything. When I came down stairs a half-hour ago, she was sitting in the parlor with a drink. I have no idea how long she'd been home or if she'd even been gone. Her hair looked like a steel beehive, but it's always like that."

The waitress placed huge platters in front of them. The delicate smell of fish made his mouth water. Golden fried shrimp, scallops and a piece of haddock, all nestled next to a mound of French fries. Individual bowls of cold slaw rounded out the meal.

Jillian placed a scallop in her mouth, chewed and groaned. "I think I've died and gone to heaven. Seth, this is delicious."

"When it comes to food, I know all the best places. I lack cooking skills and eat out most of the time." He dipped a shrimp into sauce and popped it in his mouth. "Did the letter from your aunt contain any information that would be of interest to others?"

"Nothing I'm aware of." She cocked her head to one side. "Say, do you think this letter might be what the thieves were hunting for when they broke into my lawyer's office?"

A burst of laughter from the other side of the room filled the air. The interlude gave Seth a moment to think. "When was this? What was missing?" He sat taller in the booth, his dinner forgotten for the moment.

"The night I arrived in town, I guess. Mr. Bannerman didn't exactly mention when. I helped him straighten up a little until we found my aunt's file. Didn't you see a police report on the break in?"

He didn't want to tell her he was on special assignment, tracking drugs to her house, at least not yet. "No, I don't see the daily reports unless they pertain to a case I'm working. I'll definitely check the paperwork when I go to the station tomorrow. Do you know which officer answered the call?"

"No officer had come to take a report by the time I left." Jillian finished the scallops and ate some slaw. "Do you think it would help if you read the letter?" Her eyes were luminous in the dim light.

Seth took a drink of beer to wet his dry mouth. "If you want to trust me with the information it contains."

She didn't say a word, simply reached into her purse and offered him a lavender envelope.

He scanned the letter quickly, then started at the top, reading it again to make sure he grasped all the details. The only thing to catch his eye was the information about an item hidden in the house. Drugs? But Felicity had concealed it over twenty-five years ago. There didn't appear to be anything in the letter of interest to anyone but Jillian.

Jillian was fiddling with her wineglass when he looked up.

"Now you know all my secrets, Seth. I'm not only weird-looking, but possibly illegitimate, too." She ducked her head, intent on smoothing the napkin on her lap.

Weird-looking? He couldn't imagine how she came to that conclusion. Didn't she ever look in a mirror? He thought she was one of the most beautiful women he'd ever met.

The smiling waitress came to their table. "You folks want some dessert? Coffee? More wine?"

It took Seth a few seconds for his mouth to work. "Coffee for me, please. Jillian?" She nodded in agreement.

"I'm so sorry about your mother. Why don't I check out the accident report in our old files? They should at least have her last name. But...why would you think you're illegitimate?"

"I'm not sure. I suppose because my mother showed up at Aunt Felicity's house alone with me in tow. I sort of assumed she became pregnant, her parents kicked her out, she had nowhere else to go. Clearly the man in the photo is my father, but what happened to him? Did he leave her too?" She picked up her spoon and made lazy patterns on the tablecloth. "I don't know." A busboy picked up their empty plates, making way for coffee.

"But, then who was chasing you? Perhaps it was your father and he'd changed his mind, wanting you after all."

"I have no idea." She shrugged. "I want to talk to RaeJean and perhaps some other people who knew my aunt. It sounds like she was confused at the end. Perhaps it was all in her imagination. I—I really don't believe there were any men after my mother. I think Aunt Felicity didn't know what to do with a child. When my mother died, she took the easy way out by relinquishing me for adoption." Bright tears sparkled in her eyes. Seth's heart ached to hold her.

"Were the photos in with the letter?"

"No. My aunt had them in a safety deposit box."

"May I see them?"

She gave a rueful chuckle. "Silly me, I had hoped to find a bunch of money in there, or at least enough to fix up Thornton House. The box was empty except for this packet of pictures." She gave the packet to Seth.

He shuffled through the photos. "The woman is obviously your mother. She's beautiful." Seth glanced up at Jillian. "You resemble her."

Her eyes grew large, her face reddened. Seth stopped to wipe his sweaty palms on his napkin. He picked up the pictures and riffled through them again more slowly.

"The guy has to be your father, all right. The eyes are identical." He handed the items back to Jillian. "What do you think is hidden in the house?"

"I have no idea, but I'm going to tear the place down board by board until I find it. I'm moving into my aunt's apartment."

"No you're not! You can't stay in that house alone."

Jillian ground her teeth together. "I beg your pardon?" Just when she'd decided to trust the policeman, he had to go and get bossy. Why did he have to be possessive? She was glad now she hadn't mentioned the sleeping bag to Seth.

"I said you cannot live in that house alone."

"You have no authority to tell me what to do. I'll live where I please." Jillian had had enough of men giving her orders. She tossed her napkin on the table, grabbed her jacket and purse. "Thank you for the lovely evening, Detective Falconer. I'll see myself home."

She stomped out of the restaurant and stood at the edge of the curb. She had no idea where she was or how to get back to Cantrell's. Before she could decide which direct to go, Seth came up beside her.

"I'm sorry, Jillian. I didn't mean it to sound the way it did." He took her elbow. "The rain has stopped. Let's walk along the ocean for a bit. I guess I'd better explain."

Jillian hesitated for a moment, but knew she needed help. Who better than a member of law enforcement, even if he was a jerk? "Okay, start talking."

As they strolled along the sea wall, she filled her lungs with tangy salt air. Overhead clouds played tag among the sparkling stars. The closer they walked to the marina, the louder the sound of the wind singing in the rigging of the boats anchored there.

"Okay, first of all, I don't want you living alone in the house because I think a gang is using it to hide drugs, or did at one time."

"What?" Jillian jerked away to face Seth. "That's ridiculous. I've been all through the house. It's empty; there's nothing there."

"Hold your horses." He smiled and took her hand. He placed it in the crook of his arm and started to walk again. "You haven't been in the attic have you? The basement?"

Jillian's mind flashed to the dungeon-like basement. The attic couldn't be that bad, could it? "No, but from what I've seen, no one has been inside for months, if not years." She bit her lip, knowing she should tell him about the old sleeping bag she'd found in the house. Jillian waited, wanting to know what he had to say first. "Why do you think there are, or were, drugs in Thornton House?"

He paused for a moment. She saw him swallow hard. "My involvement started about two years ago, when my sister died."

As they continued to walk, he recounted the story of his sister's drug overdose and death. Jillian thought the connection to Thornton House tenuous at best. She felt sorry for Seth. He'd obviously loved his sister very much.

"I've seen that old guy lingering around the house before," Seth said. "The night I met you was the closest I've ever come to nabbing him. I'm not even sure he has anything to do with drugs, but I wanted to talk to him to find out why he keeps going back there."

"Perhaps he's homeless, needed shelter. He might have been inside at one time. Heaven knows it's easy enough to crawl into the house. Most of the windows are broken or boarded up."

Jillian's heart bumped in her chest and she felt sweat dot her upper lip. He was right. Thornton House was like Swiss cheese but what choice did she have?

Seth stopped and rested both his hands on her shoulders. His eyes were two pools of ebony, dark and fierce. "All the more reason for you not to be there alone." He stared at a distant spot over her shoulder and cleared his throat again. "I wasn't going to tell you this because I didn't want to alarm you, but, someone has been following you."

Fear stabbed Jillian's heart. "Following me? Was it the man with the camera? The one who took my picture?"

"I'm not sure." She grew lightheaded and swayed. Before she knew what was happening, Seth took her in his arms. His coffee-scented breath was warm against her cheek.

"I'm so sorry. I didn't want to scare you." He hugged her, rocking her like a child.

Without thinking, her arms encircled his solid body. He smelled like soap, warm laundry and vanilla. He was so comforting, she didn't ever want to let go.

She tilted her head so she could see Seth's face. "Who? Why?" She bit her lip to keep from crying. All she'd wanted to do was start a new life here on Amelia Island, but now everything was falling apart.

"I don't know." He kissed the tip of her nose, sending shock waves through her body. "You're cold. Let's go back to my truck and I'll drive you to Letty's place."

She wanted to scream, don't stop now. Kiss me, I'll be plenty warm, but of course, he only felt sorry for her. He kept his arm around her. As they walked back toward the restaurant parking lot, she nestled close to the warmth of his body. She was afraid if he let go she'd fall over.

Once inside the truck, Seth cranked up the heat before turning in his seat to face her. "Is it possible someone from home is pursuing you? You said you were alone, but did you perhaps leave someone on bad terms. A man who's come south to find you?"

Jillian could see genuine concern on his face. She couldn't help but laugh. "No, Seth, there is no one in Denver who will miss me. I had a relationship with a man there, but he replaced me with another woman. I can't say I blame him. He wanted to have kids, and with me being adopted, he said he couldn't be sure of what his children might inherit, other than strange eyes." She turned her head to gaze out the window. When she looked back at Seth she saw his jaw clenched in anger.

"That bastard! How dare he treat you so badly?"

Amazement flooded Jillian. "I guess I can't blame him. Craig thought perhaps my mother had been a..." the words stuck, "...a prostitute or something."

"What on earth does your ancestry have to do with you? You're a unique individual, and Jillian, you have the most beautiful eyes I've ever seen. There's nothing wrong with your eyes. So they're two different colors! What kind of an idiot is this guy?"

Before she could answer, Seth reached across the seat and drew her into his arms. His mouth covered hers hungrily. His kiss sent the pit of her stomach into a swirl. She'd never felt anything like this with Craig in all the years they'd been together. Jillian reached up to tangle her fingers in Seth's thick ebony hair while she returned his kiss.

He quickly broke off the kiss, burrowed his face in her neck murmuring, "Jillian, Jillian."

She heard someone rap on the driver's side window. A bright light pierced her eyes. She blinked. A cop stood shining his flashlight in the window.

Seth jerked away from Jillian, turned and started laughing. He rolled down the window.

"Hey, Denny, what's up?" She felt heat flood her face.

"Jeez Seth, sorry, I didn't know it was you. The window in your truck was starting to fog up. I thought some kids was in here...you know?" The young man's face turned the shade of ripe tomatoes. "You might want to move somewhere else. Right now you're giving everybody in Captain Jack's a good show." He touched the tip of his flashlight to the brim of his hat and sauntered off.

Still chuckling, Seth rolled up the window, put the truck in gear and started off.

Jillian wanted to be back in his strong arms, safe, but she was certain she could never again let a man have any kind of power over her. Seth could be a good friend, but nothing more. She would have to erase the thought of his kiss from her mind, at least until she knew she was emotionally strong enough for a relationship.

* * * *

"Thanks for the dinner, Seth." Jillian said when Seth came to a stop in front of Cantrell's. She turned to go.

"Wait a minute. What are you going to do tomorrow? I'll check out your mother's accident report first thing in the morning and let you know what I find out. Why don't you stay here until I call?"

Her chin came up; her mouth formed a straight line. "I'm going to call Mr. Bannerman and ask him to have the utilities and phone turned on at Thornton House. Then I'm going to clean my new apartment, buy groceries and move in."

"You can't. It's not safe."

"The door to the bedroom is reinforced with steel. Once the phone is turned on, if I need help, I'll dial 911." Even in the dim light she appeared pale and frightened. He had to think of a way to keep her out of the house. A pint-size woman, she'd get lost in such a large house.

"What about fire? A wooden house that old would go up in minutes."

"There's a fire ladder by one of the windows." She touched his cheek. "I appreciate your concern, Seth, but I have to find out what's hidden in the house. The best way to do it is to be there to search every room." She smiled, and deep dimples jumped to her cheeks. "I'm a big girl. I can take care of myself."

Seth didn't think either of them believed that.

"Okay, how about if I bring a cot and leave it in one of the rooms, sleep there at night?" Seth reached out and tucked a stray piece of hair behind her ear. "Only until we find out who's been following you."

"And taking my picture, don't forget." A wobbly grin decorated her face.

"Don't you think it's the same man?" Seth said. She was so lovely he was surprised she didn't have a parade of men following her.

Jillian gnawed on the ragged cuticle of her right forefinger. "I've been thinking, Seth. Maybe the guy is a real estate agent, farming for houses to sell or someone who heard I'd inherited Thornton House and wants to buy it, turn it into a B-and-B." She turned toward him, her eyes sparkling. "Sure, it would make sense. He photographed the house, not me. I only got in the way."

Seth remembered the long black car that had almost run over Jillian. Some agents were ruthless, but he didn't think the thought of a good commission extended to killing homeowners for their property. "I still think it would be safer with me staying in the house with you."

She sucked in her lower lip then shook her head. "No, it's not necessary, but thanks for the offer." She stroked the side of his face. "Thanks for everything, Seth. Will you come to Thornton House and let me know what you find out about my mom?"

"Sure." Before he could kiss her again, she opened the door. "You're a good friend." She fled up the walk into the house.

* * * *

Inside Cantrell's, Jillian tiptoed though the dim front hallway then up the stairs to her room. She didn't close the hall door until she'd made a thorough examination of the room, but nothing seemed out of order. Once again, she settled the chair under the doorknob.

"Ohmigod, if I'm scared to be here in a house full of people, how am I ever going to spend the night alone at Thornton House?"

She should have asked Seth about buying a gun. Somehow she knew what his answer would be. Jillian brushed her fingers across her lips, remembering his sweet kisses. Then she headed for the bathroom to wash up. She had to slow down and not depend too much on the hunky cop. She had fallen fast for Craig and where had her undying love gotten her? Besides, how did she know Seth wanted to protect her instead of using her to come into the house to search for his imaginary drugs? No, from now on, she would be an independent woman; she would stand on her own two feet.

With a sigh, she reached for her toothbrush. She couldn't bring herself to tell Seth the real reason for moving. Jillian only had a few hundred dollars left. She'd have to find a way to replenish her funds, and she had less than two weeks in which to do it. Time was running out.

Chapter 8

Jillian sat back on her heels and pushed her damp hair out of her eyes. She'd spent most of the morning cleaning her aunt's apartment and still hadn't finished. She needed to have the water turned on before she could complete the job and move in, and hoped Bannerman had come through for her. Wet wipes and paper towels just didn't do a thorough enough job. Good thing she hadn't checked out of Letty's place yet, she'd need at least another day to make this apartment habitable. She wanted to spend a few hours searching too, before it got dark.

Last night's storm had passed and she had all the windows open to let in fresh air. Most of the musty smell had disappeared from the apartment. Somewhere nearby, a dog had been barking all morning. It had stopped for a while, but now from the woods behind the house, the dog resumed its frantic barking. The poor animal sounded panicky and it bothered her.

Jillian stretched her arms over her head. Her tummy made rumbling noises, reminding her it was getting close to lunchtime. She wandered into the kitchen area to take a short break. The refrigerator door stood propped open with a box of baking soda resting on the shelf. Jillian sniffed and smiled. Then with fingers crossed, she walked to the kitchen sink.

When she turned the knob, a gush of rusty water shot out of the spigot.

"Yes! Thank you George Bannerman."

She let the water run until it cleared. She wouldn't have any hot water, but she could warm some on the electric stove. There were plenty of pots and dishes. Wiping her fingers on a paper towel, she sat on the edge of the naked mattress. She had removed the linens for her trip to the Laundromat. She picked up the black rotary phone and held the receiver to her ear. The dial tone sounded like a heavenly choir.

When she'd spoken to George Bannerman from Letty's house this morning, he, too, had tried to dissuade her from moving into the house. Once he encountered her stubborn streak, he agreed to make the calls to activate the utilities.

"I think if I vouch for you, there won't be any need for deposits even though it will only be for a couple of weeks."

Jillian prayed it would be for longer, perhaps years. "Thank you so much for all your help, Mr. Bannerman. I appreciate it."

"Nonsense, and please call me George. Once you're settled, will you go out to dinner with me?"

Surprise ran through Jillian and the memory of his plain honest face made her grin. He wasn't her type, but had been very kind to her. One dinner wouldn't hurt. "That would be very nice, George." She'd only been on Amelia Island for a few days and already had more friends than she'd had in Denver for years.

The dog kept barking, but sounded hoarse and exhausted. She had to find out why. Jillian locked the apartment door behind her, walked down the stairs and through the gloomy hallway. The back door creaked in protest when she opened it. She'd have to remember to buy some WD-40. Every darn door in the place squeaked, and most of the drawers too. This house sucked up money like a big leaky sponge.

Outside, warm moist air eddied around her. Jillian could barely see the worn path drifting from the back door toward the woods. Here and there wild flowers poked up through the earth. The square patches had been flowerbeds at one time, but neglect had turned them back to weeds. The closer she moved to the trees, the louder the barking became.

She stopped part of the way across the tall grass to look around. At one time the back lawn must have been large and well cared for, but now the trees and wild grasses had narrowed its scope. Jillian squatted and ran her fingers along a ridge of faded white wood. Somewhere in the back of her mind, a bell of recognition clanged. She remembered a gazebo that had stood here at one time. She could almost see a line of dolls sitting on a bench, and feel the cool moistness of a glass of lemonade held carefully in her small hands.

She stood and continued to the edge of the line of trees. The minute she entered the thick tangle of trees, the breeze died and the bugs dive-bombed her damp skin, tangled themselves in her hair, and generally made her miserable.

"Okay, WD-40 and bug spray." She spit out a black thing. The bug wiggled all the way to the ground. *Yuck*. She kept her mouth shut, breathing through her nose. Wending her way ever deeper into the woods, Jillian heard the dog's frantic barking closer now. She stopped to wipe the sweat from her brow. A tree branch crackled not far away. She froze. Her eyes scanned the dense foliage while she fanned the bugs away from her face. Slowly, Jillian turned in a circle, didn't see anyone, but still felt a presence. Sweat trickled down her sides.

Maybe this hadn't been such a good idea. Jillian spotted a thick stick and picked it up. She shivered in spite of the heat.

Swinging the limb from side to side, she moved forward and peeked through the moss-covered oaks. Bannerman had been right. The copse of trees wasn't that large and very quickly she came to an opening. A one-story shack sat in the middle of a clearing. Its bare boards had been weathered to an uneven gray, and most of the windows sported plastic instead of glass. A stocky white dog was chained to a stout tree. The animal had become entangled in the chain and couldn't move. Once more he lifted his head and howled.

Fear fled. Without hesitating, Jillian hurried through the underbrush and ran to the dog. His neck was puffy and red where he'd struggled to free himself. His large pink tongue lolled out, but his gums were ashy from dehydration. A large pail nearby held only a few inches of filthy water topped with scum and dead bugs. Out of the dog's reach was an empty food dish.

She hesitated for a second. He was a medium-sized, unfriendly looking dog, looked like part Pit Bull and part who knows? The animal tried to bare his teeth and growl, but only whimpered with exhaustion.

"Oh, sweetie, here, let me help you." Jillian studied the chain. She held out her fingers and the dog sniffed, then licked them. She patted his square head. Running her fingers along the metal in an attempt to figure out how to untangle the critter, she found it had a padlock on the end. She finally settled for guiding the dog back and forth around the tree until he had some leeway.

Then she glanced around and saw a hose connected to the back of the shack. She grabbed the water container and hurried over. After rinsing the pail quickly to wash away the worst of the pests, she filled it with clean water and, with liquid slopping over the top, hauled it to the dog.

The animal almost dived headfirst into the water in his haste to drink. "Easy, sweetie, not so fast. You'll be sick." Sure enough the pooch gagged and brought up a frothy gob of water. He dove back into the bucket and drank again.

"What the hell do you think you're doing?"

Jillian let out a squeak, tripped on the chain and flopped on her butt. The sun flamed out behind the large figure standing in front of her. She couldn't make out his features, but saw a rifle pointed at her head. She scrabbled around on the ground until her fingers connected with the piece of wood she'd dropped.

Now without the sun in her eyes, she could see him clearly. The man looming over her wore bib overalls over his bare chest, Paul Bunyan without the blue ox. His dirt-brown hair and full beard were filthy and uncombed. He took a step closer and squinted at her.

She scrambled to her feet, sliding the club behind her back. She barely came up to the middle of his chest. Jillian opened her mouth to speak and gagged. The man smelled like a sewer. She stepped back, fumbling around for the dog's solid body behind her. He gave her courage.

"What am I doing here? Giving your dog a drink. I've been listening to him howl all morning and finally came over to check on him." She reached back to pat the head of the animal. She didn't want the man to see her shaking. "He didn't have any water and he's all tangled up."

"He's a wuss. I give him a bowl full o' grub and bucket of water 'fore I went away. He's jist a pig, probably et it all the first day." The man shifted the rifle, scanning the woods behind her through squinted eyes.

"What do you mean, before you went away. How long has this poor animal been alone?"

He hoisted the rifle onto his shoulder. With grease-imbedded fingers, he scratched at his hairy face. Jillian shuddered. She thought she saw something move in there.

"'Bout two days, if'n it's any of your damn business." His eyes wobbled in their sockets. "Where you come from, anyhow?" He leaned over Jillian. "You know it ain't safe for wimon to wander around in these woods too much." He leered at her, exposing blackened rotted teeth.

"I live on the other side of the woods. With my husband," her mind searched for the proper name, "Hoss. And our children, boys, all five of them. Huge, they're all really enormous." Her chin came up as she clamped her mouth shut, trying for a fierce look.

He snorted and spat tobacco juice at her feet. He reached a grubby paw out for her. "Hell, if'n they ain't 'specting you for a while, maybe the two of us will have us a private party. We can—" His head came up, his mouth slammed shut. Both of them heard the sound of a heavy body crashing through the brush.

"Someone's out there. You best git back to your house, girl."

Jillian stood her ground. "What about the dog?"

"Snowflake? I'll bring him food, don't worry none." His narrowed eyes probed the forest behind Jillian.

Jillian touched the dog's head once more. Snowflake? The sturdy dog rippled with muscle. He looked about as fragile as a Mack truck. "I'll be watching you. If you don't care for this dog better, I'll call animal control and report you."

He made a grab for her. "Why, you—" Before he could finish, she fled across the ragged grass out onto a narrow dirt path. It would be shorter to go back the way she'd come, but she was sure there was someone out there. Overhead the tops of large trees met, leaving Jillian in a gloomy tunnel. She ran.

After a few minutes she popped out of the forest and found herself on a paved road with a narrow strip of beach on the other side of it. Beyond that, the ocean stretched out like a calm blue carpet. Jillian had the prickly feeling of eyes on the back of her head. She whipped around, staring at the line of trees, but saw nothing. She continued walking with the trees on her left side, but wasn't comfortable until she saw other houses. With a sigh of relief, she turned onto Broome Street, heading for Thornton House.

* * * *

Seth sneezed, then fumbled in his back pocket for his handkerchief. Overhead a single dim light bulb cast vague shadows around the room. He'd been grubbing in the old files in the basement for over an hour without results. He still hadn't found the file he'd been hunting for amid the stacks of moldy cardboard boxes. A hump of damp cartons beckoned to him from the corner. He shoved his way through the mess to reach them.

"A friend, she thinks I'm only a friend." All morning long the word had been picking at Seth's ego like a kid at a scab. He wanted to be more than a friend, but he had no choice. Jillian wasn't ready for anything more right now, even if he was.

"About time." A third of the way down, he found a file marked 'Brown' on the tab. Tall red letters stamped across the front screamed, *Case Closed*. He flipped it open to check the date. He'd finally found the right file.

Too depressed to spend any more time in the cellar, he turned out the overhead light before fumbling his way toward the square of light at the top of the stairway.

"Where you been, Seth? We got crimes going on here, you know." The phone rang again before Murphy could continue. He snatched up the receiver, scowling at Seth.

Pink telephone message slips littered the top of Seth's desk, almost, but not quite obscuring the pile of files. Seth flopped in his chair, and fanned through the heap. He snatched one piece out of the middle. It contained a reply to his request on the license plate of the black car. It was registered to a JBS Corporation of Savannah. At least part of John Smith's story turned out to be true.

The file containing all the information on his sister's death glared at him from his IN basket. He only had one more day to find some concrete information. Should he even bother to go on? He'd been working the case for over a year and so far nothing had turned up. Better to concentrate on a living woman and attempt to help her He didn't have the time or energy to follow up now, so he shoved everything to one side and opened the dusty file.

The police radio on the shelf behind Murphy's head crackled to life.

"Any car in the area respond to a two-forty-five at 743 Front Street. Possible one-eighty-seven. Proceed with caution."

Before the dispatcher could repeat the message, both Murphy and Seth jumped up and headed for the door.

"Your turn to drive, partner." Seth grabbed a set of keys out of his pocket and tossed them to Murphy.

Seth's mouth grew dry, hot blood gushed through in his veins. He whipped out his Glock, and checked to make sure he had a full magazine before settling it back in his holster. A domestic disturbance, possible homicide. He hadn't encountered this much police activity in months.

"Jeez, Seth, how many times we been there? I knew that butthead would kill his old lady one of these days."

"Yeah, and we both know what his excuse will be." Seth hit the back door to the station parking lot and ran for the black Crown Victoria he and Murphy shared on duty.

"The bitch deserved it," they chorused in unison.

By the time they returned to the station with a very drunk, unrepentant prisoner, the last light of day was gone. The adrenaline rush had faded, leaving Seth limp. No great detective skills needed on this one. Both husband and wife had been falling down drunk. She said something to irritate him. The perp, one Elmer Babcock, had grabbed his shotgun and fired two shots into his wife's body. True to their prediction, while handcuffed he was led away, shouting to the assembled onlookers that "the bitch deserved it!"

Seth gave all the pertinent information about the crime to the assistant DA then returned to his desk. Although tired and hungry, he wanted to scan the Brown file so he'd have something concrete to tell Jillian when he saw her later in the evening. And see her he would. He had to talk her out of moving into Thornton House.

He shuffled through the meager stack of papers until he reached the coroner's report. Cause of death had been listed as accidental drowning; she had water in her lungs. The report listed her name, Melody Brown, no married name, her age twenty-five. There were no obvious signs of foul play, only wood chips embedded in her right cheek from when she fell out of the boat, hitting her head on the side, fracturing her skull. There had been some question as to why she was out in a small boat with her child during a storm, but no one had come up with an answer. Seth gazed into the distance as he thought, but nothing came to him either. He wondered if Jillian might remember what they were doing in that boat. Once more his eyes focused on the file contents.

The morgue photo didn't provide much help. The picture showed a lifeless young woman who would never laugh again. The poor woman had died before her life had begun.

One paper listed the personal items that had been turned over to her adult surviving relative, Felicity Thornton. Among them, a plain gold band—a wedding band.

"So, either she had been married or she had pretended to be." He lounged back in his chair. The interview notes stated Felicity took possession of the body for burial in the family plot. He'd have to tell Jillian so she could visit her mother's grave. Poor kid.

Seth stood and stretched. He tossed the file into his out-box. He'd return it to the basement in the morning. Right now, he needed a cold beer, something to eat and, more than anything else, the sight of Jillian Bennett's dual-colored eyes.

* * * *

Jillian unscrewed the cap on the water bottle and chugged. Rivulets ran off her chin and down onto her sweaty T-shirt. The warm liquid tasted awful, but it quenched her thirst. She grabbed the rest of the six-pack off the counter and walked over to the refrigerator.

"Well, that wasn't too smart." Anger had outweighed her good sense when she'd seen the dog. Even now, locked safely in her room, Jillian couldn't stop shivering.

She bent over, shoved her nose in the fridge and sniffed nothing but sweet-smelling air. Jillian turned on the fridge and set the bottles inside.

"What I need is a glass of iced tea." First she'd have to make some ice cubes. Soon, she'd have to get a dog or cat to talk to instead of herself, or folks would question her sanity. Smiling, she opened the freezer compartment and removed the old-fashioned metal trays stacked one on top of the other. When she took them to the sink to wash, Jillian heard a rattle in the bottom tray. They were probably corroded and no good after all this time. She set them on the counter. She'd buy some plastic ones at the drug store.

This time when she turned on the faucet the water ran clear. Fresh air blew in through the tiny window over the sink. Outside only a gentle breeze whispered through the branches. Things were definitely looking up.

Jillian couldn't get the dog out of her mind. "Poor pooch." She'd felt his back when she'd patted him, but hadn't encountered any sores or welts and he had a nice thin pad of fat on his ribs; still, he shouldn't have been alone for days at a time. It wasn't right.

She started to place the top tray in the stream of water when something caught her eye.

"What on earth?" A key and pair of huge sparkly earrings rested in the bottom tray. They looked like diamonds. Stunned, Jillian stared at the items until she realized the water continued running. She cranked off the faucet.

"Omigodomigodomigod!" Her gaze flew around the room, expecting someone to come and snatch the baubles away. They couldn't be real, could they?

Gingerly, Jillian lifted one of the earrings to eye level. A beam of light bounced off the diamond, sending flashes of fire around the room. She ogled the stones, estimating each of the studs at a good two carats in weight, maybe even three. Now what on earth had her aunt been doing with them? So poor she didn't have furniture yet here were gems worth thousands of dollars. They must be fake, CZ's or something similar.

Jillian went into the main room and snatched a tissue from the box by the bed to carefully wrap the jewelry before depositing it in the pocket of her jeans. She didn't dare hold them up to her own ears, in case they didn't belong to her. The temptation to wear them was too great.

"But they were in my house; they must be mine!" Jillian pirouetted around the room. If the rocks were real, she could sell them, pay the taxes, insurance, then buy some paint, and start to redo the downstairs; but first she'd call George Bannerman. He would know her rights. Or should she? She needed to think about the earrings for a minute. The ice cube trays sat on the counter, unfilled.

Jillian wandered between the bedroom and kitchen, her mind in a whirl until she finally remembered the key. She plucked it out of the tray and walked into the hallway. It appeared about the right size. Sure enough, when she slipped the key into the locked door to the attic, it turned easily. Might as well explore while she decided what to do next. Maybe RaeJean could tell her more about the jewelry. She would stop at Cantrell's on her way to the Laundromat and find out what the housekeeper knew.

Rusty hinges creaked when the door opened, revealing a long dusty set of stairs. Jillian centered her foot on the first tread, setting off a whirlwind of dust. She sneezed. The sound echoed up the stairs and disappeared into the shadows. She flicked the wall switch, but nothing happened. If there had been a bulb upstairs, it probably burned out long ago. Since she didn't have much light, only what filtered through the dirty attic windows, it would be silly to start exploring now. She paused for a moment, but curiosity got the best of her, and she started up. Somewhere in the distance the sound of sirens split the air. She paused to listen. The sound came closer, then growled to a stop; silence filled the air once more.

Step by cautious step, Jillian kept going. She feared the wood beneath her feet might splinter at any moment to send her hurtling to her death. She reached the top, peered over the rail, and felt her jaw drop.

A pair of mahogany end tables sloped against a horsehair sofa like two friendly drunks leaning against a light pole. A huge travel trunk kept company with an antique horsehair couch, while lamps without bulbs hovered over boxes, barrels and bags crammed with goods. So many things crowded the space, Jillian didn't know where to look first. Excitement sizzled through her body like a bolt of electricity in a summer storm. This could be a great source of income. She could sell most of the pieces; some might even be worth big bucks.

No time to start exploring now. She walked back down the attic stairs, her shoulders hunched. This was shaping up to be a much bigger project then she'd anticipated. The furniture would be there when she returned. She could catalog everything later. She carefully locked the door behind her.

Jillian picked up her bundle of washing from where it waited by the apartment door, and headed out.

Ten minutes later she walked in the front door of Cantrell's and found RaeJean standing there.

"Mercy, Miss Jillian, what you toting? I thought I'm the one supposed to be the slave here," RaeJean said with a laugh. Her merry brown eyes danced.

"Ho, ho, very funny. It's linens from Thornton House. I'm going to move into my Aunt Felicity's apartment there, but first these need to be washed. I'm heading for the Laundromat in town."

"No you're not. You wash those things right here. The washing machine is out on the back porch. Come on back. We can have a nice cup of coffee while they're cycling."

Before Jillian could protest, RaeJean snatched the bundle and took it to the porch.

"There's a pot of fresh coffee, help yourself."

Jillian poured two cups, found sugar and cream, and set everything on the table.

"I just took cookies out of the oven. Want one? How 'bout a sandwich. You have lunch?"

"Cookies will be fine." Jillian's mouth watered when RaeJean placed a plate of warm chocolate chip cookies in front of her.

"Letty said you were planning on moving into Thornton House." RaeJean's dark face pinched with worry. "You think it's safe there, honey?"

"I hope so. The bedroom door has been reinforced. I had the phone turned on so I can call for help if I need it." The very thought of spending the night in her aunt's room gave Jillian the purple meanies. "I'll be careful, RaeJean."

"If you need money, I have a bit squirreled away."

Jillian placed her vanilla hand on top of RaeJean's chocolate one. "I appreciate your concern, but I'll be okay." Jillian nibbled her lower lip while glancing around the sunny kitchen. "Please don't tell anyone." She pulled out the diamond studs out of her pocket. "I found these in the ice cube tray at the house today. Do you think I should keep them?"

"Oh, my heavens! Those are Miss Felicity's earrings. She wore them all the time—never saw her without them." RaeJean's head came up. She put her finger to her mouth to quiet Jillian, stood and walked to the door to the hallway.

"Sorry, honey, I thought I heard someone. Yes, of course they belong to you, but you're ought to be careful about who knows. They're worth a lot of money."

"There's something else, RaeJean. I found a key to the locked attic. When I checked up there I discovered the whole place full of furniture, trunks, all kinds of lovely things. Why do you suppose my aunt had it up there?"

RaeJean paused for a moment. "Now, honey, it's none of my business, but since you found Thornton House in such a dilapidated state, I can't help wondering. What happened to all her money?"

Chapter 9

"Are those cookies I smell?" Malcolm Winters stood grinning in the kitchen doorway.

"Yes, sir, Mr. Malcolm. Coffee's fresh, too." RaeJean cupped Jillian's hand containing the earrings, a subtle signal to shut up. "Sit yourself down. I'll pour you a cup."

Jillian's fingers closed around the diamonds and she pushed them into the pocket of her jeans.

Malcolm sat in a chair. "I hope I'm not disturbing your coffee klatch."

RaeJean poured his coffee, busied herself at the kitchen sink, then slipped out to the back porch. Jillian could hear the washing machine spinning and thunking against the wall.

"RaeJean kindly offered to let me do my laundry here," Jillian said.

"Letty said you'd be moving into Thornton House. My, it must have been a fine old house in its day." His strong white teeth crunched a cookie. A flake of chocolate hung for a second at the corner of his mouth before falling off, drifting to the floor. In contrast to her grubby appearance, he looked like he'd just stepped out of a shower into clean clothes. Jillian could see comb marks in his still damp hair. Even his fingernails were manicured, shiny and buffed to perfection. She peeked at her own fingers where they rested on the table, their nails chopped, the cuticles ragged. She sighed. He might be attractive, but something about him made her skin crawl.

"And it will be again, I hope," she said.

He seemed startled, but quickly composed his face. "Once you settled in, would you mind if I visited you and explored the place a bit?" Malcolm's eyes crinkled boyishly. "Part of my book is about the old houses on Amelia, their history, *et cetera*. I know Thornton House has been here for years; I'd love to see it. The dining room chandelier alone would be worth a look."

Jillian's spine stiffened. "How—" A movement caught her eye. She glimpsed RaeJean in the doorway, moving her head from side to side. She cleared her throat. "When would you like to come? Actually it might be best to wait a while. The place is filthy. I'm in the processes of cleaning it up." She placed her clenched fists back onto her lap. "I want to restore it, room by room." What the hell could he be up to?

Jillian smelled gin and turned to find Letty behind her chair holding a half-full glass of clear liquid.

"There you are, Mal," the woman said.

He came out of his chair so fast it almost fell over. He hurried over to stand by Letty.

"Do you have time to come help me with something in the den?" She took a sip, aware of Jillian for the first time. "Hello, Jillian. How are things coming at your house?"

"It's a lot more work than I thought. I'll be staying here for at least one more night, maybe two. Will that cause a problem?"

Letty waved the glass, splashing liquid on the back of her hand. Her pink tongue darted out to lick it off. Dark red lipstick was smeared on her lips. Flecks of it had bled onto her teeth. "No, 'course not." She meandered back down the hall.

"Let RaeJean know so she can plan meals." Her voice drifted back into the room.

"Thanks for the snack, RaeJean. I'll see you ladies at dinner," Malcolm said over his shoulder. His lips turned up, but the smile never reached his eyes. Malcolm followed Letty down the hall.

Jillian felt relieved once he was gone. She sneaked a peek at her watch. It was pretty early to start drinking. The sun definitely hadn't dropped behind the yardarm yet.

"RaeJean, how did Malcolm know—"

The woman held her finger to her lips to halt Jillian's words. Her eyebrows were knitted in a frown, her mouth turned down. She picked up the plate of cookies, the cups, took them to the sink, then walked over and squinted down the hallway.

"What's wrong?" Jillian had a fluttering feeling in the pit of her stomach.

"Maybe nothing, sugar. There's something 'bout the man I don't trust. What's that saying? He's so slick he could pick your pocket over the phone. That's Mr. Malcolm." She made a hurrumphing noise. "Supposed to be writin' a book but he doesn't have a typewriter or computer in his room, just a bunch of papers littering the place. He's been here for months, and none of them has been moved."

"How can you be sure?"

A deep chuckle rumbled in RaeJean's throat. "I put one of my hairs on a pile of paper. It was there the next time I cleaned. Read about that trick in a mystery book."

"How do you think he knew about the chandelier in the dining room? Do you suppose he's already been in the house?"

"Could be. Ms. Felicity had a habit of takin' in strays. She always had a house full of people. Heaven only knows who they were or where they came from. Prancin' in and out all hours of the night. Some stayed there for a spell, too. So he might have been in the house at sometime." She started to rise. "Now, I'd best start on dinner."

"Wait, RaeJean. You said something before, about wondering how the money had disappeared. What were you talking about? What money?"

With a sigh, the woman settled back in the chair. "Like I said, it's none of my business, honey, but Thorntons have always had money. The family was super rich even before the Civil War. They owned most of this Island at one time. They had property near Jacksonville, and all over the state, from what Ms. Felicity told me. Now, what I'm wondering is, what happened to it all?"

Confusion buzzed in Jillian's head. Had they worked, had professions? Or been lazy dilettantes. She knew nothing about her real family. Jillian slumped into her chair, staring off into space. "It could have dissipated over the generations for supporting the Thornton's."

"I guess." RaeJean didn't look convinced. "Ms. Felicity was always very generous. Matter of fact, she loaned my husband Harold and me money for the down payment on our first house." RaeJean smiled at the memory. "She didn't even want us to repay the loan, but of course we did, with interest."

"That's the answer then. She gave it all away."

"Honey, I don't think she could have given it all away in her lifetime." She ran her finger through a trail of cookie crumbs on the table. "Once I started having babies, taking care of my own family, I sort of lost touch with Ms. Felicity. Then Harold had a job offer up north—Detroit. We lived there until he passed three years ago. I always hated cold weather, so I came back here to live."

The two women sat in silence until the washing machine beeped it had finished with its job.

"I'll load the stuff in the dryer." Jillian went to the porch.

As she stood in front of the spinning dryer, Jillian's thoughts tumbled like the sheets she had stuffed in the metal bin. When she returned to the kitchen she found RaeJean peeling a mound of shrimp onto a newspaper. "Want more coffee, honey?"

"No, I'm going up to my room and clean up before dinner. Unless I can help you?"

Surprised flitted across the woman's face. "Why, thank you, but no. I've got things under control. Jambalaya for dinner, I hope you're hungry."

"Not yet, but I will be. I'll be back in a while to fold the sheets." Jillian had never eaten jambalaya, but she loved shrimp and, judging from the pile of fat pink seafood on the counter, she'd have her fill tonight.

"Be sure and hide you know what in a safe place or keep them with you. I'd hate for them to go missing." RaeJean glanced toward the front of the house.

Jillian nodded. The diamonds felt like hot coals burning a hole in the pocket of her jeans. Once inside her bedroom with the door locked, she held the diamonds up to her ears. They caught the late afternoon light from the window, shooting prisms of colors around the room. She couldn't help herself. She unscrewed the back of one earring and pushed it into the hole in her lobe.

A soft knocking sounded on the door. Jillian's heart took off galloping in her chest. Quickly she snatched the diamond out of her ear and shoved the pair back into her pocket. When she opened the door, she found RaeJean standing there.

"Sorry to bother you, but Mr. Seth is downstairs. He'd like to see you."

"Tell him I'll be right down, RaeJean. Thanks." She closed the door and leaned against it. She hurried into the bathroom to make sure there were no errant streaks of dirt on her face. A touch of lipstick, a comb through her tangled curls completed her beauty regime.

The timing couldn't be more perfect. She could ask Seth to help her find out about her family, and if money had been hidden in the house... Jillian took a deep breath. No. It was time to stand on her own two feet. She couldn't keep turning to the nearest charming man for help. The very thought of Seth's hard body and smiling face made her mouth go dry. Maybe someday after she'd straightened out her own life she would be ready for a serious relationship again. But right now, she wanted to find out about her past.

Excitement thundered in her chest. She locked the door and started down the hallway. She was dying to find out what, if anything, he'd discovered about her mother.

* * * *

Seth watched Jillian hurry down the stairs, anxiety written all over her face. He only hoped the meager amount of information he'd brought would bring her a measure of peace, a place to start searching for her family.

"Hi, Seth. Did you find anything?" She looked at him with her gorgeous eyes. He wanted to crush her body to his, hold her tight and never let her go.

"Yes." He glanced over and saw the silhouette of someone standing in the parlor, out of sight. "Do you have time to go for a ride?"

"Sure, but I have to be back in time for dinner. RaeJean's making some dish with shrimp. I don't want to miss it."

He took her arm and drew her toward the door. "I'll get you back on time. RaeJean invited me to dinner, too."

Outside long shadows stretched across the sidewalk, announcing the arrival of darkness soon. "You warm enough?"

"Yes. Where are we going?"

Seth started the truck and pulled away from the curb. "The cemetery, to see your mother's grave." He heard her gasp beside him, but she didn't speak. He concentrated on driving until he maneuvered through the slow moving traffic in town.

"I found the accident report on your mother. There were some pictures from the morgue, but I didn't think you'd want to see them."

"No," she murmured, her voice soft as evening fog. "I'd rather remember her from the photos I have, when she looked happy."

"Maybe your father is alive somewhere. It's possible."

She turned her head toward the window so he couldn't see her eyes. "He's dead. I'm sure of it." When she turned back to him, her face was shiny with tears. She remained quiet until they arrived at the town cemetery.

Seth helped Jillian out of the truck. He felt her shoulders trembling. Thank goodness he'd driven over earlier to find the Thornton family plot. Jillian didn't need to be tramping around a graveyard in her present state. She resembled a wounded bird. He wanted to hold her in his arms until she healed and became whole again. He led her up the hill to where an alabaster angel stood guarding a huge mausoleum.

"Take your time, Jillian," he said and walked a few paces away. The beautiful spot on top of the hill had a perfect view of the ocean, not that any of the permanent residents could enjoy it. Acres of lush emerald lawn undulated in the sighing breeze. The smell of fresh-cut grass tickled his nose.

A spark of light caught his eye. He whirled. It flashed again on the far side of the grassy turf near the forest. Seth reached automatically for his gun and froze. Could someone be standing there with binoculars, or worse, a rifle with a scope? His eyes searched the tree line. Keeping his hand on the butt of his gun while walking toward the flash, he suddenly stopped. He didn't want to leave Jillian unprotected. He moved closer to her.

A soft breeze ruffled the leaves on the top of the trees. He heard the raucous sound of sea gulls fighting over their dead fish dinner. Nothing seemed out of place. Seth couldn't shove the thought of John Smith from Savannah out of his mind. He'd have to go back to do some further checking on the man. Why had he been stalking Jillian Bennett? There had to be a reason.

Seth remained alert, observing the thick trees surrounding the cemetery. He didn't see anyone and after a few minutes, he stared out to sea once more. Standing in this peaceful place, he couldn't help but think of his own sister, buried in the hard rocky earth of New England. Perhaps this wasn't such a bad place to live after all. And, he couldn't deny his growing attraction to Jillian.

He felt Jillian's presence, and smelled her light airy perfume before she spoke. He squinted once more at the tree line before he dropped his hand from his gun butt completely. The light was fading fast. She leaned her head against his shoulder. He slid his arm up around her waist. She melted into his body like warm butter on a roll. They stood together, in silent communication for a long time. Seth saw headstones marked, "Thornton" dating from the early 1800's up to Felicity Thornton's name—the last and most recent. Finally he heard her sigh.

"Thanks for bringing me, Seth. I feel more connected now. Not like an unwanted orphan."

"Ready to go back?"

She wiped the back of her hand across her eyes like a child, and smiled. "Yes."

They walked back to the truck, shoulders touching. He felt better once he had gotten her safely inside.

"I'm going to stop my housecleaning for a while. I think I'll go to the library tomorrow and get on a computer to do some Internet research. They buried my mother under her maiden name, Brown. I want to see if I can't find some of her background. Maybe even the name of my father."

"Did you find anything in the house yet?" Seth turned out of the cemetery onto the main road.

"Oh, yes!" She wiggled in her seat until she managed to pull out a pair of spectacular earrings.

"Wow!"

"RaeJean said these belonged to my Aunt Felicity and they're real. They were hidden in an ice cube tray of the freezer." Excitement colored her voice. Out of the corner of his eye, he saw her blush. "I found the key to the attic there too and went up. Seth, it's full of furniture, trunks, tons of other stuff."

"Maybe we should start up there," he said.

The words startled her, and Seth thought, *We? Did I actually say we? Why not?* His drug investigation had stalled, but if there was any connection to be found at Thornton House, it might be in the attic. Besides, he wanted to stay close to Jillian in case the stalker came after her again. He couldn't bear the thought of her alone in the house in the daytime, and certainly not at night. Somehow, he had to talk her out of moving into Thornton House. Or into letting him stay there with her.

"Seth, if anything is hidden in the house I could search years before I find it. I can't help but wonder if Felicity needed money, why she didn't sell some of those things. I can't be sure, but there might be antiques up there."

"Maybe she didn't need the money that badly." Seth parked a half a block from Cantrell's B-and-B, shut off the motor and turned in his seat to face Jillian.

"That's another thing. RaeJean grew up on the island and knew my aunt years ago. Seth, she said the Thornton's had always been very wealthy. There should be money left, a lot of it."

"What did your attorney say?"

"Only that she'd run out of assets. What money she had was used up finding me." She tilted her head, staring off into the distance. "Wouldn't there be tax returns to analyze?"

"Of course. The attorney, what's his name?

"Bannerman."

"Yeah, Bannerman should have copies. Unless the money had all been spent before he took over the estate."

"Could be. But he told me he'd only been her attorney for the past couple of years. She trusted a different lawyer to help with my adoption, but that was twenty-five years ago. If that person was Felicity's contemporary, he's probably long gone."

Seth's stomach growled, causing them both to smile.

"I guess it's time for dinner. Why don't you go to the courthouse in the morning," Seth said, "get copies of the tax records. They're open to the public. You might learn something and it would be quicker than starting on the Internet. I have to wrap up some paperwork on a murder in the morning. How about if I come to Thornton House around lunchtime? The two of us can make like Columbus and go exploring."

Jillian's exotic eyes widened. "A murder! Here on Amelia Island? What happened?"

"No need to be frightened, it's the first one I've encountered since I started on the force. Let's go into the house, I'm starved. I'll fill you in over dinner."

* * * *

Jillian paused in dishing up the rice to listen to the end of Seth's story. She felt better now than she had at the cemetery, standing there in front of the grave of a woman she didn't remember—her mother. In terms of relatives, she had no one but herself to rely on. She tuned back into the conversation.

"By the time we locked him in a cell, he was blubbering how much he missed his wife." Seth lounged in a kitchen chair while Jillian helped RaeJean with the final preparation for dinner. "They lived in a shack in the woods behind your property, Jillian."

"I heard sirens at the house today." She couldn't help but shudder. "I'm glad I didn't see anything."

"Silly fool. I knew one of them would kill the other some day," RaeJean said. "It's a mercy they didn't have any younguns." She wiped her fingers on a blue striped kitchen towel. "I grew up with him. Booger always did have a temper."

"Booger?" Jillian couldn't help but giggle. "How on earth did he get that nickname?" Sitting in the warm brightly-lit kitchen, Jillian felt happier than she'd been in a long time.

"Honey, you don't want to know, especially before dinner. You grab the bowl of rice and go sit down in the dining room. I'll round up the other folks and bring in the rest of the food."

The honeymoon couple came into the dining room, gazing into one another eyes, oblivious to the rest of the world. Jillian felt a twinge of jealousy. In all the excitement she'd almost forgotten that Craig was on his honeymoon, too.

Malcolm and Letty were already seated with their heads together, whispering. The minute Jillian entered the room they stopped talking. They stared at her, then one another before shifting their gazes. Letty seemed more wide-awake than she'd been earlier. Her hair had been combed, and she'd applied fresh lipstick. Perhaps she'd had a nap. All at once, she became the gracious hostess.

"Seth, Jillian, these are two of my other guests, Biff and Cindy Lawson. Jillian Bennett, Seth Falconer."

"You want me to serve or should we wait for the other guest?" RaeJean stood next to the steaming tureen of jambalaya. Jillian could smell the spices and green peppers. Her mouth watered in anticipation.

"Oh, dear, I'm so sorry. She went out to dinner with friends. I guess I forgot to tell you," Letty said.

Jillian could see RaeJean shrug. She must be used to her capricious boss.

"Good, more for me," Seth said. "I've had RaeJean's jambalaya." He heaped his plate with rice before passing it on to Jillian.

Conversation lagged until Malcolm asked Biff if he golfed. That's all it took. Both Lawson's were avid golfers and soon the talk around the table buzzed with birdies, bogies, courses they'd played as well as the advantages of various clubs. Jillian tuned out to concentrate on the delicious food and her thoughts.

She'd forgotten to tell Seth about the disgusting man who lived behind her with Snowflake. Poor dog, Jillian hoped he hadn't gotten tangled in the chain again. Tomorrow she'd ask Seth to go with her to... No; she could take care of this herself.

"Have you ever lived in the south?" Jillian bumped back to the present to find Cindy Lawson staring at her from across the table. "Atlanta, Savannah, Charlotte?"

"No. I grew up in Colorado and have never lived anywhere else. Why?" No need to mention her brief childhood stay on the Island.

RaeJean placed a steaming pan of hot peach cobbler in the center of the table. "Coffee?"

There were murmurs of agreement around the table, along with groans of satisfaction.

"No particular reason. You just seem so familiar for some reason," Cindy said. "Maybe it's your eyes. They're gorgeous." She took a sip of coffee then smiled. "Just my imagination, I guess."

Jillian saw RaeJean watching her from behind Cindy's chair. Instead of dropping her head with embarrassment, she held it high. "Thank you, Cindy." Relief flooded through her body. Accepting a compliment hadn't been all that hard after all. Jillian decided she might as well make the most of her eyes, play them up to the hilt. RaeJean had been right when she told Jillian her eyes were beautiful. Most people would love to have such an unusual feature.

The dinner chatter wound down with the last bites of cobbler. The Lawsons said their good nights and headed off to town to check out a local nightclub. Malcolm mumbled something about going over his notes, and Letty invited Seth and Jillian into the parlor for after dinner drinks.

"Not for me, Letty, I have a busy day tomorrow. Thanks for dinner. Tell RaeJean it was delicious." Jillian stood up. "Walk out with me?"

In the hallway, when he took her hand in his it felt so comfortable, so right. She sauntered outside with him to the side of his truck.

"I'll come by around lunch time tomorrow and bring some sandwiches, then we can go poke around in your attic, okay?"

Jillian nodded. "Sure, I'd appreciate the help." Shards of moonlight behind Seth's head highlighted a few strands of gray in his hair. His dark eyes shone like liquid coal. He bent forward, bringing his lips to hers. They were eager, soft and tasted of peaches. The kiss sent a wild swirl into the pit of her stomach.

A groan of desire escaped from deep in Jillian's throat. She reached up to push her fingers into his thick, raven hair. The tip of his tongue probed her mouth, setting her on fire. He pulled his lips away and crushed her against his hard body.

"Jillian, Jillian," he whispered against her hair. She circled his body with her arms, melting into the embrace. If only she could stay here in the protection of his closeness forever. She felt the heady sensation of his lips on her neck, the hard knot of his manhood pressing against her thigh. He kept murmuring her name between light kisses on her face. Slowly his lips came closer to hers until she wanted to scream with longing. Their lips met once more. Her eager response startled Jillian. She had never felt like this with Craig.

Abruptly, Seth pulled away. "I have to go, now." His voice grumbled hoarsely, rough with longing. His large hands held her gently by her upper arms. "I'll see you tomorrow." He leaned over once more and planted a kiss on her nose, soft as angel wings passing by.

Jillian leaned against the picket fence, watching the tail-lights of Seth's truck until they disappeared into the darkness. Her mind tumbled in turmoil. She had enough decisions to make without the complication of falling for Seth.

House, money, job...what was she going to do first? Off in the distance, she heard the lonely wail of the train whistle crying in the night. Once again, it stirred an ancient memory in her brain.

Chapter 10

Jillian sprinted the last few feet up to the porch of Thornton House, dodging puddles of muddy water. It had rained again all last night, leaving the air cool but filled with moisture. Gray clouds skittered overhead, ripe with wetness, ready to dump again. The inside of the house wasn't much warmer than the outside. She heard the wind moaning through loose planks of siding, crying to come inside. She'd barely stepped inside when rain splattered against the windowpanes and slithered in between the boards.

Thank goodness she'd dressed warmly. The huge University of Colorado sweatshirt she'd pulled over her long sleeved T-shirt hugged her like a heavy rug. Jillian had even remembered to wear an extra pair of socks inside her disreputable tennis shoes.

She set her bag of groceries on the floor and cocked her head to listen. No creaking boards, no slamming doors, not even a wailing ghost. Other than the patter of rain, silence filled the house. Hands on hips, she did a slow turn in the foyer. Then in her best Bette Davis accent she declared, "What...a...dump!"

Chuckling, she bent over and picked up the bag. Jillian shouldn't be this happy, but a good night's sleep combined with the memory of Seth's kisses woke her at six-thirty, ready for the day ahead. One of the best, perhaps the only good thing Craig had gifted her with was the joy of early rising. Jillian loved nothing better than hauling out of bed before dawn to start her day. Unfortunately, nothing in town opened until at least nine o'clock except the supermarket that opened at six, so she had some time to kill. No matter. The extra hours would allow her to continue searching the house for treasure.

After making sure she locked the front door, Jillian scooted up the stairs. She unlocked the door and went in, setting the groceries on the table. The day before she had pushed a window open a few inches at the end of the hall. Now the air smelled fresh and clean. A bit of rainwater had seeped in, but she quickly disposed of it with a paper towel.

"Let's go see what's in the bat cave." Jillian flicked on the heavy flashlight to make sure the beam burned steady, then took the key and made her way up the stairs to dig in the attic for a while.

At the top of the steps a canopy of spider webs halted her progress. Dead bugs dotted the web like raisins in rice pudding. The air smelled of mold, dust and ancient mouse droppings. She shot her light beam around the cavernous space, sweeping up toward the ceiling. There were no apparent leaks in the roof. Shifting her light back down, she saw a faint pathway through the piles of furniture with barely an inch of extra room on either side.

"Now why in the name of heaven did she stash all this up here and leave the rest of the house empty?" Jillian swept the attic with her light. Under the eaves an upright piano cowered beneath a dusty, paisley shawl. Ten years of piano lessons, recitals and endless hours of practice made Jillian's fingers itch. She knew the perfect spot for the instrument downstairs.

Turning sideways, she sidled between an enormous steamer trunk covered with decals from exotic locations around the globe, and a mahogany desk. She set the flashlight on the desk and tugged at the top desk drawer. The wood shrieked. Unbalanced, the flashlight rolled to the edge and onto the floor with a crash. The light blinked out. Murky shadows pushed in around her. At the end of the attic, Jillian heard the angry rattle of wind buffeting the wooden slats over the louver.

She stood, quaking, trying without success to control her ragged breathing. Behind her in the shadows, a mouse squeak was abruptly cut off mid-squeal. The sound sent a chill down her back. With fingers crossed, she slowly bent over to pick up the light. She stabbed at the button with shaky fingers. A steady beam lanced the gloom.

This time before Jillian pulled at the sticky drawer she wedged the flashlight in her right armpit. The drawer still refused to move. She tugged again with all her strength. The whole thing flew out. Jillian landed on her backside on top of the steamer trunk.

"Ouch!" One of the rivets gave her butt a nasty pinch. After rubbing the spot to set the blood flowing again, she aimed the beam of light at the contents of the drawer strewn at her feet. It consisted of the usual assortment of desk paraphernalia: pencil stubs, paper clips, and rubber bands. Slips of paper and a mixture of coupons from the Sunday supplement, years out of date, fluttered in the wake of her man-made breeze when she stepped closer. She should have brought a grocery bag up here to gather some of this stuff for later reading. She shoved the whole mess back into the drawer and tried the one on the other side. This one came out more smoothly.

A faint noise echoed up the stairwell. Jillian couldn't be sure...was it the wind or had someone called out a name? It almost sounded like a man calling for Felicity, but who was it? It was way too early for Seth to arrive and he wouldn't use her aunt's name. She stood frozen, waiting. She heard nothing. As quietly as possible, she walked to the top of the steps. The lump in her throat grew to the size of a boulder and her breath escaped in shallow gasps. After what seemed like an hour but was probably only seconds, Jillian relaxed a bit. She hadn't heard any more sounds; it must have been her imagination. The front door was locked, after all. She resumed her tasks, but kept one nervous eye on the stairwell.

Beneath a pair of scissors, rusted along the edges, a book with a worn purple cover was trapped. Excitement almost curdled the breakfast eggs in her stomach. It was the right size to be a diary. Feeling a bit like Nancy Drew as she pulled it loose, she eased her bottom back onto the trunk and aimed the light at the book. With great care, she pried open the front cover.

Faded purple ink on the inside proudly proclaimed this to be the private diary of one Felicity Antonia Thornton. The words had run into illegible smears. Jillian's heart sank. The pages were cemented together from dampness. Fuzzy gray mold grew across the tops.

Jillian's fingers dove back into the drawer and scurried around until they touched a letter opener. "Come on, come on." She managed to insert the tip a few millimeters, but the sheets remained glued. She sat staring at the offending layers, willing them to separate; all thoughts of intruders had fled from her mind. She tried further back in the book. This time, with a tiny sucking sound, the pages drifted apart.

Most of the words were lost or had dribbled to the line below. There were only a few distinct sentences.

It's happened again. Two dining room chairs disappeared last night. A swath of ink obscured the rest, then: *I don't know whom to trust or where to turn. I hired a crew to come in at night during the Shrimp Festival when everyone will be busy in town. They will help me hide...* The rest of the page had either rotted away or been torn out. From the date on top of the page, Jillian's aunt had written this part four years ago.

She turned another page. *I received my bank statement yesterday. It's gone, it's almost all gone! What have I done? Oh, dear God, what's happening to me?* The rest of the pages in the book had been ripped out.

Forgetting where she was, Jillian started to lean back. She almost fell ass-over-tea kettle onto the floor before she managed to jerk forward to her feet. Had someone been harassing the woman, or had her poor aunt been suffering delusions toward the end? The result of a stroke or merely old age? She might never know.

Jillian set the diary on top of the desk. She'd take it downstairs with her, dry it out and perhaps she would be able to read more of the words. She would like to learn more about her aunt.

After a quick peek at her watch, Jillian squeezed through the mess around the bureau. A flash from lightning bobbled across the filthy window at the end of the room. She heard the wind rising. Something appeared to move off to her right. She whirled, ducked and aimed her flashlight toward the corner. An old dressmaker's dummy stood illuminated in the beam. It was naked except for a racy red-plumed hat atop its head. The patter of heavy rain echoed Jillian's heartbeats. She took a few deep breaths to calm down.

Her chuckles echoed through the vast attic. "Sheesh, if I'm afraid of a dummy, how on earth am I going to live here?"

As if in answer to her question, the wind howled and threw the branches of a tree against the house. She should leave for town soon, but wanted to check out the bureau before she departed. The top drawer yielded an old white cotton bra, 38-D, with a broken strap, and three marbles. The second drawer down contained a wadded up ball of paper. Jillian smoothed it and found the same spidery handwriting in purple ink. *They're watching me. I have to hide everything!*

Jillian stuffed it in her pocket, turning her attention to the lower drawer. Inside rested a massive jewelry chest made of highly polished rosewood. Wrestling it from side to side, Jillian managed to extract the box. She carried the case over and placed it on top of the desk. Running her tongue around her lips, she raised the lid. A skitter of wind whispered across the back of her neck.

Marvelous things must have rested at one time on the spots of the worn purple velvet. Now, it was empty except for a rusty dime, two quarters, a gold cross on a thin chain with a tiny ruby in the center and a child's barrette, pink as the inside of a conch shell. Her fingers flew to the side of her head. Jillian was positive it had belonged to her at one time. All her earlier happiness evaporated like mist in sunlight. How different her life would have been growing up here with her aunt.

Jillian wiped her cheeks with the back of her hand and picked up the heavy box. She'd take it and the diary to her room, and decide what to do with them later. She might use the jewelry box for her earrings. A chuckle escaped at the thought of only one pair of earrings in this huge box. Frustration settled in her chest. At this rate she'd be searching until her bones rattled and her hair turned gray. Time to go wash up and head for city hall so she would be back to Thornton House in time for lunch with Seth.

She saw at least four empty light fixtures hanging from the lower parts of the ceiling. Not only would they give her more light, she wouldn't have to worry about dropping the heavy flashlight on her toes. She'd pick up a few bulbs while in town.

Jillian eased carefully down the stairs with her burden, shifted the box and turned the doorknob, but the door wouldn't budge.

"Must be stuck." She set her finds on a stair and grasped the knob with both hands. It twisted easily, but the door wouldn't open. Jillian fumbled with her flashlight, shining it through the keyhole. Only blackness stared back. The key remained in the lock. Someone had trapped Jillian in the attic.

* * * *

Seth arrived at Thornton House a little before noon with sandwiches from the deli. The door stood open, and he knew instantly something was wrong. Taking the steps two at a time, he rushed up to Felicity's apartment. That door, too, gaped, but the room was empty. He dropped the bag on the table and yelled Jillian's name. He heard frantic fists pounding wood from the other side of the attic door. The key was in the lock, so he turned it. The minute the door flew open, Jillian leaped into his arms. Her face was covered with dirty tears. He held her and soon she stopped shaking.

"Jillian, what happened? How did you manage to lock yourself in the attic?"

She shoved him back and glared at him. "How did I... Wait right here." She hurried into the bathroom. She came out dabbing at her face with a peach-colored towel. "Sorry, I've been locked in there for over three hours."

"You really have to be more careful about locking the front door when you're here alone," Seth said.

"I did! I know I locked that door. Someone must have opened it and come in, and trapped me in the attic." She crossed her arms and rubbed her palms up and down the sleeve of her sweatshirt. "I heard a voice down here, too."

The cop in Seth took over. He had to get all the details but didn't want to scare Jillian. Seth eased a chair out from the kitchen table. "Here, sit down and try to relax." He helped Jillian into the chair. "Now, tell me everything." He grabbed a water bottle out of the fridge and took it to her. She drank thirstily then patted dribbles from her mouth with the towel.

"I had extra time before City Hall opened this morning, so I thought I'd poke around up in the attic."

Seth sat, leaned back, tilting the legs of the chair. He grabbed the edge of the table to balance himself. "What did you find?"

"A lot." Jillian got up and hurried out of the room. Before he could follow her, she came back and set a wooden box in the middle of the table next to the bag of deli sandwiches Seth had brought.

"Seth, the attic is jammed with furniture. I know some must be antiques." She took a ratty-looking leather book out of the case. "I also found my aunt's diary. I had hoped to read something about my parents or at least my relatives, but..." She held it up. Seth saw that the pages were gunked together and fringed with mildew.

"Were you able to decipher any of it?"

Sadness pulled at the corners of her mouth. "She must have been sick, perhaps paranoid toward the end of life. She had some men move her furniture into the attic because she thought someone had been stealing it." A crooked grin spread across her lips. "You don't think insanity is inherited, do you?"

The chair thumped against the floor. Seth reached out and took her hand between his. "No, I don't. Why are you so intent on finding out about your past?"

She lowered her eyes to their joined hands. With her fingers, she drew lazy circles on the back of his hand. "Because I was adopted, I've never felt whole, or connected or..." Her fingers fluttered up. "…something. My parents were good people, but I think they adopted me so they'd have someone to care for them when they grew old." Her head came up, their eyes met.

"You grew up in a loving family, surrounded by siblings, cousins, a big family." Jillian brushed a dark curl from her forehead. "You're so lucky." She started to say something else but bit her lip to keep the words contained. "I don't know anything about my medical background. I might harbor some genetic disease I could pass on to my children. Certainly my eyes…"

Seth rose from his chair and pulled her into his embrace. She had been terribly hurt and it made him furious. "Your kids will be lucky to inherit your eyes."

She leaned into his body, circling his waist with her arms. He kissed the top of her soft curls. She smelled like soap or flowers, something light and refreshing.

Jillian pulled away and reached for the water bottle on the table. Seth missed the warmth of her body. He wanted to reach out to bring her close again. "Did you find anything else in the jewelry box?"

She turned the open box toward him. "Only some rusty coins and a child's barrette. I think it belonged to me. Oh, and this cross." When she held up the delicate chain, Seth thought his head might explode. Without thinking, he shot his hand out and grabbed the chain.

"This is Melinda's! My sister's." He would always picture her the way he'd seen her last—laughing. "My parents gave it to Melinda for her first communion. She never took it off. The stone is a ruby; her birthday was in July."

Jillian curled his fingers around the piece. "Now we know for sure your sister spent time in this house. You keep it, Seth."

He took a clean handkerchief from his back pocket and carefully wrapped the icon in it. He'd send it to his Mom. When he looked up he saw Jillian hovering next to the table.

"Wait a minute." She turned around in a slow circle, staring at every aspect of the room. "Seth, someone has been in here."

"In the apartment? Are you sure?"

"Yes. For one thing, I remember setting the bag of groceries on the table, now it's on the kitchen counter." She walked over to peek into the bag. "Everything's here. 'Course, why would a thief want toilet tissue or dog cookies?"

His mind did a double take. "Dog cook—"

"There's something else," she interrupted. A frown marred her perfect pale skin. "The voice I heard when I was in the attic was a man calling out for Felicity. At first I thought I was imagining it. I didn't recognize the voice and kept quiet. I didn't want anyone to know I was up there."

"Are you sure it was a man?" Seth asked

"Yes. He sounded so sad or lost."

"Who else has a key to the front door?" This damn place was to busy for his taste.

"Who knows? I'm the new kid in town, remember?" She walked over to look out the window. Over her shoulder Seth saw the sun playing hide and seek in the clouds, the rain over for a while. "Maybe it's your mysterious drug dealers," she said, "or, oh, I almost forgot. George Bannerman, Felicity's attorney, he kept a duplicate key. 'Course he wouldn't be calling my aunt's name." She tilted her head. "And, it didn't sound like him."

Seth didn't know the attorney but reminded himself to check up on him.

Jillian strode to the phone. "There's one way to find out if he was here. I'll call him." She pulled her purse onto her lap, rummaging around until she came up with a wrinkled business card. "I can ask him for copies of Felicity's tax returns, too."

Seth roamed about the room while she sat and dialed.

"It's his answering machine... Mr. Bannerma, this is Jillian Bennett. Please call me when you return." She rattled off the phone number before hanging up. "He's gone to the Bahamas for a few days of fishing."

"First things first," Seth said. "Let's eat, then I want to cruise through your attic. My Uncle Nick owns an antiques business up near Battleboro, Vermont, and I learned a bit about heirlooms the summer I worked for him. Who knows? Maybe you're a rich heiress after all."

Jillian retrieved sodas from the refrigerator while Seth unwrapped the sandwiches. "Turkey or tuna?"

"Both," she said with a grin.

Jillian put half of each sandwich on a plate and set them on the table along with sodas and napkins.

Seth barely got his teeth around the turkey on rye when he heard a soft voice drifting up through the window from the yard.

"Felicity?"

Seth dashed over, jerking the window all the way up. The swollen wood screamed in protest. "Hey you! Stop!"

He ran for the door. "You go out the front," he called to Jillian. Don't let him by you. It's the old guy. I have to catch him."

* * * *

Jillian choked down the half-chewed mess of tuna in her mouth. She thundered down the staircase after Seth, jerked open the front door, slammed it shut behind her, ran outside and stopped. Which way should she go? There were scruffy broken brushes to the right, so she turned that way. By the time she rounded the side of the house to the back, Seth was crashing into the trees.

"Wait for me!" Jillian followed the faint trail. Angry clouds scudded overhead. The wind had picked up again, and cold air moved around her. "Seth! Where are you!" She saw a blur of movement to the right, whirled, but only saw branches wavering in the wind.

She moved forward as fast as possible in the dense underbrush. A plop of cold water dropped from a leaf, hitting her square on the nose. "Great, it's going to rain again." Up ahead it sounded like a herd of angry rhinos were taking tango lessons. A mad thrashing ensued, then silence. Jillian halted in her tracks. Had Seth found the man? Should she go call for help?

"Seth?" Jillian said in a voice barely above a whisper. "Did you find him?"

"No."

Jillian whipped around. Seth stood behind her, panting. Dead leaves and brown grass covered his clothes. He looked a bit like the straw man from *The Wizard of Oz*. He bent at the waist, palms on his knees, sucking air into his lungs.

"You let him slip away." Jillian had been anxious to meet the old guy to make sure she hadn't hit him the night she came to town.

"I let him slip away? Where the hell were you?" Seth's eyebrows almost met in the center. "I thought you were right behind me."

"I thought so too. He must have gone out the other side of the forest. It's not that deep."

"Yeah, I guess. It's easy to become confused in these woods. Sorry I snapped at you. Here, give me your hand, I'll take you back to the house." He held out fingers covered with mud.

She ignored his outstretched hand. "I know exactly where I am. I'm perfectly capable of finding my way home, Mr. Falconer." Jillian marched by the cop, pushing a branch aside.

"Going the long way? Because you're headed for the ocean."

Jillian gritted her teeth, stomped off in the other direction, and promptly fell over a dead log. Her palms slid over the rough bark, sizzling with pain, and she bumped her head on a rock.

"If I hear laughter coming from anywhere in these woods, I will kill you!" She flopped on her bottom and started pulling twigs out of her hair.

"I wouldn't dream of laughing at you."

Jillian looked up and saw a lop-sided grin decorating Seth's face.

"Now will you let me help you home, miss?"

She extended her arm. He grasped it, swooping her up with ease.

"You're mighty feisty today," Seth said. "What happened to the scared mouse who only blew into town a couple of days ago?"

Jillian swatted the dirt off her butt. "I guess she's tired of chasing everyone else's cheese. Now she's going to find her own."

Chapter 11

"I think you'd better disinfect that scratch." Seth cupped Jillian's elbow with his strong grasp. "Don't want it to become infected; it might leave a scar on your chin." He let go and they mounted the front steps and walked into the house.

"It'll be fine. Right now I'm more interested in lunch." Jillian started up the narrow staircase to the second floor ahead of Seth. "Seriously, what do you think the old guy is doing around here?"

"I have no idea. I've only spotted him a few times at night. Never was able to catch up with him. He keeps disappearing into the woods." Seth couldn't keep his mind on the old man while he watched Jillian's cute fanny ahead of him. He took a handkerchief out of his back pocket, swiping at the worst of the grime on his hands. "Maybe he's—" Up ahead he saw Jillian standing frozen in the doorway to the apartment. She turned to him, her eyes wide.

"Seth."

He flattened himself against the wall and reached for his gun. In one swift move, he sprinted forward, shoved Jillian aside, rounded the doorjamb and dropped into a crouched shooting position. There at the kitchen table sat the old fellow they'd been chasing. He was happily munching on Seth's turkey sandwich.

"It's good," he said before pausing to sip from the can of soda. He saw Seth's gun and dropped the can. He buried his head in his arms. A soft moan escaped from his throat as he sat cowering in his chair.

"Hands in the air, now! Let me see those hands! Who are you? How the hell did you get in here, why—"

He felt a gentle touch on his arm. "Seth, you're scaring him."

Before he could stop her, Jillian walked over to hunker down by the man. "It's okay. We won't hurt you." She patted his arm. "Why don't you finish the sandwich?"

Slowly, his head came up, inches from hers. "Felicity?" he said. "I've been hunting all over for you for the longest time. Why did you go away?" He rested his gnarled bent fingers on Jillian's soft white arm. Then the man seemed to forget her and went back to eating. Jillian ripped off a paper towel to mop up the spilled soda before taking a chair opposite the man.

"My name is Jillian, what's yours?"

He stopped mid-chew, his eyes drifting up toward the corner of the room. He fingered the plastic card suspended from a cord around his neck. "Fred, I'm Fred. When is Felicity coming back? I miss her."

"May I see your card?" Jillian asked.

When he nodded, Jillian flipped over the plastic square. "Seth, he's an Alzheimer patient. There's a phone number to call."

Seth went and picked up the receiver. Jillian read off the numbers while he dialed.

A woman's voice answered. "Marymount. May I help you?"

"This is Detective Seth Falconer of the Amelia Island PD. I have one of your patients here named Fred."

Seth heard a sharp intake of air. "Is he dead?"

"Hardly. Right now he's eating my lunch. I assume you knew he'd traipsed off."

"Oh, yes. Are you sure he's okay? He's been gone for hours. Where are you?"

"Slow down, he's fine. Can you send someone to pick him up?"

"Not right now. Everyone's out searching for him."

Seth turned to watch Jillian and Fred. She sat opposite him, murmuring softly to the old man. "Where is your facility? I can bring him back."

"Thank you, officer, that would be wonderful. We're right off Sadler Road, 74 Marymount Street."

"Off Sadler… How in the hell did he walk way up here?"

A low chuckle floated across the phone lines. "It's a mystery to us, too. Once these Alzheimer folks start walking, they can go amazing distances. We'll be waiting for you. Thank you so much, officer."

Seth hung up. "Did you find out anything?" he asked Jillian as she gave him a half of the tuna sandwich. He ripped into it like a rabid wolf.

"He told me his name is Fred and he's engaged to Felicity. They're getting married on Saturday." Jillian patted the old man's shoulder with a smile. "Did he wander off?"

"Yeah, I said we'd bring him home. Did you find out how he got into the house?"

"Yes, I think so. Fred said it's a secret but he'd tell me because I'm so pretty." Her dirty face turned pink. "He keeps saying two down, three over. I have no idea what it means."

Seth grabbed a fresh soda out of the fridge to wash down the remains of his sandwich. "If you ask me, there are far too many secrets associated with this house. Ready to go?"

"Sure. Want to go for a ride, Fred?"

Fred sat for a moment then hauled his body up. “Are we going to find Felicity? Did she go to Miami?”

“No, sweetie.” Jillian took his arm. “First you’re going to show me the magic spot you mentioned, then we’ll drive you home.”

“Your eyes are beautiful.” Fred smiled. He shuffled out the door holding Jillian’s arm. Seth locked the apartment.

When they stood on the front porch, Jillian made sure the door lock clicked. “Now, where’s the magic spot, Fred?”

He stood staring at the house in obvious confusion. With bent, scarred fingers, he scratched at his tangled gray hair. Then his face lit up. “Two down, three over.” His hands fluttered in front of his chest. He reached for the siding on the right side of the front door. Carefully he pushed a panel of siding away. There in a niche rested a duplicate key to the front door of Thornton House.

* * * *

Jillian watched with astonishment as Fred plucked the key from the hollow and deftly opened the front door before returning the key to its hiding place.

“Always a meal and warm bed, she said.” Fred stood on the porch, fists in his pockets, waiting.

“Jeez, I wonder how many other people knew about this?” Seth pushed the panel aside, took the key and put it in his pocket. He thumped at the boards around the inside of the hiding place.

“Lots of folks,” Fred told him. “My Felicity is a wonderful woman. We’re getting married on Saturday, did I tell you?” He frowned, and then his eyes searched the front windows of the house. “Where is Felicity?”

Jillian used her key to re-lock the door. “We’ll go find her now, Fred.” She took his arm, leading him down the steps.

"He's very tired, Seth. Time to go. Perhaps they'll have some answers for us at the nursing home."

Jillian checked her front pocket to make sure the diamond earrings were still there. They were her insurance she couldn't lose. Then the three of them climbed into Seth's truck. Fred fell asleep, his head resting against the door, and started to snore loudly. The journey only took ten minutes by car, but Jillian was amazed the old man had been able to walk the distance, more than once.

"There it is." Seth pulled up in front of a medium-sized stucco building. Ramps and railings along the front left no doubt about the purpose of this building.

A woman wearing a crisp white blouse, severe black skirt and matching no-nonsense shoes came hurrying out the door before they'd come to a complete stop. Loose gray hairs had escaped from the tight bun at the nape of her neck and flew out around her anxious face.

Fred snorted himself awake. "Are we in Miami already?"

Seth jumped out of the truck and came around to help Fred and Jillian out.

"Is he all right?" the woman asked. "Where did you find him?"

"Seems to be fine. He was at Thornton House—over on Broome Street...I'm Seth Falconer and this is Jillian Bennett."

"Virginia Trent. I'm the supervisor here at Marymount. I do appreciate you bringing him home." She took Fred's arm, steering him toward the front door. "Come along Fred. We've all been so worried about you."

She spoke to them over her shoulder while walking. "We lock our doors and try to keep an eye on our patients, but sometimes they escape." She patted Fred's arm. "We found out today one of Fred's old fishing buddies had a key hidden in his room. He didn't want to stand in the way of true love and has been letting Fred out."

"I'm tired. It's time for my nap." Fred wandered in the front door and disappeared down a hallway.

"Can he find his own room?" Jillian asked.

"Yes, he's fine inside the facility. Thank you again." She turned to go.

"Ms. Trent, I would like to ask a few questions," Seth said.

Jillian could see the woman stiffen. She turned to face them again, her lips pressed together in a straight line. "What?" she asked.

"Actually we need your help." Seth smiled at the woman, showing a deep dimple in one cheek. Jillian could almost hear the ice melt. "Miss Bennett is Felicity Thornton's niece. She never met her great-aunt. Fred's been showing up at Thornton House more than once. Today he told us he's going to marry Felicity. We, I mean Ms. Bennett, would like to know more about her aunt." A lock of dark hair had fallen over Seth's forehead, giving him a decidedly boyish appearance. He flirted with the older woman outrageously. "Is there any information you can share with us?"

"I knew Felicity Thornton well. I'll be happy to tell you what I can, outside of patient information, of course. My office is down this way, if you'll follow me. We can be more comfortable there." She walked down the hallway, her sensible black shoes squeaking on the immaculate tile.

Jillian and Seth trailed behind her. They passed a large recreation room where seniors were playing cards, Ping-Pong, or watching television. The facility smelled of boiled vegetables, pine cleaner and gentle decay. The patients appeared to be happy and well cared for.

"The building is very nice, Ms. Trent." He wiggled his eyebrows at Jillian. "This must be a wonderful place for these elderly folks to live."

"Here we are." She stepped aside for them to go into her office. "Yes, we try to make the place comfortable, like home. We're able to do it in part thanks to Felicity Thornton's generosity." She walked around behind her desk and sat, crossing her fingers on top. "Now, then, what can I tell you?"

Glancing at Seth, Jillian licked her lips. He gave her a slight nod, so she spoke. "I only recently found out about my inheritance. I know nothing about my aunt, but I want to find out more about her. Several times Fred told he intended to marry Aunt Felicity. Is it a fantasy or had they planned to wed at one time?" She sat back in her chair.

"Oh, I expect most of us older residents of the area know the story. You see Fred and Felicity were sweethearts long ago. They fell in love in high school and wanted to marry. Fred spent his life at sea on a shrimp boat. Felicity's father, Horace, wouldn't allow her to marry a shrimper. He wanted something better for his daughter, someone more in keeping with their social status." Virginia paused before continuing.

"Of course, Felicity obeyed her father. Many times she sat right in that chair, Miss Bennett, and told me how much she regretted her decision. She never did marry, you know." She glanced down at her own bare fingers. "Even after her father died, she couldn't defy him. She and Fred remained great friends for years but they never married. When he became sick, she cared for him in her home. When that no was longer possible, she arranged for him to live with us." She hesitated for a moment and seemed to come to some decision.

"Felicity loved Fred so much she set up a trust fund for him here. There's more than enough money to see him through until the end, then the remainder will revert to

Marymount. She would have moved here herself, but died before she had the chance."

Tears pooled in Jillian's eyes. Now, more than ever, she regretted not having known her aunt. "What a wonderful thing to do." She reached into her purse for a tissue to dab at her eyes.

"Oh, yes, Felicity was known for her generosity. She spent her days caring for others, feeding, clothing and housing young people. She treated them like the family she never had. She even took in some drug addicts to clean them up, make them healthy again."

Jillian saw Seth sit forward on his chair; his mouth opened, then snapped shut. He'd been right all along about addicts in her Aunt Felicity's house, but not about the reason they were there. She reached over and touched his hand to keep him quiet until the manager finished speaking.

"I told her more than once it wasn't safe to have strangers in her house, but she never listened," Virginia continued. "She simply kept doing for others."

Before the woman could go on, Jillian heard a rustling sound at the doorway.

"I can't find my baby! Where's my baby!"

An elderly woman stood in the doorway to the office, pulling at her skirt, with tears streaming down her wrinkled face.

"Why Catherine, don't be upset." Virginia Trent hurried to the woman. "I've been babysitting, remember? Here's your precious baby." She cradled air and gave the invisible baby to the woman.

"Oh, thank you dear. I couldn't imagine where she'd gotten to." The elderly woman shuffled away, cooing and patting her nonexistent child. "Come now, darling, time for your bath."

Jillian stood. "We've used up enough of your time, Ms. Trent. I do appreciate your helpful information."

A knot twisted in her stomach. Fear clutched at her heart. What would happen to her when she got old? She'd be alone, with no money, no relatives, and no home. She couldn't think about that now.

"If Fred comes for another visit, I'll bring him back," Jillian told Virginia Trent.

"Here, take one of my cards. It has my cell phone number on it too. We're moving Fred to a more secure wing after today's adventure, so hopefully he won't wander again, but," she smiled gently, "they do find ways to escape."

Seth remained silent until they were outside in the truck. Once they were on the road to town he spoke up. "When did the lawyer say he'd be back?"

"He didn't. The message on his answering machine said he is spending a few days fishing in the Bahamas. Why?"

"You really need to obtain a copy of your aunt's tax returns. If she funded Fred's old age, she might have used her money for others. You said you thought she had been declining mentally in her later years, having slight strokes." Seth signaled a turn onto Beech Street. "You might be able to contest the trust and get some of the money back."

"No, Seth. Felicity Thornton knew what she wanted to do with her money. I have no right to it." When the truck came to a stop in front of Thornton House, she sat with her mind in a whirl. "I'll have to make some decisions in the near future. I don't have a lot of money. If I don't find what's in the house in the next week, I'll have to apply for a job." Her gaze traveled around the miserable house. "In the meantime, I have no choice but to stay here until I discover what my aunt and mother hid."

* * * *

Seth hunched in the driver's seat, listening to the cooling engine ping. He'd tried for so long to prove his sister had been given drugs in this house, but he was wrong. Felicity Thornton had only tried to help Melinda. Surely the ruby cross Jillian had discovered proved his sister had been in the house, and he'd never found any sign of drugs. He tasted the remains of tuna sandwich. Would he ever lessen the guilt of letting his sister down?

"I don't know. There has to be another alternative. This house isn't secure." He raked his fingers through his hair. "I wonder how many other keys Felicity hid around the place?"

Jillian wiggled her fingers into the pocket of her jeans. "I guess I'll have to sell these." The diamond earrings caught the late afternoon sun and shot colored lights around the cab of the truck.

Seth ached for Jillian. She had so many decisions to make, and no one to help her. "Keep them. Those belonged to your aunt and who knows how many generations of Thornton women." He folded her hand around the gems with his fingers. "I have a few extra bucks in the bank for a rainy day. Let me help you."

Jillian caught her lower lip between her teeth. He wanted to taste her mouth, wrap his arms around her to keep her safe. He reached for her but she held him off, a grim look on her face.

"I appreciate your offer, Seth, more than you can imagine. But, I have to stand up for myself." She glanced at her watch. It was four-forty five. "Too late to go to town now. I don't know about you, but I'm dying for a cup of coffee."

He could see determination in her eyes. Her lips trembled when she tried to grin.

"Yeah, me too." They walked up to Thornton House side-by-side, comfortable as a pair of old slippers. "Didn't you say you thought some of your aunt's furniture might be worth money? Might be antiques?"

She brightened immediately. "Yes. Perhaps I can find an appraiser to give me a price, maybe buy some pieces." She unlocked the door and stepped inside. "It would free up some cash for the property taxes, allow time to continue searching for what my mother and aunt stashed." She stood with her head cocked to one side. "Aren't you curious? I sure am. I doubt it was money, but I wonder what they hid?"

"Only one way to find out. We start digging around. First, coffee, then I want to go up into the attic with you. I only worked one summer in my uncle's antique store." He draped his arm around her shoulders. "I'm no expert but I picked up some knowledge about old stuff."

"I have a good feeling. I'm going to find something, I know it." Her slim body trembled with excitement beneath his fingers.

Back in the apartment, Jillian nuked hot water for instant coffee. "I hate to suck up all your time, Seth. Will you get into trouble?"

"Nah, I'm pretty independent. I have to be in court tomorrow when they arraign Elmer Babcock, but I'm free the rest of the afternoon."

"Let's carry our cups up to the attic with us. I'm anxious for you to see what's there." Jillian grabbed her mug and headed for the attic.

They climbed the dark stairs after Seth pocketed the key to the door.

He stood in the narrow space at the top sipping his coffee. "I wonder how they moved this stuff up here?"

"Couldn't have been easy. The bureau, huge chest, and the piano, they're all bulky and heavy." Jillian walked between the stacks of furniture and stood in front of a dusty chest, the front festooned with many tiny drawers. "Is this a desk?"

"Hard to say." He moved in to stand behind her, close enough to smell the coffee on her breath and feel the warmth of her skin.

"I wonder..." She pointed her finger at the top middle drawer handle on the chest and counted, "two down, three across." Seth squeezed in beside her. She nibbled at her lower lip when she slid the drawer out. Jillian clasped an object with her fingertips and pulled it out. A silver broach garnished with purple stones lay in her palm like a dead bug. Seth could see excitement ripple across her face.

"Look!" Jillian cheeks were flush, her eyes bright.

"Calm down. It looks like costume jewelry." He ran his fingernail across the flaking green tinged metal and bent prongs. "Can't be worth much."

"Of course not, but it meant something to Felicity, so she hid it. Seth, I've been finding all kinds of odd things—scraps of paper, old children's barrettes, coupons and recipes. At the time she concealed them, they were precious to her. I'm excited because I think we've cracked part of the puzzle."

"Okay, I give up. What am I missing?" he asked.

"Two down, three across!" Her fingers fluttered like Fred's had on the front porch. "Seth, she knew her memory was slipping away. Fred had been off mentally for a while, so she secured everything she wanted to keep in this house in safe spots. In order to recall, she used the same combination, two down, three across." Jillian moved closer to Seth. He could feel the heat of her body; excitement emanated from her slender frame. "We have to start searching downstairs. The cabinets in the kitchen, panels in the den, bricks in the fireplace...oh, all over!"

He grasped her upper arms to hold her down. "Okay, but I don't want you to be disappointed. This is a huge house. Why, some of the shelves might have collapsed. Stuff would slide between the walls, disappear." His looked toward the window. "The light's starting to fade. Let me look around while we're here, then tomorrow we can start downstairs—really tear into the house. Okay?"

"Oh, all right." A wave of disappointment flitted across her face.

He bent down and dropped a kiss on the end of her nose. They stood toe to toe, his hard thighs pressed tightly against hers. Jillian tipped her head back. His lips met hers, softly at first, then with more pressure. He wrapped his arms around her body. She snuggled close to him, returning the kiss. He could feel her soft breasts pressing against his chest. A groan of desire churned deep in his throat.

He broke away first. "Jillian, you do wicked things me." The huskiness in his voice echoed in his ears.

"I'm so sorry, officer. Is that against the law? I promise never to do it again."

"Oh, I wouldn't want you to do that. I might have to come and arrest you, put you in handcuffs, and—" He wiggled his eyebrows at her. She blushed and giggled.

Time to stop this game, he thought. As he hugged her once more, he stared off over her shoulder. "Hello, what's this?"

The instant she turned to follow his gaze he missed the warmth of her body. "What, Seth?"

"The lamp, on the floor over there, see? Where's your flashlight?"

"I put it on the desk." She twisted through the narrow space and grabbed the light. "Got it."

He squirmed between the furniture pieces. "Shine it over here." Seth squatted in front of a table lamp. A geometric tangled color of glass caught the light, sending prisms of brilliance up to the rafters.

"What is it, what did you find?"

"I'm not sure." With great care, Seth flipped the lamp base over. "Can you come closer?"

She managed to make her way to him. Standing behind his back, she angled the light at the metal base of the lamp.

"If this is what I think it is, and if it's authentic, your worries might be over."

"What?" Jillian asked in a voice barely above a whisper.

"See here on the base, what looks like scratches? We'll have to clean it up and have it authenticated but, see the name?"

Seth's fingers trace the name: L. C. Tiffany.

Chapter 12

Musty air closed in on Jillian, making it difficult to breathe. She licked her index finger and wiped the dust off a panel. Beneath the dirt, the strip of glass was the color of a May summer sky. "Wow." She hauled a tissue out of her pocket and cleaned off another space. "Supposing it is real, how much do you think it's worth?" She started to polish the entire surface.

Seth grabbed her wrist to stop the motion. "I hope for your sake it is real, but please don't get your hopes up. There are a lot of fakes floating around, good ones."

"Okay, but if it's not fake?" She pulled her damp T-shirt away from her sweaty skin.

"Could be fifty thousand, maybe more," he said.

Jillian would have fallen over if Seth hadn't kept hold of her. "Fifty..." She licked her dry lips and blew out a puff of air so hard her hair shivered. She'd been hoping for a few thousand bucks to tide her over. "I can't leave it here. What should I do with it?" She turned in a circle, searching for a good hiding place. Visions of Thornton House restored to its original beauty flew through her mind.

"It's been safe up here for years, I say—"

Before he could finish, a male voice drifted up the stairway. "Hello! Anybody home?"

Jillian stared at Seth. This house was busier than Grand Central Station on a Monday morning. At least this time she knew the front door was unlocked. They'd left it open to get some fresh air inside.

Seth placed his finger on his lips then pulled her through the maze toward the stairwell. "Don't say a word," he whispered in her ear. "Leave the lamp here." His hot breath sent ripples down her spine.

"We're on our way down," Seth yelled. He preceded Jillian, guiding her down the last few stairs.

"Sorry to bother you all, but I've been dying to see inside this house. The door was open so I walked in." Malcolm Winters stood in the hallway, hands shoved deep into the pockets of his fresh khakis. "Hope you don't mind."

"Of course not. Actually there isn't much to see, Malcolm. The house is run down." Jillian pulled the attic door closed behind her. Seth reached over and locked it before handing her the key.

"What's up there?"

"'Bout a million spider webs and a lot of dust," Seth said, taking Jillian's elbow and starting down the hall. "We were getting ready to leave. Perhaps you can have a tour another day."

Malcolm didn't move. "Why are you locking the door if nothing is up there?"

"Why are you being so damn nosy?" Seth took a step toward the man.

"Please, gentlemen, stop! All the testosterone floating around here is giving me a headache." Jillian looped her arm through Seth's and pinched his skin. "I'm keeping the door locked for safety, Malcolm. There are boards missing everywhere, the roof leaks. I don't want anyone rummaging around up there getting hurt." Her nervous giggles sounded phony.

She could see skepticism written all over the man's face. "I'll be happy to show you around some other day. We were on our way out." She started toward the stairs with Seth at her side. Malcolm had no choice but to follow them.

When they entered the main foyer, Jillian hesitated. "You mentioned wanting to see the dining room chandelier. Why don't you go catch a peek now? We'll wait." When Seth opened his mouth to say something, she squeezed his arm again. At this rate poor Seth would be sporting bruises all over. Maybe not. Underneath his smooth skin lurked hard ropy muscles.

"Thanks, I'd love to see it." Without hesitation, Malcolm chose the correct archway and disappeared into the dining room.

Seth's eyebrows drew together; he tilted his head to one side.

She pulled his face close to her until her lips touched the edge of his ear. "He said he'd never been in the house and wanted to see the dining room chandelier. He lied. How else would he know which doorway to choose?"

Before Seth could reply, Malcolm walked out of the dining room, wiping his fingers on a handkerchief. "Beautiful, simply beautiful." He wandered across the foyer and out the front door, Seth and Jillian apparently forgotten.

"How weird," Seth said. Jillian trailed behind him as he retraced Malcolm's footprints into the dining room. She could see where the man had cleaned off one of the prisms. Even in the dim light, it sparkled.

"I'll definitely have to have an antiques appraiser in here for the chandelier, too." She stroked one of the prisms and watched in fascination as it twirled. "It could be Baccarat crystal."

Seth glanced at his watch. "Yeah. Let's go to Letty's. You can call your lawyer again from there. There might be an old inventory of household goods or something." He waited while Jillian locked the front door. "Probably wouldn't hurt to check up on Malcolm either. There's something about him I don't trust."

They scrambled into Seth's truck to drive the few blocks to Cantrell's B-and-B.

"You coming in, Seth?" Jillian asked when he stopped in front of the house.

"No, it's getting late. I'd better check in at the station." Smiling, he reached over and brushed a curl off her forehead. "Will you call me at my place later; let me know if you've gotten hold of the attorney?"

"Sure." Still she sat, reluctant to leave his comforting presence. Why had he had clammed up all of a sudden?

"Okay, I'll talk to you later." Maybe it was for the best. Jillian didn't need any entanglements right now. But before she could leave the truck, Seth pulled her to him and brushed his lips against hers. The touch of his lips sent tingles all the way to her toes. She tilted her head back, wanting more, but he'd already pulled away. He confused the heck out of her.

"Take care of yourself," his voice rumbled out, thick with desire.

* * * *

Seth clenched his jaw. His body screamed with frustration. He had used every ounce of his willpower to act natural and not say anything to Jillian. He'd wanted to sweep her into his arms and carry her off to the nearest bed. But first he had to keep her safe.

The minute his truck had rounded the corner near Letty's, he'd seen the man from Savannah, John Smith, leaning against the hood of the long dark car parked half a block down the street. Time to confront the man to learn why he had been following Jillian.

Seth gunned the engine and angled his truck in front of the car. In one swift motion, he jumped out, gun in one hand, badge held out in the other.

"All right, hands up where I can see them."

Instead of being startled, the man grinned, then casually lifted his hands, palms forward, to shoulder level. Today he wore a different version of the same loud print shirt. The garment clashed with the large diamond pinky ring on his finger. "What did I do, officer?" The words flowed out of the man's mouth like warm molasses.

"How about stalking, for starters." Seth shoved his badge back into his pocket and stepped closer. "You want to tell me why you've been following Jillian Bennett?"

"I'll be happy to explain, officer, the instant you stop pointing your gun at me."

Seth lowered his weapon, but kept his finger on the trigger.

"Now, first of all, I am carrying a gun but I have a permit so it's legal," Smith said. "I'm going to reach into my back pocket for my wallet." Seth wanted to wipe the insolent smirk off his face with his fists. "Then I will produce my private investigator's shield where upon you will holster your gun, return to your truck and leave me alone."

The man's face grew hard. He extended his wallet to Seth.

Seth slipped the gun back into its holster and examined the documents. The current license had been issued in the state of Georgia. "Your name really is John Smith." He also found Smith's permit to carry a concealed weapon.

"You've been a busy boy, checking up on me. Yes, my parents had a bit of a sense of humor." He held out his hand.

"Now, if I might have my credentials back, I do believe I'll head to town for one of those delicious seafood dinners at Captain Jacks."

"Not so fast. You didn't tell me why you've been following Jillian."

"Nor will I, officer," he said. "Unless you're prepared to arrest me, I don't have to say a damn thing."

He was right. Seth didn't have probable cause to arrest the man for anything right now. He clinched his fists to keep from popping the arrogant jerk in the nose. "What's JBS Corporation."

"Tut, tut, officer," he actually waggled his finger under Seth's nose, "same answer."

Rage boiled in Seth's veins.

"Please return my property to me or I'll be forced to report to your superiors you held out for a bribe." His gray eyes, free of their sunglasses, were like chips of dirty ice.

"Why, you—"

"Temper, temper." Smith pocketed his wallet. He opened the car door, bent and maneuvered one foot inside, then hesitated. "All will be revealed, officer. Your companion is perfectly safe, believe me." He gave Seth a two-finger salute, slid into his car and turned on the engine. He sat there staring until Seth climbed into the truck. Seth gritted his teeth, revved his engine and waited. Finally John Smith gave up, and pulled out around him. He drove the big car sedately down the street, headed for town.

* * * *

Jillian stood in front of the bathroom mirror and ran a comb through the dark tangles of her hair. Her cheeks were pink with excitement, her eyes sparkled. She bent closer to her reflection. Why had she thought her eyes were ugly? Unusual, to be sure, but certainly not unappealing.

Scrambling around in her cosmetic case, she came up with dark brown eyeliner, barely used. Jillian carefully outlined her eyes, the tip of her tongue protruding between her lips. Next she brushed on a coat of black mascara and a touch of glossy pink lipstick. She stepped back to survey her handiwork. A lovely young woman stared back at her.

"Eat your heart out, Craig Hamilton. Not only am I beautiful, I'll soon be rich." She pirouetted, dancing back into the bedroom. "Rich, rich, rich." She tucked her purse containing the letter and photos away behind the headboard of the bed, grabbed her key and hurried down to dinner.

She'd have to make a list of things to do in the morning before moving into Thornton House. A shiver of fear shot through her at the thought of living alone in the creepy old place. Maybe, if she could have the furniture appraised, if it turned out to be worth some serious money, she'd stay here, or move to a motel. So many decisions she had to make.

"Good evening, Jillian." Letty seemed to be observing her in a very strange way. An empty wineglass sat before her. Her hair was neatly combed and her lipstick on straight. For once she appeared to be quite sober. Malcolm merely nodded, his eyes refused to meet hers. He took a sip of water. Biff and Cindy sat with their heads together, whispering.

"I don't believe you've met our other guest yet, Jillian. This is Mrs. Severin," Letty said.

Jillian smiled at the older woman. "Jillian Bennett."

"Nice to meet you, Ms. Bennett," she said in a frail voice. A perfect French twist corralled her cottony white hair. Tiny pearl earrings matched a string of creamy pearls resting on the yoke of her plain black dress. The woman's eyes were obscured behind a pair of dark, nearly opaque sunglasses.

"Evenin,' Ms. Jillian." RaeJean placed a steaming pan of lasagna in the center of the table. "My, aren't you all spiffy this evening." She smiled and winked. "Did you have a good day?"

"Yes, thank you, RaeJean." She helped herself to some salad and snagged a piece of garlic bread. Words of excitement bubbled up in her throat. She tamped them back down with difficulty.

Conversation ebbed and flowed around the table while the guests consumed another of RaeJean's delicious dinners. To Jillian's amazement, Malcolm hadn't mentioned her house or the chandelier. Letty kept glancing between Jillian and Malcolm all through dinner. Biff and Cindy fed one another bites of food in a haze of self-indulgent love, ignoring the rest of the guests. Mrs. Severin nibbled on a few tiny bites and she pushed the rest of her food around the plate.

While they were waiting for RaeJean to serve coffee and dessert, Jillian excused herself and went to the parlor to use the phone. It was after business hours, so she wasn't surprised when she heard George Bannerman's voice on the answering machine. She didn't leave a message. Instead, she consulted the business cards he'd given her with his home number on the back and tried that one. She gave up after ten rings and returned to the dining room.

The Lawson's declined dessert and moved away from the table, cooing to one another. Letty and Malcolm followed along behind them.

"Could I have a rain check on dessert, RaeJean?" Jillian asked. "I'm stuffed."

"Sure. The rice pudding will be in the fridge. Help yourself when you get hungry."

Jillian sat in silence, sipping her hot coffee. The older woman did the same. When she couldn't think of a topic of conversation, she placed her napkin beside her empty plate and stood. "Goodnight, ma'am. I hope you sleep well."

"Ms. Bennett, would you mind helping me to my room?"

The woman's voice startled Jillian because she hadn't uttered a word all during dinner. It would only take a moment to help the woman then she could call her attorney again.

"Of course." She circled the table to help the woman up. She leaned heavily on Jillian's arm. The two women made their way slowly out of the dinning room and down the hall in the opposite direction of the kitchen. Jillian hadn't been down this way before. Apparently there were only two rooms in this wing.

Bent and thin, Mrs. Severin continued to lean on Jillian's arm. Her long fingernails were covered with pale pink polish. The diamond solitaire on her left finger had to weigh at least five carats. Instead of old-lady lace up shoes, her long narrow feet were shod in black alligator pumps. She smelled of lilacs.

When Mrs. Severin fumbled with her door key, Jillian took it from her. "Here, let me."

"Thank you, my dear.

"Is there anything else I can help you with?"

"Yes. Please come in. We need to talk."

Jillian clenched her teeth to keep her mouth from dropping open. While she watched the elderly woman's demeanor change, she straightened her back, her head came up, and she thrust out her chin. The fragile old lady disappeared. In her place stood an arrogant, imperious woman.

"Close the door and sit down."

Too startled to disobey, Jillian complied. She shut the door and went over to sit on the only chair in the room. Mrs. Severin continued to stand.

"I know you've been through quite a lot these past few days and I apologize for not coming forward prior to this evening." She clasped her blue-veined hands at her waist. "You see, I had to be sure before I approached you, but now I've seen you up close, there can be no doubt."

In one swift move she snatched the sunglasses off her face. Jillian grew lightheaded; she had to grab the edge of her chair to keep from falling on the floor. The older woman stared at her with two different colored eyes, one blue, and one green.

"I am your grandmother."

Chapter 13

When Seth pulled up in front of the police station he saw an EMT truck idling there. Fear clutched at his gut. He checked his beeper, realizing he'd forgotten to turn it on—again. As he headed inside, he had no idea how long he'd been out of contact. Sounds of commotion emanated from the rear of the building where the holding cells were located.

He found Captain Burgess, along with three uniformed officers, standing in the hallway. Two paramedics knelt on the floor, working on a man.

"Seth, where have you been? I've been trying to reach your for over an hour." The captain's silvery eyebrows scrunched together across his forehead.

Embarrassed, Seth fingered his beeper, then thought fast. "Interviewing a suspect in another case. What happened?" He didn't lie often and did a poor job. He knew his face had turned red. Fortunately, Burgess didn't notice.

"Elmer decided he didn't want to live without his wife." The man shook his head. "He didn't have anything in the cell to kill himself with, so he commenced to bash his head against the wall."

Inside the cell Seth saw spatters of blood on the concrete blocks.

The paramedics rolled Elmer onto a stretcher and pulled it into an upright position.

"Is he going to make it?" Seth winced when he saw the wound on the man's forehead seeping blood.

"Oh, yeah, but he's going to have a hell of a headache for a while. We're going to transport him to the hospital, let the doctors check him out. Gotta make sure he didn't crack his skull."

"I miss my honey bun." Fat wet tears leaked from Elmer's eyes. "I don't want to live."

Seth had no pity for the man. "Jeez, Elmer, it's your fault she's gone, you killed her." Elmer hadn't bathed in a few days and the odor wafting upward almost knocked Seth over.

"You can call me Booger, everybody does. I know I done it man, I know. She just made me so damn mad! Wanted to start selling that crap again, them drugs. Always bitching we was too poor, didn't have no money." He reached out to clasp Seth's forearm. "You'll tell them, won't you, man? It weren't my fault. She drove me to it with her whining."

An arctic chill flushed through Seth. "What do you mean? Selling what stuff, Elmer?" He gripped the man's fingers where they rested on his arm, subconsciously trying to squeeze out some answers.

"Hey man, easy. You're hurting me. I'm injured. I gotta be moved to a hospital 'fore I bleed to death."

Seth eased his grip on Booger and glanced at the paramedics.

"Make it quick," the man in charge said.

Seth bent over so he was level with the man's head. "I'll try to help you, if you answer a couple of questions. Okay?" The combination of rotten teeth and fading alcohol fumes made him want to puke. He started breathing through his mouth.

"Yeah, I guess. Man, my head's hurting. You got anything for the pain?" he asked the paramedic holding his IV bag.

"Sorry, no painkillers until we reach the hospital. We have to keep you awake until the doctors can assess the damage."

"Tell me, what drugs did you sell? When?" Seth wanted to beat the answers out of the man. He bit down hard on his lower lip to stay calm.

"Maybe we'd better wait with further interrogation until he sees a doctor," the captain said, his forehead wrinkled with concern. "Don't want any law suits."

"No, no, I don't care. I wanna get this offa my chest. 'Bout two years ago. Me and Betty Sue was making a nice bundle selling X...Ecstasy, outta the house. Damn, these town kids loved that shit. Had to stop, though, got scared." His voice drifted off; he turned his head away, his eyes fluttering closed.

The paramedic standing opposite Seth reached over, dug his knuckle into the man's sternum, hard, and started rubbing. "Stay awake, sir." He scowled at Seth.

Seth hurried on. "Yeah, Okay. What happened, Booger?"

"Huh? Oh, damn Miss Felicity kept interfering with my bidness. Called the cops on me more than once. But we never got caught. I got me some good stuff from a buddy in Nassau. He offloaded it practically on my front porch. Woulda kept going 'cept a girl died."

Seth had to grab the edge of the stretcher to keep from falling over. "What girl? Do you remember her name?"

"I don't know. She was one o' them rich kids what comes down here for a good time." He grinned, showing several gaping spaces where his teeth had rotted away. "She loved X, but got in way over her head. Run outta money. Miss Felicity took her in. I guess she tried to clean her up, get her offa them drugs. She was a fool. The girl came to me with a fancy pin with all kinds of colored stones in it, begging for a few hits. Probably stole it from the nosey old bitch. I didn't want the damn thing, but Betty Sue took a likin' to it, so I took it and give the girl what she wanted.

"Next thing I know, she's dancing naked in Miss Felicity's back yard, drinking water outta the hose, loaded outta her mind. I was scared she might swallow too much. I was watching from the woods. I guess she did drink too much 'cause all of a sudden she flopped over and hit the ground like a sack of wet cement. Me and Betty Lou decided it was time to take a trip, boogie on down to Disney World." His voice grew weaker, his eyelids quivered.

"I'm sorry, officer, but we have to go."

Booger still had a death grip on Seth's arm.

"When we got back, I decided it weren't worth the possibility of goin' to jail, so I decided to go legit. But I couldn't find no work. I gotta bad back, you know," he sniveled.

"What was her name? The girl." Seth pried Booger's fingers off his jacket.

"Don't know, man. She never said, but she talked funny—like you."

* * * *

A range of emotions whirled through Jillian until they finally burst out of her mouth in one explosive word. "Why?" The chair felt too small for her. She launched herself and stood trembling in front of the woman.

"What do you mean?" Mrs. Severin hadn't moved.

"Why did you wait so long to find me? I'm twenty-eight years old! Why now?"

"Lower your voice this instant." The woman towered over Jillian, her odd-colored eyes shooting fire.

Rage boiled in Jillian's veins, erupting in a froth of words. "Don't you dare use that tone of voice with me. I am not a child. I will not be treated like one."

They stood toe to toe. Mrs. Severin broke the stare first.

"I am sorry, Jillian. I think we started off on the wrong foot. Will you sit down and let me explain?"

Jillian was breathing so hard she felt dizzy. "All right, but only if you stop treating me like hired help."

A crooked smile graced the woman's face. "Sorry. I've been alone for a long time. I deal mostly with servants and underlings. Will you forgive me?" She searched the room for a place to sit.

Jillian merely nodded her acceptance. "Here, use the chair. I'll sit on the bed." Jillian's legs barely carried her to the edge of the mattress. She perched on the end and waited.

"Thank you, my dear." Mrs. Severin sat ramrod straight on the chair and delicately cleared her throat. "This is harder than I'd anticipated." She sat, twisting a fragile lace handkerchief in narrow fingers.

Jillian had to bite the inside of her cheek to keep quiet. She wanted to shake the woman to make her start talking.

"Your father, Paul Severin, was our only child. Before your grandfather died, he owned several lucrative family businesses. Of course we both assumed Paul would get his degree in business then join his father in the firm." She paused to dab at her eye with the wrinkled cloth.

"I'm afraid we spoiled Paul. Whatever he wanted, we gave him. Still, he never caused us any trouble. From the time he could wrap his tiny fingers around a crayon, he loved to draw. He was quite good, actually. So, when he graduated from high school, he asked his father if he might skip college for a few years to paint and travel before he settled down. We reluctantly agreed. He took off in a scruffy old camper to see the world, paint and, I guess, find himself. We never saw him again." Glistening tears coursed down her cheeks, leaving trails in her makeup. She paused to wipe them off.

"After two years of wandering around the southwest, Jean Baptiste, my husband, told Paul to come home. Paul refused. He decided he wanted to be an artist. He broke his father's heart. I realize now, we didn't manage things in the best manner, but..." She shook her head in remembrance. "His father cut him off financially. We didn't hear from Paul for another year, then he only called to inform us you were on the way."

Jillian remained silent, her fury barely contained. She wanted to find out what the woman had to say. She needed answers.

"He told us only he'd met your mother in," she pursed her lips like she'd eaten a worm, "California. He never mentioned marriage, only wrote they were deliriously happy. They lived on the outskirts of some dessert town in Arizona. He'd started to sell a bit of his work, though not much. Your mother supplemented their income waiting tables at a truck stop on the highway near where they lived."

Mrs. Severin gazed off over Jillian's shoulder, remembering. "In spite of the fact we'd ignored him, Paul sent us some photos along with a brief letter when you were born. He was so proud of you. I wanted to go to my son, see my grandchild, but Jean Baptiste wouldn't allow it. He said Paul had made his bed with—I'm quoting him, my dear—'that tramp'. He had no intention of supporting Paul's love child. Till the day he died, he was convinced that your mother was after Paul for his money, or at least money that would come to him someday."

Jillian gasped. "How dare he call my mother a tramp! She came from a good family, probably better than yours." Unable to sit any longer, she rose, heading for the door. "I won't sit here and let you insult her memory."

"No, please wait." Mrs. Severin grabbed Jillian's arm before she made it to the door. All the lipstick had worn off her thin lips. Jillian could see dark smudges of fatigue shadowed under her eyes. "I told my husband I didn't care if Paul had married or not, but Jean Baptiste wouldn't hear of bringing a bastard into our family. He had always been so conscious of our wealth, our social position."

"If having a ton of money means abandoning your family, I'm glad I'm poor." Jillian wrenched her arm free and glared at the older woman.

"I know we were wrong. After my husband died, I tried very hard to find you, but the leads kept drying up, until now."

Terrified of the answer, Jillian had to ask, but she had to know. "What happened to my father? Is he still alive?"

* * * *

Seth watched the taillights of the EMT truck wink into the distance. He stood alone in the hallway, too stunned to move. For two years he'd been chasing the wrong shadow. He'd been concentrating on Thornton House as the source of drugs while all the time Booger Babcock had been selling crap out of his house in the woods, and Felicity Thornton had been helping the addicts. Why hadn't that been in any of the reports? No wonder her neighbors were all so tightlipped, they were protecting Felicity and her generous endeavors.

He shuffled down the street, his shoulders hunched. The soft evening breeze brought the scent of night-blooming jasmine to his nose. All his work, all his anguish had gone for nothing. His sister hadn't had many friends in the area and the few he'd found always denied she took drugs. Of course, they'd probably been into the drug scene too, and weren't about to tell a cop.

He'd lost his main reason to stay in Florida. He could go home. Off in the distance, a train whistle cried in the night. What on earth would he tell his parents? They had been so sure Melinda's death was an accidental overdose. He'd found the man who sold her the drugs, his mission was finished, but it wouldn't bring his sister back. Seth walked down to the water, sat on a bench and watched moonbeams play tag on the ocean waves.

* * * *

All the air seemed to leave the older lady like a deflated balloon. She slumped in her chair, sobbing. "I'm so sorry, Jillian. He's dead. I blame myself and my husband." She stopped to mop the fresh spate of tears off her face. "He still drove the same old camper he bought when he moved away from home. The newspaper articles reported it had over two hundred thousand miles on it. He'd gone to town to buy you some diapers and, on the way back, he blew a tire." The quiet laugh that ripped out of her mouth had nothing to do with humor. "He ran head on into the only boulder for miles around." Her words dried up, her lips quivered. Finally, she spoke again, in a low anguished whisper. "He died instantly."

Jillian couldn't help but feel sorry for the woman. She'd lost her son twenty-eight years ago and still mourned him. Somehow, in the back of her mind, she'd known her father was dead. If not, he would have found her; she believed it with all her heart.

Mrs. Severin sat with her head down, the handkerchief pressed to her eyes.

"Would you like a cup of tea? A glass of water?" Jillian knelt by the chair, looking up into eyes that mirrored her own.

"No, thank you, dear. I think I'll go to bed. I'm very tired."

Inspecting the woman closely, Jillian revised her age upward. At first, she'd thought Mrs. Severin was in her early seventies. Now she appeared older. She couldn't bring herself to think of the woman as her grandmother.

"I'll leave you then." Jillian's head was pounding; she needed some time alone.

"No, wait a moment. I want to finish." She licked her lips. "I am sorry for all the subterfuge, but you have to realize there is a lot of money at stake, a huge amount. I had to be sure." She looked exhausted and was wilting fast. "After Paul died, I hired a firm to find you. They came to a dead end, here on Amelia Island at Thornton House. You have no idea of my disappointment when I found out your mother had passed on, too. I did so want to make things up to her, help her out."

Jillian bit the inside of her cheek. She didn't believe that crap for one moment. She waited for the woman to go on.

"The detectives couldn't pry any information out of your great aunt, so I gave up. But now," she dropped her gaze to her lap before she continued, "I'm not getting any younger. I wanted desperately to know you before I died. You're the only family I have left. I hired a private investigator to locate you. He'd been monitoring Felicity Thornton for quite a while. When she died, he followed the trail of the private eye who actually found you." A faint tinge of blush flooded her pale face.

"When the private investigator I hired sent me photos of you, I knew at once you were my granddaughter." A gentle smile creased her face. "The eyes, of course."

The man with the camera, Jilllian thought.

"Mr. Smith was looking over the house. He didn't expect you to come out at that moment, so he did the first thing that came to mind. He used his flash to hide his face and record yours."

Jillian's stubby fingernails dug into her palms. She fought for calm. Too damn many people wanted to control her life. "Do you have any idea how much he scared me? When he followed me and took those photos, I couldn't imagine why."

A wobbly smile creased the woman's lips. "You gave him a bit of a scare, too, my dear. He was lucky to come close enough to shoot them. Apparently you have a guardian angel in the form of a town police officer."

Fatigue pulled at Jillian. A million questions flooded her brain, but she was too confused, too weary to articulate them now.

"Mrs. Severin, I appreciate the trouble you took to find me, but right now, I'm exhausted. Can we continue this discussion in the morning?"

The woman rose and stood in front of Jillian. "There's only one thing to discuss, my dear. When can you come to Savannah?"

"Savannah? What for?"

"In order to inherit my estate, you have to come to Savannah. There is no other way."

Chapter 14

Jillian's mouth felt like it had been filled with sand. Her palms were slick with moisture. It could be the solution to all her worries. A mental image flashed through her mind of herself standing in front of a room full of people: her staff, her business. She wore a sleek Donna Karan suit worth thousands of dollars and a pair of alligator pumps, one of several items she'd always lusted after.

Jillian glanced down at her grubby blue jeans and wrinkled T-shirt. The broken tennis shoe lace flopped loose, threatening to trip her when she walked. The dream disappeared with a poof and she smirked at the irony.

"I'm sorry, Mrs. Severin, but I couldn't possibly move to Savannah."

"Why not, child? Mr. Smith did a complete background check on you. I know all about the terrible man you were with. He betrayed you in the worst possible way. You have no job, not much money and no place to live. What could be simpler? You're my son's daughter and I want you with me. I'll add you on our payroll immediately starting at, say…eighty thousand a year?"

Jillian's pulse quickened. She stumbled backward and leaned against the wall to keep from falling over. The temptation was so great it made her stomach hurt. "I worked in a bank for seven years, Mrs. Severin. I have no skills to run a company."

"Don't be silly, of course you can. You're a smart girl, you can learn." She waved her hand in front of her face like she was shooing away flies. "If you feel better about it, you can return to college for a degree, but believe me it's not necessary. I have hoards of staff to do my bidding, and they'll be available to you, too."

Reality intruded once more. As much as Jillian longed for family, she refused to give up her burgeoning independence. "You're forgetting, I have an obligation here. My aunt entrusted me with Thornton House. She asked me to restore it and keep it in the family." Jillian had no intention of mentioning the fact that her aunt had hidden something in the house. For her own peace of mind, Jillian knew she had to find it. The hidden item might have something to do with her mother, or both her parents.

"Oh, forget that old pile of boards. Let the state have it, tear it down—leave it. Mr. Smith drove me by the place yesterday and believe me, it's not worth fixing up." She glanced at the diamond-encrusted platinum Piaget on her left wrist. "Now, I have to leave first thing in the morning. I've let too much slip at home. Can you be ready to leave at eight o'clock?"

"Mrs. Severin, I'm not going with you."

The woman kept talking, ignoring Jillian's words. She wanted to shake her, to make her pay attention, but she rattled right along.

"Actually, you might want to leave everything here. We'll take a quick trip to New York, have Mr. Antoine do something with your hair and I can buy you a new wardrobe." She took Jillian's chin with her pencil-thin fingers and gazed into her eyes. "Thank goodness you have wonderful skin and those beautiful eyes." She let Jillian's face go only to pick up her right hand. "You'll have to stop chewing your nails."

Jillian snatched her fingers back, quickly pushing them into her pockets, out of harm's way. "Are you listening to me? I have no intention of going to Savannah with you."

"Oh, all right. I can wait a week or so, until you wrap up whatever loose ends you have here." She strode to the night-stand, opened a drawer and pulled out a burgundy leather-bound day planner. "How long do you think you will need?" She opened it and stood waiting.

Jillian didn't want to insult the woman, but she had to do something to break through to her. "I'm not moving to Savannah, certainly not now, maybe never. In the future, I'll be happy to visit you, we can get to know one another better, but right now, I'm staying here and moving into Thornton House."

The older woman's lips formed a thin, tight line. "Is it the money? You want more?" The book snapped shut, she glared at Jillian. "All right, name your price."

An icy calm took possession of Jillian. "I'm sorry for you, Mrs. Severin. You think money can buy anything, including me. Well it can't. You've insulted my mother, not for the first time, and I won't stand for it. Now, if you'll excuse me, I'm leaving." She strode over and yanked open the door.

The sound of the older woman's voice echoed down the hallway. "You'll be sorry. This is your only chance. Don't think you can come crawling to me later." Jillian started up the stairs when she heard the old woman wail, "Jillian! Please. Come back!"

* * * *

Seth slathered shaving cream on his face. A stranger stared back at him from the mirror. He'd walked by the edge of the ocean for hours before dropping into bed near dawn.

He'd barely slept for thinking of his sister, his parents and the futile quest on which he'd wasted two years of his life. He should go back to New England to be with his family. But he wanted to stay here with Jillian. He simply didn't know how she felt about him.

One thing for sure, he would help Jillian find out about her past. He didn't want to leave her nearly broke and alone in that damn old house. He didn't want to leave her at all. The idea of never seeing Jillian again twisted in his gut. The funny way one side of her mouth twisted higher when she smiled. Those gorgeous, quirky eyes and that compact killer body. Besides, he had obligations at home. The last few days had driven them further apart. He finished scraping the stubble from his face.

At least she wouldn't have to worry too much about strangers breaking in, because the true drug dealer had been apprehended. And, if Fred came calling again, he wouldn't be able to get in. He still didn't trust the PI, John Smith from Savannah. He'd drive to Thornton House after talking to Captain Burgess to help her search, then make sure the lower floor had been secured. It was the least he could do.

He hunched over once more to stare at his reflection in the mirror. Dark smudges under his eyes, sprinkles of gray in his hair. He gazed into his own troubled eyes. He'd become accustomed to living here and didn't know if he wanted to leave. Seth shook his head and starting climbing into his clothes.

* * * *

Jillian shoved the last suitcase in the trunk of the rental car. True to her word, Mrs. Severin had departed in the long black car at precisely eight o'clock. Jillian had watched her from the front window. She yearned for a family connection, but couldn't think about her grandmother now. First, she had to find her legacy, whatever it might be, in the old house. Once she unloaded her things at Thornton House, she would return the rental car. She should be able to do everything on foot until she could afford to buy a car of her own.

Jillian couldn't help but chuckle. That luxury was far down on her long list of things to buy. Perhaps she should have accepted the offer from Mrs. Severin. She could almost see herself in the driver's seat of a burgundy Jaguar convertible or a cute silver Beemer.

"Those earrings are perfect on you, Jillian. I'm glad you decided to wear them."

Jillian turned to see RaeJean studying her. She reached up for perhaps the twentieth time to make sure the huge diamond studs were still in her ear lobes.

"You don't think they're too massive, do you?"

"'Course not. Can't never have diamonds too big. Besides, they make your eyes sparkle." RaeJean tilted her head. "At least something does. You seem happier than when you came here."

"I am happy, RaeJean. I feel like I know who I am for the first time in my life." She hadn't told anyone about her confrontation with Mrs. Severin. It was too new. There'd be plenty of time later. "Gotta go."

RaeJean stood by the curb, arms crossed, a frown on her face. "You sure I can't come along and help? I'm not busy right now."

"Positive." Jillian reached out to RaeJean and gave her a hug. "Once I'm settled, will you come over for coffee?"

"'Course I will." She pulled a slip of paper from her apron pocket. "Now, here's my home phone number. If you're scared or lonesome, you give me a call, hear?"

"I promise." Jillian slipped into the car, and headed down the street.

In a few moments, she pulled up in front of Thornton House. Soft morning dew sparkled on the sparse tufts of grass sprouting around the front lawn. A mound of white lay stuffed against the door of the house. She leaped out of the car, rushing to the porch.

"Snowflake!" The white dog stood quickly, panting and woofing a greeting. "What are you doing here, sweetie?"

When she bent to pat the dog, Jillian could almost swear he was smiling. His white fur, spotted with mud and gunk, stunk. In place of the heavy chain, a frayed rope was tied to his collar, the other end was secured to a porch post. A sheet of yellow paper with penciled writing had been thumb tacked on the post.

I got to leave town fast. I can't bring the dog with me. You was kind to him, but if you don't want him, leave him at the pound or shoot him. I don't care.

No signature, but of course Jillian knew it was from the disgusting man who lived the woods. The last thing she needed was another complication in her life. Jillian searched the empty street but saw no sign of the man. Still, this might turn out to be a good thing. Now she wouldn't be alone at Thornton House. First a house, now a dog. Her heart swelled with joy. What next, a husband? Jillian couldn't help but giggle. An image of Seth popped into her mind. She shoved it out.

"Snowflake, I'm going to give you a bath. You smell." She unlocked the door and hurried up the stairs to the apartment for soap. All she had was dishwashing liquid, probably not best thing for his coat, but it would have to do.

When she returned to the porch, she found Snowflake lying there with his head on his paws.

"You poor thing, I'll bet you're hungry. I'll give you some nice doggy treats and buy you kibble soon."

She untied the dog, trotting him along the side of the house to an outdoor faucet. The hose was still attached, but when the rusty water gushed out, several geysers erupted along the length, spritzing Jillian with a fridge spray. Snowflake seemed surprised by the spray. He tried to drink the water.

"You've probably never been clean before, huh, sweetie? If you're going to live with me, you need to be." Visions of the chunky dog curled up asleep by her feet on the bed flitted through Jillian's mind.

She ran her hand across the dog's stocky body. His short white fur was surprisingly soft. To her surprise he appeared to be in excellent shape. He snapped at soap bubbles and licked the water off Jillian's arms. Scrubbing his stocky body, she found no scars or welts on him, only a thin layer of fat. His black nose had areas of pink. He couldn't be more than a year or so old.

"What kind of doggy are you, Snow?" His stocky body and blocky head were Pit Bull but there was definitely something else in the mix. He wasn't too big; maybe sixty pounds but very strong and muscular.

When she tried to towel him dry, Snowflake grabbed the towel and tugged. "Oh, so now you want to play." Twice he managed to pull the towel away from her and went bounding off across the lawn. They were both drenched. Jillian giggled at the goofy dog. "Okay, enough, I surrender. I have to get going! We'll play later."

Gathering up her supplies, she wrestled all her belongings into the house, depositing them at the bottom of the stairs. The dog remained at the door, whining.

"You can come in." He cowered in the doorway.

Quickly changing into dry clothes, Jillian wrapped the rope around Snowflake's neck and led him to the car. He balked, refusing to get inside. But when she tried to tie him to the porch, he whimpered and pressed his body against her leg. She ran upstairs to grab a few dog cookies.

The poor dog was a sucker for treats, and was quickly sitting next to her in the passenger seat, head out the window, tongue wagging. Within a half-hour she'd bought supplies for the dog and returned the rental car.

Jillian was tempted to take Snowflake with her to see her lawyer, but she couldn't be sure how he'd act, so she decided to leave him home. Again Snowflake refused to enter the house. She set a pan of fresh water out for him next to a bowl of kibble, and let him stay in the shade on the porch. She wouldn't be gone long.

Jillian hurried along the sidewalk to town. A stiff breeze blew cool air in off the ocean, drying the moisture on her forehead. The salty scent of the sea tickled her nose. She should have called first, but decided to chance it and see if Bannerman had returned from his fishing trip. As she approached Bannerman's building, she saw him standing at the top of the stairs, unlocking the door.

"Mr. Bannerman! Can I talk to you for a moment?"

He jumped and whirled around. "Oh, Miss Bennett, you startled me. Of course, come on up." He pulled a handkerchief out of his back pocket and mopped his face. He stood aside to let her enter.

Dismay turned to frustration when she stepped inside. The same litter filled the office as the last time she'd been here. Jillian spied a large spider web clinging to the telephone sitting on the desk. How did the man stay in business?

"Sorry about the mess. I became so overwhelmed after the robbery, I decided to leave it for later, take a few days off to go fishing." He shrugged. "Stuffy in here." He walked over and opened a window. "I returned a few hours ago." He seemed to see her for the first time. "My, your earrings are lovely."

"These were my aunt's." Once again, Jillian's fingers strayed to her lobes.

"Did you find them in the safety deposit box?" A cool breeze wafted across the office from the window, but the man continued to sweat profusely.

"No, I found these at Thornton House." The minute the words popped out of her mouth, Jillian wanted to kick herself. She didn't want anyone to know there were things worth money in her home.

"In the house? I thought it was empty? Did you find anything else of value?" While he waited for an answer, his lips formed a grim line, his eyes narrowed.

"No." Jillian bit her lip.

Silence filled the room. Bannerman capitulated first, sliding his gaze off to one side. He fiddled with the front of his shirt, removing an invisible piece of lint.

He took a deep breath before he spoke. "What can I do for you today?"

Jillian wondered how he managed to avoid sunburn on his pale pasty face while fishing in the ocean. "I'd like copies of Felicity Thornton's tax returns for the last ten years or whatever you have." She brought her chin up a notch. "And any other papers pertaining to my inheritance and Thornton House."

Bannerman remained quiet for a moment. "Sure, but may I ask why? I mean there's not much information in tax returns. Miss Thornton had very few assets to declare."

"Yes, you told me." Jillian wiped her palms along the sides of her jeans. "I'm curious. I'd like to find out when she set up the trust fund at Marymount and how it's funded."

Jillian could literally see the man blanch. "Marymount? I'm not sure…what is kind of facility is Marymount?" He walked over and flopped on the couch.

Now it was Jillian's turn to be surprised. "A nursing home. My aunt established a trust account for a friend and herself. I have no intention of breaking it. I only wanted to find out how long ago she set it up." She didn't want to mention there'd been plenty of money at the time.

"I've been her attorney of record for five years, but…" His eyes scanned the room like he'd never been there before. "I sure don't remember anything about a trust. Are you sure?"

Jillian tried to keep the astonishment out of her voice. Either the man was totally inadequate or…"Yes, I'm sure. I've spoken to the director of Marymount. The only reason I'm asking is I'd like to find out if my aunt has any other trusts."

"But, she didn't have any money." Bannerman's freckles stood out on his cheeks like lumps of coal in a snow bank.

"I've been poking around, asking questions, I know at one time my aunt had a great deal of money. I'd simply like to find out what happened to it all."

"Certainly." He looked down, folding the cloth he held into increasing smaller squares, until finally his head came up. "I have boxes, reams of paper from Brogan, Miss Thornton's previous attorney. I flipped through them, of course, but most of the records are very old. I have the whole mess in a storage locker." He jumped up and scurried to the desk. "I'll clean up the office and find the information for you in a few days."

Jillian could see a thin line of moisture on Bannerman's upper lip. A knot of tension twisted in her gut. There was something off about this guy. "I'd like the information by tomorrow, Mr. Bannerman. I'm running out of time." She walked to the door.

"Yes, yes, of course. I'll call you when I gather everything together. Are you still staying at Cantrell's?"

"No, Mr. Bannerman, I'm living at Thornton House now. I believe you have the number. Please call me there when you have the paperwork." Jillian nodded and walked out, feeling pleased that she'd stood up for herself. She would become her own woman yet.

All the way home, the conversation she'd had with the lawyer kept pinging around in her mind. She wanted to talk to Seth, to find out his thoughts on the matter. Something seemed off about the lawyer. He had to be lying, but why?

The idea of Seth made her face flood with heat. She wouldn't be leaning on the man, she only wanted his advice. That, and more of his kisses. No, she had to banish those thoughts from her mind. Seth was a friend, period. Still, she couldn't wait to tell him about her grandmother.

Back at Thornton House Jillian found her new companion waiting patiently by the front door. Before going inside, she led him around until he lifted his leg on a scrubby dead tree, then praised him to high heaven. This time he only balked a bit before accompanying her into the house.

They both stopped in the gloomy foyer. The immense house seemed to press down on Jillian. Where to begin? Snowflake started sniffing along the floor, his toenails tapping on the parquet. Jillian followed him into the library. He followed his nose around the edge of the room and sniffed in every corner. He made Jillian nervous, so she pulled a raw hide chew out of her pocket and gave it to him. "I guess this is a good a place to start."

The dog grabbed his treasure, scampered to a corner and started to gnaw.

"I think it's time to test my theory." Blank dusty shelves stared back at Jillian. She walked to the row nearest the door and counted two down, three across. She pushed. A panel moved.

Chapter 15

Excitement bubbled up inside Jillian. She pushed her trembling fingers into the space and touched paper. Carefully, she pulled it out and slumped against the wall. It was a coupon for bread, sixteen years out of date. "At least I was right about the code. I can't give up now." She moved to the next section and counted again.

She discovered three more secret panels in the library. More recipes, a few coupons, bits of paper with figures or telephone number on them. A couple of scraps she set on a shelf for closer reading later, along with a long list of some kind with numbers on it, teeny tiny numbers. She'd have to find a magnifying glass in order to read it tonight.

She found a packet of letters from Fred to Felicity spanning years of unfulfilled love, a charming bracelet of small amethysts set in tarnished silver. It was pretty, but not worth much. She snapped the bangle on her wrist so it wouldn't become lost and stacked the letters to take upstairs with her. Jillian couldn't wait to read them.

She thought she'd found all the secret panels in the library and it had used up the entire morning. "At this rate I'll be sixty before I find what she hid." Living on public assistance, if she didn't find some money or items to sell to replenish her cash. The dog supplies had depleted her funds seriously. Her hand flew automatically to the large diamond studs in her ear. They would be the last item she'd sell. She prayed the lamp was worth a lot of money. That would go a long way to solving her financial problems. She sighed. Snowflake twitched in his sleep, rolled on his back to expose his tummy and started to snore.

A headache crawled up Jillian's neck, settling at the base of her skull. Time to stop, go upstairs to her apartment to fix lunch. She'd taken Snowflake outside twice to relieve himself, and he seemed to be getting the idea. Snowflake grasped the rawhide chew in his powerful jaws and followed her up the stairs. She added the stack of letters to the contents in the jewelry box on the bureau.

Jillian had just finished her bologna and cheese sandwich and was slurping the dregs of her diet soda when a loud buzzing pierced the quiet of the afternoon. The dog flipped onto his four legs. The two of them stood staring at one another. The buzzer sounded again, setting Snowflake into a frenzy of woofing. Before she could stop him, he charged out the door, heading for the stairs.

"Wait up, Snow!" Jillian thundered down the steps behind the barking dog. She grabbed him by the collar, holding on with all her strength. Somehow she managed to wrench open the door. Seth Falconer stood on the threshold.

Snowflake growled, bared his teeth and leaped at Seth. Seth staggered back, holding his crossed arms in front of his face for protection. "What the hell is that?"

Jillian screamed, "Sit, sit, Snowflake, sit!" The dog continued to jump and bark; foam flew off his snout. She could barely hold him so she dropped to the floor and wrapped her arms around the quivering dog. "He's a friend, he's okay." Finally, the din subsided, but the animal remained alert. The fur at the back if its neck stood on end, his ears were flattened. His eyes never wavered from Seth.

"Hi Seth, come on in."

"Do I need my gun?"

"Not for Snowflake. He's a pussycat." Jillian kissed the blocky head and stroked the dog until his fur smoothed out. "He won't hurt you, I promise." She had her fingers crossed under the dog's belly.

Seth stepped gingerly into the foyer. A deep grumble from the dog's chest vibrated through Jillian's arms.

"And here I've been worried about you staying in this house alone."

"He is kind of over protective." Jillian held on to the dog while Seth proffered a trembling hand for Snowflake to sniff. Satisfied, the animal took two steps backward and leaned against Jillian's leg.

"What kind of dog is he, a canardly?" Seth patted the dog's square head.

"I'm not sure. I do believe his mama was a bit promiscuous." Jillian stroked the dog's fur. "What's a canardly?"

"You know, you 'can hardly' tell what he is." Seth gave her a wicked grin.

Jillian rolled her eyes. "Did you ring the doorbell? I heard a buzzing in my apartment then Snowflake went nuts."

"Yes, I knocked first then figured I'd push the bell to see what would happen. Your aunt was a clever woman, having it rigged up to ring in the apartment."

Seth stroked the dog's massive head. "Okay, I give up. Where did you find this monster?"

"It's kind of a long story. Can I pour you a cup of coffee or soft drink?"

"Yeah, coffee would be great. I have a few things to tell you, too."

Seated at the table with a cup of instant coffee, Seth waiting for Jillian to begin.

First she related the meeting with Snowflake's owner and how she'd come to the dog's rescue. "The poor thing was so thirsty and frantic. I thought he'd been abused, but now, I'm inclined to believe the owner." Snowflake had gone to the corner to resume his nap. "I have no idea why the man gave me his dog."

Seth twirled his untouched cup around. "He probably heard Elmer Babcock shot his wife and decided it might not be healthy to stay around here." He took a sip. "I have to go to Jacksonville this afternoon to take a statement from Babcock. I wouldn't be a bit surprised if the dog's owner was his drug partner."

"Drug partner? Did you find out who killed your sister?"

"She killed herself, basically."

Jillian saw a flash of pain dart through his eyes. "I've been so foolish, Jillian. I never believed my baby sister would use drugs, but she did. She spent time at this house because your aunt tried to help her." A crooked smile wiggled onto his face. "I'm sorry I ever thought you or your aunt were involved."

"Nonsense. How were you to know?" She wanted to hold him in her arms to help cushion the pain. "What are you going to do now?"

"My job is finished, there's nothing more for me here, Jillian. I'm going home, back to New England."

* * * *

Jillian's face changed and smoothed out, her lips formed a tight slim line. She turned her head away, but not before Seth saw tears pooled in her eyes. She looked so disappointed. He shouldn't have blurted his intentions out quite so fast. Still, what difference did it make? He had no place in Jillian's life; he'd planned all along to return to his family in New England.

She would be staying on Amelia Island, she had no where else to go.

"I'll be sorry to see you leave, Seth." Her dual-colored eyes met his. "How much longer will you be here?"

"Couple of weeks, maybe a month. I have a lot to do, of course, but I still should have time to help you search the house. Have you found anything yet?"

"Enough to know we were right about the code. I searched the library today, but found mostly junk, some love letters, this bracelet." She held out her slim arm circled in silver and purple. "I'm sure the articles meant something to my aunt at one time but I have no idea what."

She fiddled with her coffee cup before slumping back into her chair. "I guess we both had enlightening conversations yesterday. I met my grandmother last night."

Seth jerked upright in his chair. "Is she the one who hired John Smith?"

"Yes, how did you know?"

"I had a run-in with him after I dropped you off at the house. He told me everything would be revealed. So, what did she have to say?"

Jillian launched into her story. She stopped once to replenish their coffee and grab some cookies from the cupboard. Every time she moved, Snowflake lifted his head to watch her.

"Seth, I have a feeling she still doesn't think I'm good enough somehow, but she's alone and wanted me to come and live with her. I know she doesn't believe my parents were married." Jillian paced across the floor. A gust of wind flew into the room, bringing the scent of the sea with it. "I have to admit, the idea of a great deal of money tempted me, but only for a minute. I still want to find a way to stay, at Thornton House. I've been on the Island for less than a week, but have already found friends." The smile she gave him almost melted his heart. "One way or another, I'm staying."

"I'll help you all I can while I'm here." Seth stood up. "Do you want to search for your pot of gold some more? I have an hour or so before my meeting with the captain."

"Great." Jillian took their cups and set them in the sink. "Do I dare ask you for one more favor?" she said over her shoulder.

Seth couldn't help himself. He walked up behind Jillian and slid his arms around her slim body. "Of course, anything. Well, short of murder. I do draw the line there."

She giggled and turned in his embrace. "I have my killer dog for protection." Her arms circled his waist. He felt the heat of her body, her hair smelled like coconut. The diamond earrings caught sunlight from the window, flashing a rainbow of color around the room. He dipped his head toward her lush lips, barely stopping himself in time. He had no right to lead Jillian on when he'd be leaving in a few weeks. He hesitated, then stepped back and thrust his fists into his pockets.

"What can I help you with?"

Her smile disappeared and she was clearly disappointed. He wanted to hold her again, but didn't. She picked up a dishcloth to wipe the countertop. "Would you mind taking the lamp to Jacksonville with you? I'd love to have it appraised."

"Sure. I should have thought of it myself. I know there are galleries and antique shops near the hospital. Let's get it now, and I'll take it with me when I leave."

She dug the attic key out of a drawer, unlocked the door and they both went up. Seth looked around the attic. "After we search the house, we need to go over this stuff. There might be something of value here." He saw a faint stain of pink flood her cheeks.

"I hate to sell anything, but I need the money."

"Yeah, I understand, but how will you move all the furniture downstairs?"

"I'll worry about it when the time comes." She brushed the worst of the dust off the lamp with a tissue.

Carefully Jillian unscrewed the finial and Seth lifted off the glass top. He carried the heavy piece and she trailed behind with the base. They set pieces down on the kitchen table and reassembled it.

"There's a cardboard box and some old newspapers in my truck. Why don't you clean it off while I go grab them?"

"Okay." Jillian heard Seth thundering down the stairs as she stroked the lamp with a damp cloth. More brilliant colors emerged. He was back in less than five minutes.

"Sure is eye-catching." Seth stood in the doorway with his arms full.

"Yes, I almost hope it is a fake, then I can keep it." She touched a wedge of crimson glass with the tip of her finger.

"You hold the box, I'll pick the lamp up."

"Seth, wait, there's a label on the bottom."

"Don't pull it off. Can you read it?"

Jillian bent sideways. "Yes, it appears fairly new. I wonder how long it's been there? It's from Chasen's Fine Furniture and Antiques."

Seth studied the label. "I know where that is. I'll stop there on my way to the hospital." He pulled a notebook out of his back pocket. "What's the phone number here? I'm not sure I'll have time to drive back to the Island tonight. I want to call you if I find out anything."

After Seth stashed the lamp in the cab of his truck and locked the doors, he met Jillian in the foyer of the house.

"Okay, we'll go search the living room." He started toward the front of the house.

"I thought we'd go to the music room. It's smaller," Jillian said.

"Good idea, why don't you start in the music room, I'll start in here. We can cover more territory that way." Without waiting for an answer, he walked into the middle of the huge room. Where should he begin?

* * * *

Jillian went to the nearest wall in the small room, stood in front of a panel and started thumping. She'd been pounding and pushing using the two/three code for almost a half an hour when Seth wandered in.

"I haven't found a thing, you?"

"Nope." The sun had started its slide into the horizon, making the room dim and murky. Somewhere off in the distance, a low grumble of thunder signaled more weather on the way.

"I have to meet with the captain and get on the road before this storm hits. I heard on the radio coming over here that it's going to be a pretty good one. Let's walk through the first floor before I go. I want to make sure the house is secure."

"Good idea. I checked by the back door earlier, no key hidden there. The rest of it seems tight, but an extra set of eyes never hurts." Jillian wiped her damp palms down the sides of her jeans. The idea of spending her first night in Thornton House gave her the willies. Sensing her discomfort, Snowflake sidled over and leaned against her leg.

After a fast tour around the first floor, Jillian followed Seth outside. Snowflake wandered off to sniff and piddle, never straying too far away from her.

The smell of rotting fish and salty water assailed Jillian's nostrils as the wind blew in off the sea. "Does it always rain this much here?" In the slate-colored sky, puffy clouds roiled and bumped into one another.

"Yeah, spring weather is a bit unsettled around here." Seth took a step toward her then seemed to change his mind. "Be sure and lock yourself in the apartment at dark. Don't come out for anything."

"Yes, Daddy, I promise." Jillian held up her hand, three fingers extended, in a Girl Scout salute.

"It's not funny, Jillian." His eyebrows almost came together in a straight line when he frowned.

"You caught the drug dealer." She waved her arms. "And there are houses around. I promise to go upstairs and stay there after dark."

"You have my cell number. Don't hesitate to call or if you're worried, dial 911. I'll tell the captain you're alone."

"Seth, I'm perfectly capable of taking care of myself. Don't worry. Go." She watched him climb into his truck and drive away before she scurried into the house, with Snowflake at her heels, slammed and locked the door, intent on continuing her search. Apprehension made her palms sweat and her breath come in short shallow gasps. This was shaping up to be the longest night of her life.

* * * *

Seth forced himself to drive more slowly after he nearly ran a red light on Center Street. He wanted desperately to guard Jillian, but knew she'd never allow it. Besides, he still had obligations to his present job. He locked the lamp in the cab of his truck and hurried into the station.

Captain Burgess waved Seth into his office. "Come on in. Congratulation on solving the case."

"I didn't do anything, sir. Elmer is his own worst enemy."

"I'm adding a commendation to your file anyhow. It will be good to have you working full time on regular cases." He sat, shifting his bulk in the squealing chair until he was comfortable.

Seth sat on the edge of the chair in front of the desk. "That's what I wanted to talk to you about, sir. Since the case of my sister's death has been resolved, I'm going back to New England. I'll write out a formal resignation, if you like."

The captain's face clouded. "Have you given this a lot of thought, Seth? I'd hate to lose you. You're the most experienced man on my squad."

Seth paused, taking a deep breath before he plunged ahead. "I've spent so much of my time pursuing the people who were responsible for my sister's death I never felt like Amelia Island was home. I've always felt somewhat alien, distant. I think my place is back in Massachusetts, with my family."

The captain remained silent. He leaned back, his wooden chair squeaked in protest. Finally he spoke. "I want to tell you something in confidence, Seth. I've been having some problems with my heart and have decided to retire in the fall." A deep chuckle rumbled in his chest. "The wife and I want to do some traveling, spend time with the grandkids. Hell, I'm nearly sixty-four, it's time."

"The force won't be the same without you, sir."

"I sorta doubt it. The only reason I'm bringing it up now, Seth, is I kinda thought you could be my replacement when I retire."

Too surprised to speak, Seth sat for a moment before opening his mouth. "That's very nice of you, sir, but..." He couldn't help but remember Jillian standing in front of Thornton House waving goodbye. The ebony curls whipping around her face, her beautiful eyes sparkling in the waning light. He didn't have to leave her, wasn't sure he wanted to.

"Don't make a decision now, think about it. Amelia Island is a nice place to live, and the department has good benefits. If I appoint you to be my successor, you shouldn't have any problems being re-elected when the time comes." He chuckled. "Unless you mess up." He stood, signaling the end of the discussion. "I have a lot of confidence in you son, you know."

"Thank you, sir. You've given me a lot to think about." He almost bumped into the doorway on his way out, his mind a kaleidoscope of thoughts. Of course he had wanted to move up the ladder when he was with the Braintree department, but then his sister's death had intervened and he focused solely on solving the case. After a peek at his watch, he hurried to his truck. He'd have plenty of time to think during the two-hour drive to Jacksonville. He glanced up at the dark sky.

Chapter 16

After Seth left, Jillian decided to take a break to play with the dog before it got dark and the rain started—again. She pulled out one of the tennis balls she'd bought, took Snowflake outside and tossed it at him. It plopped on the grass. He cocked his head and looked at the ball and then her.

"You poor baby. Hasn't anyone ever played ball with you before?" He rested on his rear, woofing with frustration.

"If you going to be my dog, you're going to learn to play." She started by rolling the ball at him, until he finally figured out the game. For twenty minutes the woman and dog played and frolicked in the yard. Snowflake would have kept going for hours, but rain sprinkled down on them, ending the fun.

"Okay, let's go back to work. It will be dark in a few hours, and there's no way I want to be on this first floor without light." Snowflake slurped noisily at the pan of water she set down for him.

Jillian thumped at the walls in the dining room for half an hour, but they were solid and unyielding. "Maybe Seth was right. Let's go check out the living room some more."

The dog trotted behind her, careful never to let her out of his sight. Jillian shivered in the cold damp space. The wind had picked up, and it wiggled in through the cracks in the boards and shattered windowpanes. Darkness crept across the floor in a relentless flood of shadow. She could see smudgy fist marks on the walls where Seth had pounded, searching for hiding places.

"What I'd love to do is start a fire in the fireplace." She ducked under the massive stone mantel, but couldn't see anything but old spider webs, desiccated bugs and soot. The inside of the chimney loomed black as a catacomb. While she had her head halfway inside, she flicked on her flashlight and shined it around. From the layers of dirt, she could tell the passage hadn't been cleaned in years. Most of the stones were smooth, evenly fitted together, except one that jutted out a bit from the rest.

Her heart started a mad fandango in her chest. Carefully she counted the dirty stones, three down, two across. She wiggled the rock. It shifted.

* * * *

Seth's shoulder muscles screamed with tension when he finally pulled into Jacksonville, two long hours after leaving the island. The entire way, he'd thought of nothing but Jillian, the captain's offer, and what to do about both, and still was no closer to a solution. He found Chasen's, then had to drive around the block three times before a large minivan stuffed with kids pulled out of a slot right in front of the antique store. He parked the truck and yanked the door open.

He dashed for the front door, shielding the lamp from the rain with his body, praying he wouldn't drop the whole thing. A man inside saw him coming and rushed over to hold open the door.

"Let me help you, sir." The distinguished-looking man smiled with a mouth full of straight even teeth. His razor cut slate hair molded perfectly to his head. "We can set it right here." He gestured to an empty marble table.

Seth placed the box on the table and pulled out his handkerchief to mop his face. "Storm coming in again. Tag end of a hurricane they're reporting on the radio."

"Unusual for this time of year. I heard it's headed up the coast." He held out his hand. "Peter Chasen, at your service. What can I do for you?"

"This lamp belongs to a friend of mine. I'm wondering if you might be able to give her an appraisal. Actually, it's been here before. One of your stickers is on the bottom."

Chasen parted the crumbled newspapers. "Oh, my. Yes, I remember this lovely." He lifted the lamp out of its nest of papers with great reverence before setting it gently on the table. "Did the lady decide to sell it after all?"

Confusion muddled Seth's thoughts for a second. Could Jillian have been here already? Then it clicked. "An older lady, probably wearing a purple outfit?"

"The lady didn't bring it in herself." Chasen's eyes remained on the lamp. He kept stroking the glass, like a man caressing his mistress. "If I remember correctly, she didn't drive or didn't have a car or something, so she sent one of her minions."

"Who? Can you describe him?" Seth thought it must have been Fred.

Finally Chasen stopped drooling over the lamp and gave an elegant snort. "My dear boy, this was two, no closer to three years ago, I believe. I remember the lamp distinctly because of its pristine condition." He took a snow-white handkerchief out of his pocket and whisked a minute speck of dust off the finial. "Perfect."

"Please, make an effort to remember. It's important," Seth said. Any information he gathered would help Jillian, even after all this time.

Chasen cocked his head to one side, squinting his eyes. "I'd say young, thirties. I'm more apt to remember a young woman than a man, you understand." Seth wasn't too sure about that.

"I do recall he seemed to be in a terrific hurry for some reason. He wanted an appraisal on the spot, said he had to return the lamp to the owner the very same day." He patted the lamp like you would a child, and stepped back to admire it. "I gave him a written appraisal and begged him to ask the owner if I might have first chance at selling the lamp. He told me he'd ask the owner, took my appraisal and went away." Chasen tsk-tsk'd a bit, shaking his head. "I'm sure I still have a copy. Would you like to see it? Maybe he gave me his name, I simply don't remember."

"Please, if it's not too much trouble." Chasen nodded once and hurried off. Seth checked at the time once more and bit his tongue. He'd be late getting to the hospital to document Booger's statement, but hell, he had a badge, they'd let him in.

Outside a flash of lightning brightened the sky. Chasen returned in a minute, rifling through a file folder.

"Yes, here it is. Owner, Miss Felicity Thornton of Amelia Island." He flipped the paper over. "Hmmm, doesn't give the name of her intermediary.

"I remember I called a few customers, in case the owner decided to sell. As I suspected, any of them would have snatched this piece up in an instant." Chasen couldn't seem to keep his paws off the lamp, and touched it again. "It's not often one sees an original Tiffany lamp in this good condition. Perfect, actually."

"So, it's worth money?" Seth held his breath.

"My dear fellow, three years ago I quoted a price of one-hundred-and-fifty to two-hundred thousand. It's worth more now, less my commission, of course." He gave Seth his Cheshire grin.

Seth felt like he'd been hit in the chest by a stray bullet. His surprise passed quickly when he realized what this meant for Jillian. She'd be able to sell the lamp, restore the house and achieve her goal of turning Thornton House into a business. The feeling fled when he realized she might do it without him.

Seth could almost see Chasen drool at the thought of acquiring the lamp. "Do you think Miss Thornton might be ready to sell now?"

Seth knew Jillian wanted to sell the lamp, but he couldn't speak for her. "Unfortunately Miss Thornton passed away. The lamp belongs to her niece now, but I think so. May I have your card? I have another appointment, but I'll phone Ms. Bennett, have her give you a call."

"Wonderful! I can't wait to meet her." Chasen's eyes were bright and Seth was afraid for a moment the man might clap his hands like a child.

"Can't you just sell it? Why do you have to meet her? Why does she have to drive all the way to Jacksonville? You have the lamp."

"Yes, yes, of course, but I'll need her to sign a contract and give me the provenance."

"I'm a police officer." Seth reached for his shield and held it out to the man. "I can vouch for Ms. Bennett. I know the lamp belongs to her."

"How lovely for you, detective, but I still need the provenance. Where it came from originally, a bill of sale would be divine, and of course, a copy of the will so Ms. Bennett can prove she inherited the piece."

An elderly couple walked in, she swathed in mink, he in an aura of distraction. They zeroed right in on the lamp.

"Peter, darling, is this for sale?" The woman stood in front of the lamp.

"Hello, Cecelia. I believe so, but it might be a few days before I collect all the paperwork. May I call you?"

She walked around the table, actually licking her lips. "Yes, yes, let me know the price. I'll pay anything. Simon, this will be perfect in our Charleston house, in the den. Don't you think?"

The man grunted and wandered off. His wife hurried after him. "Call me, Peter… Remember, I saw it first!"

"Of course, darling." The minute they were out of ear-shot, Chasen leaned over to whisper too close to Seth's ear. "We'll start a bidding war. Might even bring the price closer to three-hundred thou."

Seth took a step back. The man had terrible breath. "I'll let Miss Bennett know. I have to run. May I have a receipt for the lamp?"

Peter Chasen's lips came together like he'd been sucking lemons. "We are a very reputable firm, sir."

"I'm sure you are, but hey, once a cop always a cop."

Chasen went to a desk near the wall and opened a drawer. He pulled out a receipt, filled it in and gave it to Seth.

"Please tell Miss Bennett time is of the essence. I'm having an auction next week and would adore featuring the lamp." He carefully picked up the lamp, cradling it like a baby and headed for the rear of the store. "I'll keep it on our vault until I hear from her."

* * * *

"Damn." Jillian pulled her head out of the fireplace and sucked on her skinned knuckle. It stung like crazy and tasted like ancient soot and salty blood. She gagged and spit the mess out on the hearth next to her then wiped her mouth on the shoulder of her T-shirt. She'd already broken two fingernails and now had ripped a gash in her knuckle. Jillian was not having fun. At the sound of her voice, Snowflake whined and rested his head on her knee.

"I'm okay, sweetie. I need to locate something to pry this rock loose. I have to find out what's behind it—if anything."

She shot the beam of light around the stone tunnel and stared up into the inky space. The sound of rain on the top of the chimney echoed and bounced around the inside. A bent piece of metal hung down between two bricks. She barely grabbed it before it fell into her hand, its sharp edge glinting in the light.

"Perfect."

Once she had the flashlight positioned, she dug around the edge of the rock. A tiny avalanche of sand rained down onto her face and into her mouth.

"Yuck." Again she wiped her mouth on the shoulder of her T-shirt. Snowflake crowded closer to her, his hot body adding to her misery. "Okay, okay. Let me give it a whirl one more time." She used all her strength to pull at the stone. It flew out, bounced on the opposite side, and then dropped, barely missing her head.

Excitement and fear boiled in Jillian's blood. She strained to slither closer to the opening. Her shoulder muscles screamed in agony. Finally, she managed to shove her hand into the hole until her fingertips brushed hard, smooth metal.

* * * *

Seth wrenched open the door of his truck and dove inside. The rain slashed down around him. Cars crept down the street, their high beams cones of light piercing the deluge. Street lamps swayed, dancing at the end of their poles. All around him people hurried to find shelter. Snapping on the radio, he heard the tail end of an announcer's voice exhorting everyone to move off the roads, to find shelter.

"A freak spring hurricane heading up the East Coast has turned toward Florida. Winds are in excess of ninety miles an hour. I repeat. Seek shelter immediately and stay off the roads."

Seth flipped open his glove compartment and reached for his cell phone. His finger trembled so much he almost dropped it. He had to reach Jillian, tell her to leave the house and go somewhere safer. She could go back to Letty's or even to his house. Why on earth hadn't he thought to give her a key?

He stabbed the buttons, his fingers felt fat and numb in his effort to hurry. The phone rang and rang, but no one answered.

Seth turned the key in the ignition and pulled carefully out into the street. Up ahead a trashcan rolled down the middle of the tarmac. A gust of wind picked it up and tossed it against a car like a toy. He gripped the steering wheel and sat there, afraid to move into the maelstrom. A horn tooted behind him, so he touched the gas and inched forward.

He'd drive to the hospital and spend the night there to be safe. He would call Jillian again, and urge her to vacate the house, even if she had to go to the police station for safety.

Seth found a spot near the hospital's front door in the nearly empty parking lot. By the time he entered the lobby, water dribbled off his saturated clothing. He patted his pocket, realizing instantly he'd left his cell phone in the truck. His gaze flew around the lobby until he spotted a bank of phones, and reached into his pocket for change. This time when he dialed Jillian's number, the phone only rang twice, then died. Growing more frantic by the second, he jiggled the handle until his quarter dropped. Quickly he dialed the police station on the island, but that phone never rang.

He stared at the receiver. Had all the lines gone down? Could Jillian be lying in a pile of rotting boards, injured or worse? An image of his world without Jillian flashed through his head. He glanced once at the elevator. He didn't want to disappoint Captain Burgess by not going to record Booger's statement, but he also couldn't leave Jillian alone on the island. She'd grown up in the mountains, and had no idea of the coastal wind's fury. Without hesitation he pulled out his keys and headed for the door. He had to use both arms to muscle it open. He had to get to Jillian and prayed he wouldn't be too late.

The wind rocked his truck from side to side. He aimed it towards the freeway out of town, heading for the coast. The needle on his gas gauge hovered around the half way mark. He'd search for an open gas station on the way, but wasn't optimistic. Trees along the road were bent, their tops kissing the pavement. A huge branch snapped off and bounced across the road in front of his truck. Seth swerved, barely missing the obstacle, the truck tires screamed in protest. He wiped sweat from his forehead to keep the moisture out of his eyes.

Seth didn't think he had enough fuel to make it all the way home, but he had to go for it. He hadn't been able to save his sister. He'd be damned it he'd let someone else he cared about die.

Chapter 17

Jillian was back upstairs and locked safely behind the thick door of the apartment when a loud boom echoed throughout the house. It sounded like a giant banging his fists on the roof. She stroked a cool cloth across her face to wipe off a few layers of soot. The metal box she'd managed to pull from the fireplace squatted on the kitchen table like an ugly black toad. Jillian had spent a futile half-hour poking at the thing and there it still sat, its secret safe inside. Frustrated, she picked the thing up and whacked it against the table, then beat it a couple of times with the knife. Snowflake yipped at her antics and scuttled under the table.

Jillian surrendered for the moment, and spread antibiotic cream on a new gash on her thumb, made when the knife she had been using to pry open the box had slipped. Her shoulder muscles ached from the strain of wiggling around inside the fireplace. Jillian would love to have a nice hot bath, but if this storm grew worse, she'd rather not be naked. She felt vulnerable enough already. She snapped on the radio to hear some news, but the airwaves were filled with static.

"I guess we're in for the night, huh sweetie?" Snowflake pressed against her leg. He'd refused to move from her side since they'd come upstairs and Jillian had locked the door. She struggled to put on a brave front for the dog. It wasn't working. She had to admit the storm terrified her, too. She had no idea what she'd do if he had to go outside to pee. "I guess we won't worry till it happens, huh sweetie?" The dog shivered with fear.

"Now, Snow, remind me again why I turned in the rental car? If we had it we could go find a nice warm motel to wait out the storm." She walked over to the window. It was dark outside and foreboding like the inside of her chimney downstairs. Through the wind-swept trees she could make out the ocean beyond the forest, a mass of black like the edge of the world. Nope, this was her house now; she intended to stay, no matter what.

She poured fresh water in Snowflake's bowl and filled his dish with kibble. He stood over it, too scared to eat. Jillian sat at the table staring at the metal box, racking her brain for a way to open it. Her hopes of piles of hidden cash had been dashed. The container, about the size of a cigar box, couldn't hold much. The future loomed as black as the night sky outside. She shook the box and shifted through the pile of papers she'd brought upstairs. Her fingers went automatically to her ears to feel the heavy stones. If the lamp was worthless, these earrings were the only thing of value she had left and she was terrified of losing them.

The lights blinked off, then flickered on. Jillian held her breath. They wavered once more then steadied. With trembling hands she rummaged in the cupboard until she found candles and matches. It was going to be a very long night.

Before Jillian had a chance to strike a match, the phone rang. The unexpected noise froze her in the kitchen for a moment before she dashed to answer it.

"Hello? Hello?" Crackling static rattled in her ear. "Rae-Jean, is that you?"

Jillian could only make out a few words: storm…safe…and then something garbled.

"I have a terrible connection, RaeJean. The storm's making things worse, can you repeat what you said?"

"Come to my house…storm's passed, honey… not safe there."

"I can hear you now. Don't worry, I'm fine. This house has been here for a long time. A storm's not going to blow the house down. We're fine."

"No," RaeJean shrieked. A few words were garbled again. "…much worse. Leave now it's a…" A dead silence filled her ear. The lights flickered twice and died.

"Ohmigod, ohmigod, ohmigod." Jillian clutched the dead phone. Heartbeats thudded in her chest. Darkness enveloped the room in a black cloak. Her eyes searched the nothingness for light where none existed. She took one step forward, cracked her shin into the bedpost before feeling her way along the wall toward the kitchen where she had candles. Why in the hell had she ever left Denver? That had to be the biggest mistake of her life.

Snowflake started yipping in a high stressed voice. He could sense her terror.

"It's okay, baby, we're going to be fine. Get away from my leg so I can move into the kitchen."

The two of them shuffled into the other room. Jillian felt along the counter until her fingers connected with the candles and matches. It took her three tries to light one. It took her eyes a few seconds to adjust to the dim light. The flickering candlelight cast eerie shadows that jumped and danced around the room. The illumination barely extended beyond the archway into the bedroom. It looked like a dark cave. She'd never been so scared in her life. She lined up every candle she had and lit them all. She put the flashlight in the middle of the table where she could reach it quickly.

A wisp of air blew in from the edge of the window. One of the candles puffed out. She re-lit it and moved it to another location. A different candle died.

Outside the storm's intensity increased. Jillian pulled herself into the bedroom with the dog plastered to her leg. She picked up her purse. Low on cash and not even sure where she could go with the dog, she knew staying here was no longer an option. She'd walk the few blocks to Cantrell's and hope to heaven Letty liked dogs. She'd never make it to RaeJean's house on the other side of the island.

"Okay, we're not being cowards, honey. We're being practical." The house moaned and shook in the wind, as if agreeing with her. "This storm can't last too long. Tomorrow we'll come back and stay here forever. I promise, honor bright."

Jillian found the dog's leash, grabbed her purse and made sure she had the house key and key to the apartment. Then she shoved the metal box and papers into a plastic shopping bag, wrapping another plastic sack around it to keep everything dry. The heavy silver bracelet kept catching on her pockets, so she unclasped it and set it in the cupboard. She wouldn't bother with an umbrella; from the sound of the wind it wouldn't do any good.

She located her flashlight and had begun blowing out candles when Snowflake went berserk. He threw his stocky body at the door, snarling, foam dripping from his mouth. Jillian stood frozen and watched as the doorknob turned. Someone was trying to get in.

* * * *

Seth squinted and hunched further over the steering wheel of his truck. Rain slashed across the road, turning the pavement into a slick flooded mess. Fortunately for Seth, there were very few vehicles on the road, and most of them were heading inland. Another gust of wind buffeted the truck. The front wheel caught gravel at the edge of the pavement, tilting the entire vehicle. Seth slammed on the brakes, skidding to a halt, mere inches from a speed limit sign. The engine died. He turned the key in the ignition. His palms were slick on the steering wheel and his fingers trembled. Nothing happened. Rain beat on the cab of the truck like jungle drums.

"Come on, come on." The engine moaned, chugged and finally caught. Glancing quickly over his shoulder into the gray mist, he pulled cautiously out onto the road.

The closer he drove to the ocean, the wilder the weather became. He hadn't been able to find anything on the radio for a good half-hour, but Seth knew he was in the middle of a hurricane. He'd been through enough of them. He should turn around, head back toward Jacksonville. The thought of Jillian alone in the monstrous house kept his nose pointed toward Amelia Island. As he drove, he fumbled with the buttons on his cell phone, trying to reach Jillian. After a while, he couldn't even get a dial tone so he gave up.

Surely the captain would understand why he hadn't gotten Elmer's statement. He knew this might mean not only his promotion but also the job itself. Seth straightened in his seat. He didn't want to leave Jillian or Florida and he wanted to keep his job.

A soft sigh of relief escaped his tight lips followed by a groan when he saw the sign for Marsh Bridge. Flashing red and blue lights lacerated the driving rain. He slowed and came to a stop at the Highway Patrol barricade. An officer almost hidden in a yellow slicker motioned with his flashlight to turn around. Rain slashed at his face, soaking his upper body the instant he rolled down his window. The smell of salty ocean and damp earth flooded in with the rain.

"Sorry sir. The bridge is closed. It's not safe in the middle of a hurricane. You'll have to turn back." Rivulets of waters cascaded down the man's face, blurring his features.

Anger burned in Seth's chest. He'd come too far to go back now. Instead, he fumbled for his badge and shoved it out the window. "It's an emergency, officer," he bellowed, his voice almost lost in the turbulence. His mind latched onto the first lie that drifted through. "My wife's alone, she's having a baby. I have to get through!"

The trooper shook his head, but stepped back. "Go ahead but it's your neck." He walked in front of Seth's truck and dragged the barrier aside.

Seth shifted into first gear and crept ahead. The truck crawled up the slick roadway. On both sides of the bridge Seth saw angry whitecaps raging across the black water. The truck bucked and shimmied over the metal rivets, crested and slid down the other side of the bridge. Relief almost melted Seth in his seat when he finally reached solid land.

His relief didn't last long. Fallen trees blocked parts of the road, their branches pirouetting in the wind. Overhead a streetlight twirled, crashing into telephone poles and trees. The buildings to his right were all dark. Off on a side street, Seth saw a live wire that had been ripped off the line, wiggling through puddles of water like a vicious ebony snake. When the wire snapped out of the water, sparks shot through the air. Seth had to locate a land-line phone, his cell was useless, and warn the police before someone was electrocuted.

Seth crawled forward, his nose inches from the windshield, desperate for a way around the fallen trees. He shifted into low, mounted the sidewalk, driving next to a brick building. He heard paint scraping off the side of his truck before he gritted his teeth and bumped back onto the street. Close, now he knew he could make it to Thornton House.

The deserted streets ran with muddy water. Only six blocks to go. Seth turned right onto Broome Street. The truck lurched twice and stopped. The needle on the gas gauge had dropped to the empty zone and died there.

* * * *

Panic rendered Jillian mute. Without thinking, she knelt down, holding out her arms, softly calling Snowflake's name. The dog came to her, reluctantly, a low rumble emanating from his massive chest. She looped her fingers through his collar to keep him near. Her heart was pounding so loud it took her a moment to realize someone had called out. How could it be and how did he, or she, get into the house?

While she pondered her options, a gust of wind slammed against the aging walls. The house quivered. Rain beat at the windowpane like a thousand pebbles hurled up from the beach. From somewhere below, Jillian heard a crash. A candle fell over on the counter. She jumped up to grab it a split second before it rolled to the floor. How would they escape with a stranger blocking their exit? An eerie silence filled the air as the storm took a breath before its next onslaught.

Jillian cocked her head, straining to hear. Could it be possible? She thought she heard her name. She crept to the door, pressed her ear against the metal.

"It's George! Let me in!"

Relief flooded through Jillian's limbs. Of course, he had a key to the front door. She'd forgotten. She fumbled with slick fingers until she managed to unlock the door. George Bannerman stumbled in, soaking wet, a large gash on his forehead leaking blood all over the floor.

He stumbled, nearly fell, but she caught him on the way down. Snowflake stood growling at her side. The hair along his back stood up and his ears were back.

"Snowflake, stop! He's a friend." The dog fell to his stomach but continued to stare at the man. Jillian could only hope the animal wouldn't attack.

"George, what happened?" Jillian took his arm and led him to the kitchen area. Snowflake glued his body to her leg and came along. Before the lawyer collapsed onto a chair, she caught a whiff of stale liquor. She sniffed at George again. She hadn't been wrong. He'd been drinking, a lot. He smelled like a saloon. She went to the phone and lifted the receiver, still dead. Nervous flutters filled her chest. Maybe it hadn't been such a good idea to let him in.

"I tried to call, to warn you." He was panting, out of breath. "Worst hurricane in years. Bertha. Warnings all up and down the coast. It was headed toward New England but veered off suddenly, came straight at us. Have to leave. Not safe here."

"Relax, breathe deeply." Jillian patted his arm before going to the fridge for a bottle of water. Why had she worried? This was mild-mannered George Bannerman, the Howdy Doody clone.

Snowflake hunkered in the dark corner away from the man. He watched her every move, alert, ready to jump to her defense. "Sip this and slow down." A drop of blood plopped on the table. "You're hurt. Let me find a cloth to wipe your forehead. What happened?"

George's squinted at her. "Branch hit me. Didn't see it." The words came out in a bit of a slur. He cut his glance to the bundle on the table, then up. "Hurrying here, didn't watch where I was going."

Jillian walked backwards toward the bathroom. Her eyes never left Bannerman. Something about him frightened her. He didn't seem like the mild-mannered attorney anymore. She didn't believe a branch caused the cut either, not with the black eye he sported. His knuckles were scratched raw. Obviously, he'd been in a fight.

Quickly she ran cold water over a cloth, then rummaged in her cabinet for the first aid kit. She'd patch him up, grab her bag, the dog and run. She didn't want to be around George Bannerman right now. He had to have a car. She'd make a stab at talking him out of the keys so she could go for help. Between the injury and the booze, he wasn't in any condition to drive.

"George, why don't you wait here with my dog and I'll..." She halted, dripping water from the cloth on the floor. George Bannerman stood over the pile of papers he'd pulled out of the bag. His hands were balled into fists, his mouth a thin grim line. The flickering candlelight distorted his features into a devil's mask.

"Where's the lamp, Jillian?" he asked through gritted teeth.

He didn't look like Howdy Doody any more.

Chapter 18

Seth lurched out of the truck cab. Flashes of lightning split the starless sky. Freezing rain tore at his face. He pushed buttons on his cell phone, but it was useless. He tossed the instrument into the cab, slammed the door and started walking. It was only a few blocks to Jillian's, and he hoped to find a working phone on the way. That downed line was a disaster waiting to happen.

He heard a horn beep and, through the murky gloom, saw a school bus lumbering along headed straight for the live wire snaking through the water behind him.

Without a thought for his own safety, he lunged off the curb and charged into the street, yelling and waving his arms like a maniac to catch the driver's attention. Good thing he was wearing a red jacket or the bus driver might have rolled right over him.

The bus door squeaked open. "Hop on, Buddy. We're headed for the community center."

Seth pulled himself onto the steps out of the rain. "You can't. There's a live wire down, up ahead." He gasped, out of breath. "Can you turn around?"

Worry creased the older man's forehead. "Yeah, but what am I gonna do with these kids? They're from the grade school over near the ocean. Principal didn't think they were safe, so we loaded up and headed inland."

Seth looked over the metal railing and saw a sea of large-eyed kids. A few adults clung to the children. One of the kids started to cry for his mother. That's all it took. A chorus of wails filled the bus. While the noise level escalated inside, it grew strangely quiet outside.

The driver peered through the windshield. "Eye of the hurricane. It'll be calm for a few minutes. Any ideas?" Drops of nervous sweat covered his forehead.

"Yes. I'm a police officer. You know where the station is? Over on third?"

"Yeah."

"Drive the kids over there. The building is sturdy and safe. You can report the danger here at the same time."

Relief flooded the man's face. "All right. You coming along?"

"I have someone I have to check on. Can you drop me off on Broome Street first?"

"Sure. Let's go."

Seth mounted the rest of the steps and braced himself as the driver shifted, rocking back and forth to turn around.

Seth bent over, searching the sky through the front window. Angry gray clouds shot across the sky, roiling and bumping into one another. This quiet wouldn't last long and Seth knew the second half of the hurricane would be worse, much, much worse.

* * * *

In two quick steps, George closed the gap between them. He grabbed Jillian's arm. "Where is my lamp!"

The hair on Snowflake's back stood at attention, and his legs were stiff. He growled, baring his teeth.

It took Jillian's mind a minute to wrap around what George had said. "Lamp? What are you talking about? There's no electricity, I had to light candles."

His fingers dug into her tender flesh. "Don't act dumb, bitch. The Tiffany lamp, where is it?"

Jillian set her feet and tried to pull away. "Let go, you're hurting me!" In a flash, Snowflake lunged. His solid body smacked into the back of Bannerman's knees. The man staggered, let go of her arm and reached inside his jacket. He pulled out a gun. "Get this animal away from me before I kill it."

The gun terrified Jillian. For an instant, she froze, then she grabbed the dog's collar and held on tight. She could scarcely contain him. The attorney stood between them and the hall door, the gun aimed at her head. Her gaze flew around the apartment, searching for escape. There was only one door to the hallway. With options limited, Jillian knew she had to talk her way out, or die in the attempt. She had to stall for time until she figured something out.

"I have no idea what you're talking about."

Rage suffused Bannerman's face. He gritted his teeth. Blood continued to ooze from the wound on his forehead. The gun pointed at Jillian never wavered. He stood silently for a moment, a rictus of greed spread across his face.

"You're going to tell me where that lamp is if I have to beat it out of you."

Outside the wind screamed with the sound of a thousand freight trains run amok. A sharp gust billowed the curtains into the room. The candles glued to the counter wavered, two snuffed out. The already dim room grew murkier. Understanding surged into Jillian's brain faster than a flash flood in the mountains.

"You stole money from my aunt, didn't you?"

Bannerman threw back his head and laughed. "I tried damn hard, but the stupid old woman kept giving it away! She'd sit in my office moaning about being alone, not having any relatives. She never should have let you go, blah, blah, blah." Bannerman staggered back until the back of his legs touched the table. "She paid for drug addicts' cures, sent a couple of kids to college." His gun hand collided with the table. Jillian cringed. "I needed the money more than she did! She was old, ready to die!"

Beside her, Snowflake rumbled deep in his chest. Jillian's stomach turned over with the realization that whatever inheritance she might have had was gone. She had to keep the lamp out of the attorney's greedy mitts. Along with the diamond earrings, they were the only thing of value left.

Bannerman kept staring at her. "I didn't know she'd funded a trust at the old folks home." He seemed lost in thought. "Perhaps there's a way to rescind it."

"How dare you. Haven't you stolen enough?"

An evil chuckle trickled out of his mouth. "Don't you know, my dear? There's never enough! I have this gambling habit. I owe money to loan sharks in Freeport. They aren't nice. They don't just bust your kneecaps like the shylocks in the states. They like to mutilate men in a particularly nasty way." She saw a shiver travel down his body.

Bannerman reached up and scratched his head with the barrel of the gun. Jillian flinched. She was no match for the weapon, but if she could find a way out of the room, she might have a chance. While he was distracted, she slid one step closer to the door.

"It turned out to be a sweet deal for a while. I drained what I could of the old woman's money, till only a few thousand remained. Then we scouted the furniture. Took what we could get away with, sold it." His head wobbled from side to side. "I snuck the lamp out and my partner took it into town to have it appraised, but she was already too suspicious, so we returned it. Shit, that lamp is worth more than the rest of her stuff combined. Except the land."

Jillian licked her dry lips, then his words clicked. "We? Who's we? What about the land?" Confusion made her head spin.

A loathsome chuckle rumbled deep in his throat. "The other part of 'we' is Malcolm Winters, although he's not much of a partner. Too stupid."

It didn't surprise Jillian. Winters had always seemed too slick.

"Is he a gambler too?" Thoughts of all her aunt's money down the drain made her heartsick.

"No, my dear, he's a slug. You see, Malcolm is a gigolo. He lives off women instead of working. He's been with Letty for a couple of years now, and has grown quite bored with her. He's been stringing her along, promising he could acquire the title to Thornton House, buy the property for back taxes. I was to help her obtain it, for a fee, of course. When no heirs were found we planned to take title, then sell the acreage to developers. This would be a great place for condos, in case you haven't noticed. Now that you're here, all I have to count on is the lamp."

Anger rolled through Jillian. "He's been using Letty." No wonder the woman drank.

"He's about tapped her dry. I believe he's already latched onto some rich old broad down in Palm Beach."

Bannerman swayed a bit, but managed to stay on his feet. "He used to come over here to help Felicity with all her hard-luck cases, the perfect setup. Once inside, he made a list of the furniture, and we'd come in at night and remove it. Damn old lady became suspicious and somehow squirreled the rest away."

"It's still there, up in the attic. You can have it, sell it—whatever. The lamp might still be there, too. I—I think I remember seeing one the last time I was up there. Let me go and I'll show you."

"Most of the stuff isn't worth much. We stole all the priceless antiques years ago, except for the lamp." His head came up. They both heard a garbled voice calling and loud banging, rattling sounds.

Could it be Seth? No, of course not. He'd never be able to return from Jacksonville in this storm. She held her breath and waited. The noise stopped.

"Trees. They bang against this place all the time." His attention fell to the plastic bags on the table. He staggered and bumped the table, momentarily forgetting the lamp. The liquor must be fogging his brain. He yanked open the bag and pulled out the metal box. "Now this might be interesting. What's inside?"

"I don't know. I can't open it."

"Hmm, I love a challenge. Where did you locate it by the way? I've been all over this house, except the locked attic, and couldn't find a thing. I almost started up there too, the day you decided to rescue this mangy animal, but you came back to the house before I had the chance."

"It was you in the woods! I knew I'd heard someone there."

"I'd been following you for days, or I should say following the follower who was following you." He giggled and the sound scared Jillian more than the gun. "My, you are popular, aren't you? Who was he, a disgruntled lover?"

Fear froze Jillian's brain so it refused to work for a second. "Yes, and he'll be here at any minute so I suggest you leave!"

"Sorry, honey, I know he's gone. Saw him in heading out of town in the long black beast." His fingers caressed the box. "I guess I could shoot the lock, but I'd hate to destroy any nice gold certificates or large bills."

Jillian bit her lip. The box contained her legacy, the only thing she had of her mother. She'd be damned if she let him have it.

"I saw the lamp upstairs."

He stared at her, his eyes narrowed. He waved the gun toward the hallway like a signal flag. "Okay, let's go. But believe me, Jillian. If this is a trick, I'll kill you and your stupid dog. I can bury you in the woods where no one will ever find you."

He took a step toward her. Snowflake growled and tried to charge.

"Lock him in the bathroom."

It took all the strength Jillian had, but she managed to get the animal into the bathroom. His howls of outrage tore through her heart. He threw his sturdy body against the closed door. It shook, bulging, but held.

Outside the wind died; an eerie calm invaded the room. Could it be over? Jillian had to use this time to break out. "I think the lamp is right at the top of the stairs." She pulled the key from her pocket as she walked out of the apartment and into the dark hallway to the attic door, her mind in a whirl. She took the key and scratched at the metal lock. "I—I can't fit it in the slot."

Greed overcame Bannerman's good sense. "Here, give it to me." He shoved the gun into his waistband, grabbed the key and pushed her aside.

In an instant, Jillian whirled, ran back through the doorway to the apartment, slammed and locked the metal door. Bannerman bellowed, beating his fists against the door. Snowflake's bark echoed from the bathroom.

To her horror, Jillian saw a candle in the kitchen had fallen over. Fire licked at the dry cabinets, the perfect fuel for hungry flames. A puff of air wiggled through a crack near the window. If the wind picked up, the whole house would go in minutes. This might be her only chance to escape. She dashed to the bathroom and snatched open the door. Snowflake nearly knocked her over when he flew out, wiggling to be near her.

"Come on, baby, we have to leave." Already thick smoke filled the kitchen. Jillian shoved the papers and box into the plastic bag and darted to the window where the fire rope lay curled. Her heart sank. It had been here for a long time and she prayed it would be strong enough to hold her weight. She tied a knot in the bag, hoping the papers would stay dry, and heaved it out the window. Beside her the dog trembled. Jillian knew she could make it down the rope, but what about Snowflake?

* * * *

Out of breath, panting hard, Seth trotted the last half block to Thornton House. Water dripped from his saturated clothing, his tennis shoes squished with each step. He'd slipped on the wet pavement several times, barely able to remain upright. He'd stopped twice to pound on doors of houses on his way, in a frenzy to find a phone to call Jillian, but no one answered the door at either place. The homeowners had, no doubt, sought shelter from the hurricane. He prayed someone, anyone, had contacted Jillian and gotten her to safety, but he knew in his heart, she was still there.

Through the trees at the edge of her property a flickering light caught his eye. His heart sank. Of course the electricity had gone out and she'd lit candles, but in the tinder-dry house, Jillian was courting disaster. Seth skidded to a stop. He shouldn't be able to see light from Jillian's apartment on the other side of the building.

"Oh no," he said with a groan as he sprinted up the front walk. "Jillian." He screamed her name at the top of his lungs. A gust of air snatched the words out of his mouth, hurling them into the atmosphere. Overhead the sky darkened to the color of coal. Rain slashed at his already drenched clothing, making it hard for Seth to move. The eye had passed and the hurricane roared back with a vengeance.

He twisted the doorknob and banged on the rough wood, but she'd probably followed his instructions to the letter and locked herself safely inside. Holding his breath, he checked the secret compartment, but it was empty. Seth scrambled off the front porch, calling Jillian's name again. She couldn't hear him above the roar of the wind. He rushed around the side of the house, sloshing through puddles of water, calling her name. A gust of wind brought the smell of smoke to him. His heart, already beating fast with fear, threatened to stop.

Seth picked up a fallen branch and smashed it against a parlor window. The glass shattered, but boards on the other side blocked his entry. He didn't have time to break every window. Even in the rain, this house would go up like a torch. He flew around to the back of the house. The fire was more apparent here. A zigzag stream of lightning flashed, boomed and struck not far away in the woods. Seth heard the tremendous crackle of a tree falling and felt the ground beneath him shake.

His eyes searched the side of the building but found no handholds, no way to climb up. Frustrated and terrified, he bellowed Jillian's name.

"Seth!" She stood framed in the window, her arm around the white dog—its paws on the window ledge. Dark gray smoke billowed out around her. Behind her, hungry flames leaped and danced.

"Here! I'm up here! Help me."

* * * *

Sweat mixed with tears in Jillian's eyes. She had wasted precious minutes checking for fraying or breaks while she'd uncoiled the fire ladder. The rigging looked smooth and unbroken. She used more time figuring out a way to lower the dog down. Bannerman continued to pound on the door, his fury matched only by the strengthening storm. The fire continued to spread, the fresh air flowing in from the window making it worse. Finally, she grabbed the old sheet from her bed, and ripped it into wide strips.

Snowflake pressed his terrified body against her leg, hindering her progress. "Please, Snowflake. We have to get out!" She squatted down, nose level with the dog's. "Okay, sweetie. I'm going to wrap this around your tummy and lower you down to the ground. Okay? Once you're safe, I'll climb down behind you."

The panting dog lapped at her face. Jillian didn't know if she'd be able to hold his weight, but she had no choice. If they stayed in this room, they'd die. She fastened the sheet strips around the dog's belly in a clumsy harness, then tied it to the loose end of the fire rope.

Jillian peeled the dog off her body, and managed to place his paws on the windowsill. She felt like a half-done pancake, cold on one side, hot on the other. A sound pierced her brain. She paused, and heard it again—someone calling her name.

"Here! Up here, help me!"

"Throw the rope out. Climb down! I'll catch you if you fall."

Through the pouring rain she saw Seth! Somehow he'd driven back onto the Island to help her. Jillian's heart almost melted with gratitude, but she didn't have time to think about him now. Coughing, she doubled over and grabbed the end of the ragged sheet to wipe at her watering eyes. The fabric came away black.

"Snowflake first," she yelled down to Seth. Wrestling with the terrified animal, she managed to hoist him over the ledge. His weight pulled her half way out the window. He hung limp, too scared to move. Grasping the rope, Jillian fell back onto her butt, bracing her feet against the wall to slow his descent. Agony flooded her muscles, her arms felt like they were being ripped from their sockets. The rope burned her palms raw, but she was soon beyond pain.

"Keep going, Jillian. He's almost down." Seth's words were barely audible above the rushing sound of the wind.

Jillian heard three muffled pops behind her. The door to the hallway flew open. Bannerman had shot the lock. He charged into the bedroom, hacking and swiping at his eyes with his soot-covered sleeve. A searing pain of flying white-hot ash pinched at her wrist. Fire had spread from the kitchen and now licked the floor next to her. The rope ladder went slack.

"Got him! Come on, honey, slide down the rope. Hurry!" She had one leg over the sill when Bannerman grabbed her. He whipped her around to face him and yanked her back inside.

"Oh no you don't, bitch." His red-rimmed eyes were wild, his face covered in soot and sweat. Hair on the right side of his head was singed. Behind him Jillian could see flames devouring the dry wood of the hallway. "You've caused me enough trouble." He tossed her back into the flaming kitchen area like a rag doll.

She screamed.

* * * *

It took Seth three tries before his shaking fingers could untie the dog from the wet sheet. The poor animal ran in circles, jumping at the house again and again in a frantic attempt to be near Jillian.

He yelled up at Jillian, but couldn't see anything. He was too close to the house and moved back a few steps. He saw a silhouette in the window, but the relief flooding his body was short-lived. It wasn't Jillian.

Chapter 19

It hurt to breathe. Jillian felt the sharp edge of the wood cabinet. Through the smoggy haze she saw Bannerman climb out the window. Pain shot up her back as she struggled to her feet. She turned her head. Flames lapped at her T-shirt, hot fire seared her skin. Instinctively she dropped to the floor, rolled then crawled toward the window. Her arms were blistered, her energy almost gone. Outside the storm raged and she heard her dog howling. Inch by inch, she eased her agonized body to the rope. Fire brushed at her feet.

"Too hard, too tired," she whispered through swollen lips. A gust of wind whooshed in, pushing the smoke back for a second. She lifted her face to the edge of the window and sucked in greedy gulps of air. She wouldn't give up. "Almost there, I can make it."

With a loud crackling noise, part of the wall behind her collapsed sending sparks up to the ceiling. A falling board whacked her on the back of her head. Her last thought before she spiraled into darkness was one of regret. Now she'd never have a chance to see Seth again.

* * * *

Seth had only climbed a few feet off the ground when something slammed into his head, sending him sprawling to the ground.

"Outta my way!"

A man hurled over Seth and staggered off toward the woods. "What? Who? Where's Jillian!" Seth yelled after him.

The figure disappeared into the deluge, laughing insanely.

Snowflake lay in a dirty puddle of water, panting. He growled feebly. His tongue lolled out, the whites of his eyes enormous. No time to do anything about him now. Seth wiped his fingers along his soaked pants leg, threw the wet bedding over his shoulder, grabbed the rope ladder and started up again. He felt heat through the boards and knew the fire had reached the first floor. The smell of burning wood clogged his nose, and curdled his stomach. He heard a loud booming sound from inside. The house had started to collapse.

He opened his mouth to yell Jillian's name but swallowed a mouth full of rainwater from an overflowing gutter for his trouble. Better to conserve his energy and concentrate on getting her out.

Smoke poured out of the window and slithered toward the sky. At the top of the rope, trembling from head to foot, he peered into the room. Every picture he'd ever seen of hell flashed through his mind. In the other room, flames had engulfed the bed, turning it into a funeral pyre. His heart jumped to his throat, tears mingled with rain on his face. Black oily smoke eddied through the room like an evil fog. He couldn't see Jillian.

Seth heard something. A moan? It must be the wind slicing through the trees as it crackled and howled. No, he heard it again. He poked his head over the sill. Jillian huddled inert against the wall. Blood oozed from a gash on her head. He couldn't detect any movement.

Without hesitation, Seth hoisted himself into the room. Holding his breath, he placed his fingers under her jaw. A pulse, weak and thready, throbbed under his fingertips. His back felt on fire. A gigantic crash, then a whoosh of heat knocked him sideways. He saw the piano crash through the ceiling; it opened a rent in the floor and kept going. Sparks flew, spitting fire at his face. Time to go. He threw the wet sheet over Jillian and hoisted her over his shoulder.

"Come on, honey, hang on. We'll be out of here in a second." Seth shoved his feet into the top rung of the rope ladder. The floor of the apartment fell away in a flurry of embers. The rope ladder sagged under their combined weight. He saw the fibers separating. The rope wouldn't hold the two of them for long.

Wind tore at Seth's body, pushed the two of them against the house. He shoulder took the brunt of the blow knocking him off balance. Jillian's weight shifted, nearly sending them both hurtling to the ground. Seth's feet scrabbled for the next rung, missed, then connected. He felt a sickening lurch as part of the rope snapped.

Panting and weak, he held the ladder with one arm. The ground loomed far away. Seth knew there was only one way down, but he wasn't sure they'd make it. He untangled Jillian's body from the rope. His arm circled her thin wrist. Slowly, he lowered her as far as he could, then let go. She landed on the ground like a bag of wet cement. Snowflake stood over the unconscious woman, licking her face. Off in the distance, Seth thought he heard sirens. Too late, too late. The rope split. He pushed himself away from the house, to avoid landing on Jillian. He felt himself falling through space. Pain, then nothing.

* * * *

Jillian felt the pinch as a needle pushed into her arm. "Go away," she mumbled. A knuckle rubbed her chest. She tried to swat it away but her arms didn't work. The sound of a siren pierced her brain. It took her a few minutes to realize the noise was coming from on top of the vehicle she was in.

"Come on, now. Wake up. You best not be sleeping."

Slitting her eyes, she squinted up into a smiling chocolate-colored face. "You're safe now, honey. Stay with me. You're in an ambulance on the way to the hospital."

She scrunched up her eyes against the glare of overhead lights. The inside of her head thudded. Her arms were on fire and every muscle in her body screamed with pain.

"Oh, no. Open them pretty eyes again. You have a nasty laceration on your head. We don't want you to sleep until the doctors examine you." The paramedic spread a soothing gel on her burns. "Just some singed skin here, the burns aren't bad." He made a noise in the back of his throat. "Could have been worse."

"Seth?" Her voice squeaked out, raw and hoarse. Immediately she started coughing. Pain seared her throat.

The man pulled a plastic oxygen mask from her face in order to hear her better. "Hush. He the man who pulled you out of the fire?" He put the mask back, and soothing air flowed into her air passages again.

Jillian nodded. Even a slight motion set off drumbeats in her head.

"Still alive when they loaded him into the other ambulance."

Jillian's heart contracted, tears oozed from her eyes. What if Seth didn't live? She couldn't think about it now. She jerked, trying to sit up. "Snowflake!"

"No snow, sugar. You're in Florida, remember?" Worry scurried across the man's face. He pressed her back onto the stretcher with a large, gentle hand.

She rolled her head from side to side in frustration, opened her mouth to speak, but nothing came out. She took a deep breath, coughed, and started again. "My dog." Her breathy words sounded distant and foreign.

"Oh, the dog. Fine looking animal, fine looking. We didn't know what to do with him. Lucky for you I like critters, so we brought him along." A deep rumbling chuckle came out of his massive chest. "He's up front with my partner. We'll drop him off at the vets after we get you settled. He's kinda banged up, too."

The vehicle rocked from side to side. Jillian grabbed the edge of the gurney.

"It's okay. The storm is almost over." He reached up and tapped an IV line. "It's weird to have one this early. Bad one, too."

The ambulance slowed, bumped and halted. The siren growled to stop.

"Here we are at the hospital, safe and sound. Now, there are going to be a lot of folks inside poking, prodding, asking questions, so don't be alarmed."

His face disappeared. The rear doors opened, moist cool air flowed across Jillian's face. She felt movement as the gurney was slid from the ambulance. Walls rushed by, bright overhead lights pierced her eyes.

"You'll be okay now, Miss."

The paramedic rattled off a bunch of words and gave some papers to one of the nurses.

"Wait!" she called.

He turned back and came to bend over Jillian.

"My house?"

"I'm sorry, miss. We were lucky to get you away before the whole thing collapsed." He patted her shoulder. "You're safe, that's the main thing."

"Thank you for all your help." The words taxed her strength to the max, and her throat closed up. Tears stained her cheeks. She closed her eyes and turned her face away.

* * * *

Agony like a bolt of electricity shot up Seth's leg. A moan escaped his dry lips.

"Whoa, you okay buddy?"

Seth pried his eyes open to find Murphy standing beside his bed.

"Where am I? What happened?" His voice sounded like a foghorn at low tide.

"In a hospital. You busted your ankle rescuing 'fair damsel.' Want I should find the doctor for more pain medicine?" His round Irish face twisted with concern.

"No, I'm okay. Help me crank up the bed a bit. There any water around here?" His useless hands were covered with bandages.

Murphy hurried to fill a glass. His clumsy fingers pushed the straw toward Seth's mouth. The cool water flowed down Seth's throat like ambrosia. The cast on his ankle tented the bed sheets. He took another sip.

Holding his breath, he squeezed the words out. "Is Jillian alive?"

"The Yankee Gal? Yeah, she'll recover. No permanent damage. I guess she got a fairly good boink on the head, some minor burns, but they did one of them cat scans and didn't find anything broken. She's in a room down a couple of doors from here."

Relief saturated Seth's body, and then he shot up in bed. His ankle throbbed. Nausea swam in his stomach. "I have to see her. I think someone tried to kill her. Where are my pants? Help me up." Chills wracked his body and beads of sweat dotted his forehead.

"Where do you think you're going, cowboy?" A nurse stood in the doorway, arms folded over her ample chest.

"I'm a police officer. I'm on a case." Sweat dripped in Seth's eyes, his words came out between panting breaths. "There's a dangerous man running lose. I have to find out..." His brain seemed to shut down.

"Dr. Grogan will be very unhappy if you undo all his nice ankle surgery."

"But..."

"No buts. Stay." She pointed at Seth like a trainer ordering a dog to sit.

Murphy stood wide-eyed by the bed. "Jeez, someone tried to kill her? Who?"

"I don't know. I have to talk to Jillian. Find out who he is, why he wanted her dead." Seth collapsed back onto his pillow, exhausted. "Where he might be now."

"If you're talking about Jillian Bennett, she's under sedation and won't be talking to anyone for a while." The nurse walked over to fluff his pillow and tuck the sheets tight around his chest. "Now, why don't we crank our bed down and have a nice nap?" She turned to Murphy. "You, out."

"I don't want a nap. I want to leave." The words were mere bravado. Seth felt as helpless as an upside-down turtle. "It's my job."

"Ah, Seth? There might be a problem," Murphy said.

"What do you mean?" Concentration hurt Seth's brain. Perhaps he should take the nurse's advice. A nap to clear his head, then he'd see Jillian.

"Sir, you have to leave. My patient needs his rest." The nurse glared at Murphy.

"Let him stay for a moment, please."

The nurse checked her watch, scowled as she passed Murphy heading for the door. "I'm going to check on my other serious patient. You'd better be gone by the time I return."

"I'm a police officer," Murphy said to her retreating back. "I can stay if I want to." His lower lip stuck out like a child's.

"Not in *my* hospital you can't," came the reply from the hallway.

Seth would have laughed if he didn't hurt so much. "Okay, tell me."

"The captain's right pissed you didn't get a statement from Babcock at the hospital. Why didn't ya?"

Seth scrabbled around for a good excuse. Nothing came, so he decided on the truth. "I tried to reach Jillian on the phone, and couldn't. I didn't like the idea of her alone in the house, in a hurricane. I knew Babcock would stay put, so headed back here." His voice faded with the last few words. He fought to keep his eyelids open.

"I knew…my job. Want to keep it. Stay here. But…" Murkiness crept across his vision. "…Had to save Jillian."

"I'll check on her. You rest." The words echoed through a fog, then darkness claimed him.

Chapter 20

Jillian swam up to consciousness slowly. She was lying on her side, and her head felt like it had been used as a bowling ball in a league tournament. Her entire body ached, especially her back. Pain and hopelessness bubbled up in a flood of tears that stained her pillow. Bright sunshine streamed in through the window. The storm had blown inland and dissipated there, a thing of the past. How long had she been here?

Antiseptic hospital smells crawled up her nose, increasing her stomach's distress. She heard bustling noises from the hallway, the squeaky wheel of a cart along on the tile; the intercom crackled to life and a soft female voice paged Doctor Cooper.

Alone, injured, with no money, job or family, Jillian had no idea how long she'd be laid up. Without health insurance, how would she even pay the bill? Her gauze-wrapped fingers flew to her ear. Nothing. Could the earrings still be in her house? The house had burned to the ground, with everything she owned inside.

Of course she could go to her grandmother. Jillian would have snorted, but it took too much energy. The cold, controlling woman had never been there for her before, so Jillian wouldn't dream of contacting her now. She couldn't help herself. Deep wracking sobs tore out of her chest.

"Are you in pain, honey?" A work-worn brown hand covered her bandaged fist.

"RaeJean? What are you doing here?" She glanced up at RaeJean, then tried to turn on her back, and groaned.

"Best stay where you are, sugar. Doctor said you have a few minor burns on your back. Don't you worry, though, he said they shouldn't leave scars." Her dark eyes were clouded with anxiety.

Moisture welled in Jillian's eyes and spilled over again. "My house burned, RaeJean. I have nothing."

"What do you mean nothing? You've got me, haven't you? Aren't I your friend? And Seth? Why honey, he climbed into a burning building to save your life. Once the doctor says it's okay, I'm going to bring you home with me till you're healed."

"I don't have any money, no job." Consumed with self-pity and fear, Jillian cried. RaeJean sat on the edge of the bed, held her and patted her shoulder.

"Everything going to work out, Jillian. You'll see."

Jillian sniffed a bit. "Okay, I'm done." She tried to smile. "I've decided it's a waste of time to cry. Besides, it makes my head hurt. Can you tell me about Seth? How is he?"

"He's in a room right down the hall. He's going to be fine, too. Broke his ankle, got a few burns here and there and is suffering from smoke inhalation, just like you. I'll tell you everything, but later. The doctor wants you to rest. I saw you holding your head. Lot of pain, huh? I'll ring for the nurse."

"It's not bad. I wasn't holding my head. I was feeling for Aunt Felicity's earrings. I guess they were lost, too." An enormous lump lodged in her throat. She didn't think she'd ever be able to swallow it.

A broad smile brightened RaeJean's face. "The earrings are in the hospital safe. I have the receipt in my bag. So, you aren't completely broke."

"What about clothes? Did anything survive?" Jillian had a mental picture of herself job hunting in the short flapping hospital gown.

RaeJean moved to the closet. "Nope, no clothes. Only this old metal box and a bag of," she peeked inside, "papers, of some kind."

"I remember now." Excitement burbled in her chest. "RaeJean, I found the box hidden in the fireplace. I tried to open it but couldn't." The exertion made her head swirl, so she scooted back under the sheets, covered with sweat. "I discovered the papers hidden around the house, but I don't think there's anything valuable there."

"Fireman or EMTs must have found them near you and brought the stuff along. Don't you worry 'bout nothing right now, Jillian, except getting your strength back." RaeJean closed the closet door and returned to sit on the chair near Jillian's bed.

"I am lucky. I'm alive and I have at least two friends." A strange lassitude started at her toes and crawled up her body. "I'm so tired. You'll stay with me for a while, won't you, RaeJean?"

"I'm not going anywhere, honey. Rest."

A low buzzing sound tickled at Jillian's brain. She tried to swat it away from her head, but it refused to stop. She peeled her eyes open and saw RaeJean standing in the doorway of her room, talking to someone.

"No. You ain't gonna disturb Jillian. She needs her rest."

"It's okay, I'm awake," Jillian said.

RaeJean stepped to one side and glared. Murphy, Seth's cop friend sidled into the room.

"I'm sorry to disturb you, ma'am," Murphy said, "but Seth sent me to check on you. About the man who was in your house…"

Jillian's heart beat faster. She felt sweat broke out on her forehead. "Haven't you found him yet?" Bannerman could be anywhere and he still wanted her dead.

"No, I need to find out all I can about him, his name, description, so I can put out an APB." He shuffled a few feet closer and pulled a worn notebook out of his shirt pocket. "Did he, I mean, are you…" A purple flush spread across his face. "Did he assault you, ma'am?"

Jillian took a deep breath to slow her racing heart. She should be safe here in the hospital with all the people around. She struggled to slide her weary body higher in the bed, careful not to roll on her sore back. The maneuver set off the jungle drums in her head again. The tender skin on her back sizzled with pain. "No, he didn't have time. From what I can remember, a beam or board or something fell on me." She took another deep breath. It hurt. "His name is George Bannerman. He stole all my aunt's money and tried to kill me."

* * * *

"I'm still not happy, Seth," Captain Burgess said. "Not getting that statement was a dereliction of duty." The man sat uncomfortably in Seth's stiff plastic visitor's chair.

"I know, sir. I'm ready for whatever punishment you care to give me." Depression settled on Seth. He'd decided to stick with the force here in Florida and take the promotion, have a lasting relationship with Jillian, but that seemed hopeless now.

"Ah, hell, I guess it doesn't make any difference. Babcock is still in the hospital, malingering if you ask me. I'll send Murphy or one of the other boys over to video his statement." Burgess pulled at his too-tight shirt collar. "Hell, I can't reprimand you, you're a hero."

Seth shifted uncomfortably. His broken ankle protested, sending shooting pains up his leg. "Some hero, I broke bones getting Jillian out of the house and the damn thing burned down anyhow."

"I'm not talking about you rescuing the Yankee Gal, although it was down right heroic. No, if you hadn't turned back that busload of kids, they might a drove right into the puddle of water with the downed wire. Who knows what could have happened." Captain Burgess shivered.

Seth folded back the edge of the light cotton blanket covering his body. "I don't suppose you'll want me to take over for you now."

"You made a decision and it turned out to be the right one. Hell, son, we all make mistakes." The man shifted and pulled a handkerchief out of his back pocket to mop his forehead. "The docs say with my bad heart and high blood pressure, I don't need the responsibility of command. Time for me to step down so my wife and I can retire to our house in the Keys. I already recommended you to the mayor and city council to be my replacement. Far as they're concerned, it's a done deal. Once you're fit and back on the job, I'll start turning over command to you." He finally paused for air. "How's that sound?"

Seth couldn't speak for a minute. He thought of his family, skiing in Vermont during the winter, sailing on the Cape in summers. Still, he could always go for vacations. He couldn't help but wonder what sports Jillian participated in. Mom and Pop were getting older. He might be able to talk them into moving to Florida. "Great, it's sounds great. But what about Murphy? He has seniority over me."

"Oh, I talked to him about it. He doesn't want the responsibility, said you'd do a better job." A low chuckle rumbled out of his chest. "He's a small town cop and happy to stay one."

"Good. We work well together."

Burgess shifted his bulk on the uncomfortable rigid chair. "What did you find out about the man in the house with the Yankee Gal? What the hell possessed her to live in that old derelict place anyhow?"

"It's a long story. I sent Murphy down the hall to see if Jillian's awake. He hasn't returned yet." Seth filled the captain in on Jillian's inheritance, her quest to find out about her parents and everything else that he could remember about the items hidden in the house.

"So," Seth finished, "there could have been other valuable antiques in the attic besides the lamp, but, of course, they're all gone now."

"And the man?"

"Her slime-ball attorney, George Bannerman," Murphy said, frowning in the doorway. He held a notebook open in his meaty fist. "She said he stole money from her aunt to cover his gambling debts. We'll have to sort it all out later, but right now I'm heading for the shop to put out an APB. We can arrest him for attempted murder for starters. He smacked her around then left her to burn to death in the house. First we gotta find him. He has a good twenty-four hour head start."

"No wonder he kept stalling Jillian. She asked him for tax records and other documentation regarding her inheritance." Seth shook his head. Bad idea, it made him nauseous. "He gave her some bogus story about a robbery so he didn't have to produce the paperwork. Told her he'd been out of town. I wonder..."

"Okay, gentlemen. That's enough visiting for today. My patient needs his rest." The nurse marched into the room with a diminutive paper cup on a tray.

"Come back tonight, Murph? I want an update on Bannerman."

"Sheesh, not even in charge yet and already he's giving orders." Murphy gave Seth a wink and he walked out of the room with Captain Burgess.

"Time for us to go nighty-night." The nurse held the straw for him to drink. Seth nodded off before the pill hit his stomach.

* * * *

Jillian unglued her eyelids and glanced around. Long shadows filled the empty room. RaeJean must have gone to fix dinner at Letty's. Darn, she'd been so preoccupied with her own problems she hadn't bothered to ask RaeJean about Letty's place or the rest of the town.

She smelled food and heard the sound of metal banging. Her stomach rumbled, reminding her it had been a while since her last meal. She felt better, still achy, but definitely on the mend. The burns on her back itched. Carefully, she sat up. A wave of dizziness fluttered in her head then settled down. She dropped her feet over the side of the bed, sat there for a moment, and with one careful step after the other, made her way to the bathroom.

Except for the dual-colored eyes, a barely recognizable face stared back at her from the mirror. Bright red spots covered in shiny cream dotted her face. Scratches and bruises marred her right cheek. Her lips were cracked and dry. Chunks of curly black hair had burned into uneven clumps.

She washed her face with the bandage-free tips of her fingers before making her way back to bed. Before climbing in, Jillian searched the nightstand drawer in vain for paper and a pencil. She'd have to ask a nurse for supplies. She might as well make a list of assets, options and plans for the future while she was stuck here.

"Dinner." A delicate blond teenager in a pink and white striped uniform stood in the doorway. "Are you ready to eat?"

"I'm starving."

The girl rolled the table into position and placed a steaming plate of food in front of Jillian. She dug in.

"Mercy, you are hungry. We have chocolate ice cream for dessert. I'll bring you two cups." Dimples jumped into her creamy cheeks. "Now, is there anything else I can get you?" She stood beaming at Jillian.

"No, thank you. Oh wait, yes. Can you find some writing supplies?"

"Sure. I have to finish serving patients, then I'll bring something back with your ice cream, okay?"

Her mouth full, Jillian simply nodded and kept shoveling.

True to her word, the candy striper brought back two cups of ice cream, a pad of paper and pencil.

"Now, here's the remote for the television." She carefully pointed out all the features to Jillian before finally going on her way.

Once she'd eaten every delicious bit of the creamy dessert, Jillian pushed the dishes to one side and picked up the pad of paper. Resting her head against the pillow, she stared at the ceiling, then she licked the end of the pencil and started. She had her aunt's earrings—they had to be worth at least two thousand dollars, probably more—although she hated the idea of selling them. They were the only family heirlooms she had and she would love to pass them on to a daughter some day. And there was the Tiffany Lamp. She wondered if Seth had had time to stop and have the lamp appraised. It didn't matter.

Worry over her rescuer nagged at her, even though every nurse she'd asked had told her he would be fine. She snapped on the television to check the time. She had to make sure Seth was okay, and to thank him for saving her life. But she waited until after the dinner and visiting hour. She flicked through the channels and dropped the remote next to her.

Restlessness plucked at her. She started scribbling her list. A pair of diamond earrings and a, maybe, valuable lamp? She bit her lip. Somewhere in her weary brain she remembered Bannerman saying something about the land. She made a note with a question mark. What about Snowflake? Would it be fair to the dog to have him with her when she had nowhere to live?

Jillian wiped her cheeks and brought her attention back to the list. First of all, she had to buy some clothes, find a job, then an apartment, a car. The longer the list, the more depressed she became. She closed her eyes to think.

The sound of muted gunfire woke Jillian. Sweat covered her brow. Bannerman—had he come back to finish her off? She jerked upright and stared at the television. The good guys were winning. With a wave of relief she snapped off the set. Someone had removed her dinner tray while she slept. She slipped out of bed, pulled on the hospital robe and shuffled to the doorway. Most of the patients were asleep, leaving the hallway empty and quiet. Time to sneak down the hall and find Seth.

* * * *

Seth dreamed he was on Cape Cod, lying on a dune, basking in the sunshine. Tall reeds swayed and bowed in the breeze. He wanted to sleep, but one of the stalks kept tickling his arm. Reluctantly he woke and turned his head. Jillian Bennett sat in the chair pulled up beside his bed. Her head rested on crossed arms at the edge of his mattress. A curl of ebony hair whispered across his wrist.

Somehow she'd found him. He vowed he'd never let her out of his sight again. He longed to reach out to stroke her hair, but feared he'd wake her. He wanted to pull her up beside him on the bed and hold her tight. Instead he watched the gentle rise and fall of her shoulders.

Outside his room, he saw the hallway lights had been muted. He smelled popcorn and heard feminine giggles. The nurses must be having a midnight snack.

He shifted in an effort to straighten his aching back. Pain shot up his leg. Too late he tried to stifle a moan.

"You're awake."

He turned and gazed into Jillian's gorgeous blue eye. The green one remained hidden in the folds of a swollen lid.

"I'm awake. How's my girl?" He couldn't resist. He ran his fingers through her hair. She purred like a kitten.

"Sore, tired, and mad."

Seth moved his hips to make room for Jillian on the bed. Not exactly how he'd envisioned sleeping with her but…

"Here, scoot up on the bed next to me." He opened the covers for her to slide in beside him. She snuggled against him, smelling vaguely of smoke and talcum powder. She fit perfectly next to his body. A giant yawn split her face.

"I've been asleep for hours. Have they found Bannerman yet?"

"I haven't heard, probably won't until morning." He patted her shoulder carefully. "I'm sorry your house is gone, honey. What are you going to do now?"

Her eyes were half closed but a gentle smile curved her lips. "Start over," she said and drifted off to sleep.

Chapter 21

"Are you sure this is going to be all right? Not too much trouble for you?" Jillian held open the front door of Letty Cantrell's B-and-B while Seth clomped in on crutches, his face pale and sweating. She knew his ankle hurt.

"Absolutely. Letty said to bring you both here where there's more room than my house. I'll have all my sick folk in one spot to play nurse." RaeJean had a mischievous smile on her face. She'd been grinning like an idiot ever since they drove away from the hospital. Jillian knew she had something up her sleeve.

The drive through town had been a somber one for both Seth and Jillian. They were saddened by the amount of damage they saw. Trees down, debris strewn about, and parts of buildings blown away. But now the sun burned brightly, and everywhere work crews were busy cleaning up the mess. Jillian had swallowed a lump in her throat. She had her own mess to deal with and no time to waste.

"You'll be in a downstairs bedroom, Seth. Easier for me to care for you there." The three of them made the slow journey through the house, allowing Seth to clump along on his unfamiliar crutches. Seth would be in the room opposite of the one her grandmother had occupied. Jillian didn't want to think about that woman yet.

Between the two of them, they got Seth onto the bed and propped his leg up on pillows.

"I'm going to pour you a glass of water so you can swallow a pain pill and have a nap." RaeJean bustled out of the room.

Jillian smoothed his pillow.

"Stop fussing and give me a kiss." Seth pulled her down close to him.

She dropped a quick peck on his forehead. "Doctors orders, you're not to have too much excitement."

"Hey, we've already spent the night together. Don't be shy now."

Jillian's face burned. She couldn't help but remember his hard muscular body. All the nurses at the hospital had gotten a huge charge out of finding the two of them nestled together in Seth's hospital bed, fast asleep. Before she could think of a smart reply, RaeJean came into the room with a glass of cold water.

"This will help you sleep. After you've had a nap, we'll see about opening Jillian's metal box. I'm sure you'll want to see what's inside."

"I'm all right. Let's do it now." He struggled to pull himself higher on the bed. Sweat popped out on his forehead.

"You want to go back to the hospital?" RaeJean folded her arms and frowned at him. "Sleep!" she commanded.

"Yes, ma'am." Seth dropped his head to the pillow and the two women eased out the door.

"Letty's waiting for us in the parlor, but first there's someone who's been waiting three days to see you." RaeJean hurried through the hall to open the kitchen door.

A blur of white barreled out and smacked Jillian in her midsection, almost knocking her over.

"Snowflake!" She dropped to her knees, held the dog and let him slather her face with wet kisses. He wiggled so hard, she feared his tail would fall off. She ran her fingers over every part of his body but couldn't find any obvious injuries.

"Oh, RaeJean. Thank you so much! I was afraid to ask about him. I thought you might have dropped him off at an animal shelter or something."

"Now, why would I do that? He's your dog, isn't he? Letty and me have been busy spoiling him rotten while you were in the hospital. You go into the parlor. I'm going to bring in some iced tea and cookies. Got to fatten you up a bit, girl."

Snowflake pressed his sturdy body against Jillian's leg. She placed her fingers onto his head and together they walked into the parlor.

"Jillian. How are you feeling?" Letty jumped up from the chair by the fireplace and hurried over to enfold Jillian in a gentle embrace.

"Other than being a penniless, homeless orphan, I'm doing fine." She returned the woman's hug. "Thank you so much for taking me in, and my dog, too. I'll pay you back, Letty, when I find a job and start earning money." Jillian was surprised by the woman's appearance. The once poofy hair was slicked close to her head. Her face devoid of makeup seemed thinner, but softer; she had dark pouches under her eyes.

"Here we are. Iced tea, cookies and cake. We'll have us a party." RaeJean set the tray on the coffee table and handed out frosty glasses tinkling with ice, each topped with a sprig of mint.

"Tell us everything, Jillian. How did you escape from that nasty man and get out of the house?" Letty had to use two shaking hands to bring the glass to her lips.

Jillian took cookie, bit off a piece and gave it to the panting dog. "George Bannerman, the attorney. He's been looting not only my great aunt's bank account, but her house, too, for years."

Letty gave a rather inelegant snort. "He had help."

"Yes, I'd almost forgotten, he told me Malcolm Winters was in on it," Jillian said.

The woman slumped in her chair. Her already pale face lost even more color until it turned the shade of putty. "I've been such a fool." She pulled a wrinkled handkerchief out of the sleeve of her pink sweater and dabbed at her eyes.

"When my husband Arty and I bought this house, we were so full of expectations. We moved down here from Trenton and planned on having a long, happy retirement. Instead, he dropped dead of a massive heart attack two months after we got here. I didn't know anyone, didn't have RaeJean to help. I was so lonely. Malcolm moved in and just sort of stayed." She paused to drink and found her glass empty. Jillian took the pitcher to refill her glass.

"Thank you, dear. Malcolm became a great comfort to me. He used to come and go, doing research in various parts of the south he said, but I know now he'd gone off with other women. Then somewhere, I think in Freeport, he hooked up with George Bannerman."

RaeJean had returned with the bag of papers and metal box. She had a screwdriver and pliers and set everything on the coffee table.

Letty continued. "The B-and-B has always made money, enough to support me, but never huge amounts. I know with the right management it could do better. Anyhow, after Felicity died, Malcolm told me he and George planned to appropriate Thornton House along with all its property. When Felicity was alive, I know he used to visit the house a lot, I suppose to wiggle into her good graces. Then he suddenly stopped going there. When I asked him about it, he became a little vague and just said he didn't enjoy it anymore."

"That must be how he knew about the dining room chandelier," Jillian said.

"I'm sure it is. The house hadn't been in good shape for years. Once Felicity passed away its condition worsen. They only wanted the land the house sat on. Malcolm said it was worth a ton of money. He told me George already had a buyer lined up, construction company who wanted to build condos. They had to pretend to search for Felicity's heir and when she," Letty nodded her head, "you Jillian, didn't show up, they'd buy the place for back taxes with no one the wiser. George took his time and didn't strain very hard to find you, until a probate judge put his feet to the fire."

"Fools," RaeJean spoke up. "What Letty didn't know, maybe they didn't either, the property is only zoned for a single family dwelling. Felicity told me that years ago."

"You have to realize, I'd always had a man to care for me. I leaned on Malcolm more than I should have." A deep blush tinted her face.

Jillian moved over and squatted by Letty's chair. "I know exactly how it feels, Letty. Warm and comforting, but stifling."

"Yes. I didn't have much to do and had started drinking much more than I should have. He encouraged me. When I drank, it made things easier for Mal take over my business. I realize now he'd been stealing from me, too."

RaeJean made a hurrumping noise. "Never did trust him."

"From the moment you arrived, Jillian, Malcolm started scheming to find a way back into the house. He hadn't been there in a long time and thought the lamp might still be there."

"Then he originally had it appraised?"

"Yes, he told me about it. He said Bannerman feared someone might recognize him at the antique store, wonder why he had the lamp and raise a stink. I think Malcolm realized Bannerman had been using him. Malcolm removed the lamp one day when Felicity was out of the house, had it appraised and returned it before the poor woman knew what had transpired. I didn't know any of this until later, you understand." She sat straighter in her chair. "I would never have condoned stealing, Jillian."

"I know, Letty, I know." Jillian patted the older woman's shoulder. "What happened to Malcolm? Where is he now?"

"Gone." A single tear wandered down Letty's face. "When I heard the storm warning on television I decided to check his room. Everything had been cleaned out, not a scrap remained." She grimaced. "He even took the towels. At least he had the decency to leave me a brief note. Said he'd met a woman and decided to go sailing with her on her yacht."

"I wonder what will happen to him?" Jillian asked. "And Bannerman?"

"The police are all out looking for both of them," RaeJean said, "but so far nothing. Murphy told us part of the story while you were in the hospital." She sat back in her chair, waiting. "Go on honey. Tell us what happened in the house."

"We'll get more details once the police catch Bannerman, and they have time to scrutinize his files, but basically, he took over from Aunt Felicity's attorney five years ago when the man retired or died."

Jillian paused to sip and gather her thoughts. "I believe Aunt Felicity had already had a few strokes and must have been easily confused, but she wasn't stupid. After a while, she realized furniture was disappearing. She moved everything to the attic behind a locked door. By then it was too late. Most of the expensive antiques were gone." Jillian thought of the beautiful piano and clamped her mind shut.

"Bannerman told me he'd lost thousands, probably hundred of thousands of dollars gambling in the Bahamas. He took my aunt's money to cover his losses, and to keep on playing. He stole her antique furniture and sold that. The last time he'd been in the house, the Tiffany lamp was there. He assumed I still had the lamp and decided to steal it, too."

While Snowflake snored at her feet, Jillian related the entire horrendous night of the hurricane and fire.

"If Seth hadn't returned when he did," a shudder ran through Jillian's body like quicksilver, "I wouldn't be sitting here now."

"You'll have to be sure and let the police captain know so Seth doesn't lose his job," RaeJean said.

"I guess it doesn't matter. Seth told me he'd be returning to New England." Jillian nibbled at a cookie so the women wouldn't see her pain. She'd been so worried about her own situation, she had nearly forgotten.

"Seth isn't going anywhere." He stood in the doorway, leaning heavily on his crutches.

Chapter 22

RaeJean and Jillian both jumped up and helped Seth to a chair. When Jillian lifted his foot and placed it on the ottoman, wisps of silky black hair fanned out across her creamy cheek. Even with green and purple streaks under her eye, she looked beautiful. He wanted to reach out and hug her, but three pairs of eyes watched him with expectation, so he continued.

"I already explained to the captain why I didn't go to the hospital in Jacksonville. He didn't like it, but as long as things worked out, I guess I'm off the hook and I still have my job." He didn't say anything about taking over for the captain. He wanted to tell Jillian alone first.

"Jillian, the owner of the antique store thinks he can sell the lamp for several hundred thousand dollars. The only problem might come in proving it belongs to you—its provenance." Seth drank half the glass of iced tea in several big gulps. The painkiller had dulled the ache in his leg, but made him very thirsty.

"So, it is authentic." Jillian looked stunned for an instant, and then a huge smile lit up her face. She jumped up and went to grab the plastic bag from where it sat on the coffee table. She brought it over, handed it to Seth and knelt by his chair. "I think this will help."

When Seth untied the knot and opened it, a moldy smell escaped. Inside were several pieces of paper, some glued together with moisture. "What are these?"

In spite of her battered face, Jillian's eyes sparkled. "I found a bunch of papers when I was poking around in the house and one of them is an inventory of household goods. I'm sure I saw the lamp listed on it. I hope it's still in there and hasn't been destroyed. Would it prove the Tiffany came from Thornton House and belongs to me, Seth?"

"I'm not a lawyer, but it sounds good to me."

"Things will be simpler then," Letty said.

They both turned toward Letty.

"What do you mean?" Jillian asked.

"When you sell the lamp, you'll have enough money to buy this B-and B."

"Buy your house?" Jillian sat back in her chair, stunned. "But why?"

"Because I miss my sister in Jersey. I want to go home. We never should have moved here, but at the time Florida sounded so idyllic. It is nice, but I want to spend the rest of my life with my family. I'm lonely here."

"Are you positive, Letty?" Jillian twisted her hands. "That's a huge step, not something you want to rush into."

Her head bobbed up and down. "Yes, I've been thinking about it for a long, long time. Should have sold out and gone home years ago."

The enormity of the idea overwhelmed Jillian. "I'd love to own the house, but I'm not sure I'm ready. I mean, I don't know much about running a business, let alone a B-and-B. It's a lot of work for one person."

"You won't be doing it alone." A huge smile decorated RaeJean's face. "If you'll have me, I'll invest and be your partner."

Relief flooded Jillian like a warm waterfall. "Oh, how fabulous!" Ideas whirled in her mind. "We could upgrade the web site, drop the dinners—they're too much work." Her heart thudded so fast she sure it would jump right out of her chest.

"I've been thinking the same thing. Also..."

"Aren't you ladies forgetting something?" Seth smiled at them and shifted his injured foot. "Jillian, I thought you were all hot to see what's in the box."

"Oh, of course! In all the excitement it flew out of my mind." She had a future now. It would take hard work but she knew she could do it.

"Would you bring it over, RaeJean, along with the screw-driver," Seth asked.

While he inserted the tip of the tool between the edges, Jillian pulled the papers out of the plastic bag and spread them on the coffee table. Most of the papers were useless—old recipes and scraps of nonsense. "Here's the inventory; actually it's a list and evaluation of each piece. Smart lady. She had an appraiser come out to categorize her collection." Jillian ran her finger down the rows of tiny print until she came to the lamp.

"Yes, it's here!" She could feel herself beaming. She shuf-fled through the mess. "And here's a copy of the insurance policy on the house! If Bannerman has kept up the payments, I can cash it in."

With a loud pop, the metal box lid flew open. All eyes were on the box as he studied the contents.

"I think you'll be happy to see this, honey." He held the container toward Jillian. Her fingers tingled when she picked up the box and walked to sit on the couch. Inside rested two documents: her parent's marriage license and her birth certificate. She gingerly picked up the license and read it. Tears of joy flooded her cheeks.

"They were married in Tucson, ten months before I came along." She looked up to see the others watching her. "Someday, when I can, I want to go out there and see if I can find out more about their lives, and I'd love to find some of my father's paintings." Determination stiffened her spine. She couldn't wait to make copies of the documents to send to her paternal grandmother. Too bad she wouldn't be there to see the expression on the old woman's face.

"Great idea, sugar," RaeJean said. She rested her broad hands on her knees and hoisted her body up. "Now I'd best be seeing about dinner."

"I'll help, RaeJean." Letty followed her into the hallway.

Jillian smoothed the folds out of the certificates. She couldn't stop stroking and staring at them. "There's something else in here too, Seth." Her hands were shaking so hard she almost dropped the gold ring she pulled out of the box.

"Bring it over here." He held out his arms. She stood and started toward him and happiness fluttered in her heart. Bright shards of sunlight filled the room. In the distance she heard the familiar train whistle. It no longer sounded lonely to her and, because she had a more secure future, she was ready for love. She melted into Seth's arms and never wanted to leave.

Seth kissed the side of her face, reached up and twirled a curl of hair around his finger.

"Who do you suppose they were? The men who chased you and your mother that day?"

Jillian fought to keep from stiffening her spine. "Probably private investigators my grandmother hired. They tracked us to the island, but before they could get their grubby hands on me, we escaped out to sea and my mother..."

Seth pulled her head down to his chest. "Shush, try not to think about that now."

They were both silent for a moment. Jillian couldn't help but wonder how different her life would have been if...

Out in the hallway, the phone rang.

"Nothing else matters now. I have what I wanted. Proof my parents were married and they loved me." Jillian looked up to see Seth's dark eyes adoring her.

RaeJean's voice echoed in from the hallway.

"Okay, Sargent Murphy, I'll tell them."

Jillian held her breath. RaeJean's voice sounded so serious.

"What's up, RaeJean?" Seth asked when the woman entered the room. A frown creased his forehead.

"A fisherman down at the wharf brought in a body he found floating in the bay. From the identification, it's your lawyer, Bannerman. The fool had a dinghy down at the water. He tried to row away during the hurricane." She shook her head. "They're storing the corpse down at Doc Anderson's place for the time being. Sergeant Murphy said they'd be going through his office to see if they could discover any next of kin to notify."

"Thanks, RaeJean," Seth said.

"I also told him, while he was poking around in the office to look for anything pertaining to Thornton House." She grinned. "Is it okay, officer?"

"Absolutely."

RaeJean winked as she left the room.

Seth held out his arms and pulled her down onto his lap. "You're very lucky to be able to have a partner like RaeJean. Smart lady... Now, let's see that ring."

Jillian handed the ring to Seth. "It must have belonged to my mother. It has an inscription inside, see? It says, *forever*."

She brushed the back of her hand across her eyes. "I like to think my parents are together, someplace, forever."

"I'm sure they are, honey." Seth cleared his throat. "As soon as I'm able to get around, I want to buy you an engagement ring, if you'll accept it. Meanwhile, would you wear this one?"

Words wouldn't come, so she merely nodded. Seth slipped the band on her right ring finger. "Until we can make it official."

"This is the only ring I'll ever need. Oh, Seth, I'm so happy."

Jillian snuggled down and heard a soft moan escape from Seth. "Are you in pain?"

"Only the pain of wanting you." His mouth came down on hers in a soft insistent kiss. She opened her mouth and tasted him.

"Okay, you two, knock it off and come to dinner," Rae-Jean said. She and Letty stood grinning at them from the doorway. "You'll have years to play kissy face."

Jillian's heart soared. She slipped off Seth's lap and helped him to his feet. She knew her friend was right.

ABOUT THE AUTHOR

All her life, Carlene has been a story teller. While living in Massachusetts during the early '80s, she started writing and hasn't stopped since. During her lifetime, she's worked for two International Airlines, written for a variety of newspapers, and published over 200 pieces of fiction and non-fiction while freelancing. Since moving to the San Diego area in 1986, she has published two mystery novels and a non-fiction book about her adventures as a volunteer at the Sheriff's Department. She currently lives with her husband and three huge yellow Labs and continues to write full time.

For your reading pleasure, we welcome you to visit our web bookstore